Yesterday Pill

By
Iain Benson

For
Elaine, Adam, and Thomas
Always.

Yesterday Pill

Copyright November 11th 2021 by Iain Benson
Cover Design by Iain Benson
You may reproduce no part of this book in any form or by any electronic or mechanical means, including information storage and retrieval systems, without permission in writing from the author. The only exception is by a reviewer, who may quote brief excerpts in a review.

This book is a work of fiction: names, characters, places, and incidents either are the author's imagination or used fictitiously. Any resemblance to actual persons, living or dead, events, or locales is coincidental.
One thing this book taught me: Starting again is always an option

First published November 11th 2021 on Kindle (www.amazon.com)
Second edition July 7th 2023
First printed edition November 11th 2021 on Amazon (www.amazon.com)

ISBN: 9798507901357

By Iain Benson

Dorking Review (contributor)
App World!
Fakebook.con
The Watcher
Protean
Yesterday Pill
Royal Again

The Women Trilogy
Loosely Women
Sparkly Women
Legally Women

James London Series
It's a Kind of Magic
2000 Lightyears from Home
The Man Who Sold the World
Everybody's Happy Nowadays
Spirits in the Material World
Here, There and Everywhere
London's Burning *coming soon*

Louise Sargant Series
The Case of the Half-baked Mummies
The Case of the Second Murder

1

Wade raised his wineglass.

"Happy fifth anniversary." Wade looked across the table, his voice softening. "So much has happened. I don't know what I would have done without you."

Cassandra looked so beautiful to him, with her golden hair freshly styled for the evening. Her blue eyes sparkled in the light from the candle on the table.

She clinked her glass of water against his wineglass. "I did not know when I found you on the pavement where we would end up." She rubbed her visible bump and smiled at Wade. Pregnancy made her skin glow.

He stroked her hands. Silence its own conversation amid wafts of warm Italian cooking scents.

A young girl in a black shirt came and collected their plates. She gave them both a darting glance. "Would you like to see the dessert menu?"

"Please." Cassandra rubbed her pregnancy bulge again and smiled up at the server. "Bump likes cake."

The server smiled with her mouth, but her eyes remained bored. "I'll be right back."

A commotion by the front door attracted the diners' attention. Wade looked across the low partitions towards the glass frontage. A dark-haired woman wearing a loose-fitting denim jacket pushed in. Around her, people gasped, scrambling away. Wade's eyes widened at seeing the shotgun she carried.

The weapon's dull, grey barrel may have pointed towards the floor, but her attitude oozed determination.

Wade froze in his seat as the woman bulldozed her way past servers and diners without care or concern, heading straight for their table. He had zero doubt she was coming for them. Her eyes locked onto his, unwavering.

Yesterday Pill   Iain Benson

She shoved a patron back into his seat without so much as a glance. The man collapsed backwards, grabbing at the table.

A few steps from them, she raised the gun. Wade tried to tear his eyes away from the vast black holes pointing at him. She wore her dark hair in a short curl; her Middle Eastern features looked on the edge of familiarity like a bit player in a slew of famous movies. She was attractive in a hard-looking way, dressing in camouflage trousers and stout walking boots.

The woman held the gun up to the side and pointed across the crowded restaurant.

Echoing the loud retort left an acrid smell of gunpowder billowing around the shot. The barrels jerked upwards with the blast's power.

She kept her gaze callously fixed on Wade. Uncaring if she hit anybody.

Wade looked at where the shot had gone. Despite the number of people in that direction, the only casualty had been a marble veneer pillar near the far wall. A minor miracle. Pink plaster shedding dust through an angry gouge.

"We have two minutes." Her tone held menace. "To the kitchen, right now, or I will carry on shooting."

Wade looked at Cassandra, her eyes wide, her lips thin.

"Wade?" Cassandra's voice was reedy, watered down, as scared as he was.

"We need to, Cass." Wade got to his feet. The chair with his coat on fell backwards with a clatter, filling the stunned and scared silence in the dining area.

Standing more decorously, Cassandra glared at the intruder.

"Ninety seconds, this way." The woman pointed with the gun's barrel toward the double doors in the far wall.

Wade considered going for the gun, but her gaze snapped back onto him like she read his mind.

Wade entwined his fingers into Cassandra's. Shocked faces watched them scurry across the restaurant. The kitchen's double doors had small portholes, a white and aluminium kitchen visible beyond. A young woman coming through the doors carried two large oval bowls on a black tray piled with pasta. She saw the gun; the tray dropping. The gun-wielding woman pushed the door open and gestured impatiently as the waitress backed away with wide eyes.

Warm garlic smells surrounded them, the sounds of sizzling and cooking; chefs shouting above the background noise.

"Through the window in the far wall." She kept her instructions short, her voice cutting through the commotion.

Above a metalled table, the large window did not look like it opened. He winced as the shotgun fired again, loud in the closed tiled room. Oppressive acrid gunpowder stench overrode the kitchen's warm odours. The glass in the window exploded outward. The retort provided an additional urge to follow instructions.

"I can't climb in these." Cassandra pointed at her shoes.

"There are training shoes in the car in your size," the woman said. "Leave them and your phones here."

Looking somewhat unsure, Cassandra slipped out of her favourite heels. They put their phones on the counter. Wade helped Cassandra onto the table with the woman muttering the lyrics to a song. Wade wondered how unstable she was, forcing a pregnant woman to climb through a broken window.

"Thirty seconds, hurry," the woman urged them with the shotgun barrels. Wade slid across the aluminium table and swung his legs through the window.

The drop of two metres put him on a weed-strewn alley between a white Volvo and the recycling bins for the restaurant. A waft of stale beer from the pub next door assaulted his nose. The Volvo's driver's door and rear passenger door were gaping open. Music from the stereo competed with a perplexing chopping sound of helicopters. Glass crunched under his shoes as he turned to help Cassandra down from the window. He tried to put her down in an area without shards of glass on the broken tarmac.

Yesterday Pill   Iain Benson

"Shall we make a run for it?" she whispered.

The woman landed heavily.

"If you run, you die," she said. "Get in the car. There are sticking plasters on the back seat."

A gesture from the gun prodded them back into action, clambering onto the back seat.

"Ow!" Cassandra climbed in beside Wade, wincing.

Shuddering, a shard of glass protruded from her foot.

Wade examined the wound. "It's superficial."

He found the sticking plasters in a small box on the seat.

The woman took the driver's seat. "You will need seatbelts."

With a lurch, the Volvo roared down the alley, emerging onto a busy street. Opposite the restaurant, coming over a low office block, Wade saw the helicopter sound's source. A trio of black helicopters, searchlights spearing down ahead of them, came in low over the office blocks. They looked like gunships.

Even as he watched, all three had orange bursts of fire from underneath them as they banked off in different directions. White plumes, reflecting from the street lighting, burned through the night sky, flying unerringly at the restaurant.

Almost physical, the explosion reverberated down the concrete canyon. As the Volvo fishtailed into the traffic, orange and red eruptions blossomed in every direction. Additional booms and surges of flames shot into the sky. Wade stared in anguish at where the restaurant behind had been, now a fiery war zone. The sticking plaster hung loosely in his fingers. He could scarcely believe what unfolded before him.

"My name is Anya Dogan," the woman said, turning up the radio as *Jukebox Hero* came on.

Wade could not answer. The car slewed around a corner onto the main road, throwing him sideways. Cassandra crashed into him.

Coughs resonated behind them, making Wade twist to look through the back window. A large blacked-out Range Rover chased them, flanked by motorcycle outriders. As it swerved, Wade glimpsed more vehicles further back. Flashes of light from the closest Range Rover's passenger window made Wade duck.

"They're shooting at us!" Wade found himself breathless. He struggled to process why anybody would destroy a restaurant and chase them in an armed convoy.

Anya pulled the wheel hard to the right, sending Wade and Cassandra falling across the car again.

"You've got a few seconds to get the glass out," Anya announced.

Wade complied, pulling the glass from Cassandra's foot and sticking the plaster on the wound. Gunship helicopters hovered ahead, between a shopping centre and a multistorey carpark. Anya turned a sharp corner down the shopping centre's pedestrian thoroughfare. Behind them, flames flowered where a rocket chewed up the tarmac, the chasing cars swerving around it. Lights from the shops flickered against the Volvo's windows. Anya barely slowed as she avoided small groups of benches and bushes. Fortunately, there were very few pedestrians.

"Duck," Anya said.

Wade thought they were about to go under a bridge, pulling himself down as bullets took out the rear window, holes appearing in the upholstery.

"Are you okay?" Worry filled Wade as he saw the puffs of foam on the driver's seat.

"Kevlar plates," Anya replied. "I also put them behind your seat and on the roof."

With the rear window gone, motorbikes roaring up towards the car growled louder. Anya still sang; something Wade found more disconcerting than the shops flashing past. He reached up and touched the smooth material fastened to the car roof with duct tape.

Sudden silence from Anya curtailed Wade's curiosity. "Brace!"

She slammed on the brakes, spinning the wheel. The Volvo fishtailed, rocking, threatening to flip. Through the passenger window,

Yesterday Pill — Iain Benson

Wade saw an escalator leading up. Too close, the motorcycles' front wheels hit the Volvo's front and rear. The two black-clad cyclists flew from their bikes, arcing over them in perceived slow-motion. Wade didn't have time to see them land, with Anya already slamming the accelerator to head down into a narrow run of indoor shops.

One Range Rover behind them failed the turn, clipping the escalator and flipping up and over, crashing into a coffee stand. It skidded across the tiles on its roof, spinning into a shop window.

Cassandra looked back through the broken window with fear etched into the wrinkles around her eyes.

The remaining Range Rovers and motorbikes negotiated the corner, resuming pursuit.

Anya continued to mutter the words to *Jukebox Hero* as they bounced down a small flight of stairs and onto a road lit from the streetlamps. Wade peered through the seats through the front window. A traffic-light controlled junction lay up ahead, vehicles streaming across from both sides. A small white van and a car waited for the lights to change. The crazy woman increased their speed. At the last moment, she threw the car into the oncoming traffic lane. With the red from the traffic light still fading, and no regard for other road users, Anya flew across the junction.

Wade's head snapped around, looking at their near miss. Their pursuers reached the unction as the van set off. It turned across the path of a motorbike. The crash followed them, even as they vanished from sight.

"Hold on," Anya said.

Cassandra and Wade exchanged terrified looks, but gripped the seats in front of them as she slammed on the brakes.

Two missiles punched into the tarmac, throwing up a mushroom of concrete, dirt, and dust. The windows in the buildings on either side shattered into flashing diamond shards. Angling to the left, Anya continued hurtling, bursting through the smoke and dust, leaving swirling trails etched in the air. Almost invisible through the miasma, the road doglegged to the right. Anya barely slowed to round the corner. A narrow alleyway loomed from the fog. Anya had lined the car up perfectly to squeeze through, the sound of litter crackling under the tyres.

The two remaining motorbikes followed, but the Range Rovers veered off, forced to take a different route.

Anya slowed slightly, singing a line through gritted teeth.

A car shot past the alley. Immediately after it passed, Anya erupted from the back street, spinning the wheel to join the traffic across the road.

Wade heard car brakes squealing, left in Anya's wake. They missed oncoming cars by a hair's width. Motorcycles behind them were less lucky, crashing into slewing vehicles. Anya weaved through the traffic with sickening lurches.

"You know this road well." Wade finally clicked his seatbelt fastened.

"I've driven it a lot," Anya replied. "Cassandra, when I stop in a minute, stay in the car, or a van will kill you."

Wade looked at Cassandra; she had the guilty look of when she'd snuck some secret chocolate she thought he didn't know about. She glanced at him. He minutely shook his head. Less than five minutes had passed since Anya took them from the restaurant. She had to know why helicopters, motorbikes and Range Rovers chased them. With guns.

Why had she specifically rescued Wade and Cassandra?

Seatbelt cutting into him as the Volvo screeched to a halt, Wade gasped, feeling pain across his chest. Twin blacked-out Range Rovers flashed past. A van sped past Cassandra's side, its horn blaring. It swerved, smashing into one pursuer as it, too, slid to a halt. Already reversing, Anya spun the wheel and changed gears to send them heading back the way they had come.

The heat and noise from the newly formed crater scorched the side of Wade's face, dragging his thoughts away from Anya's erratic driving. Had she not swerved, the missiles would have destroyed them along with the road. He winced as the noise pounded on his eardrums with a physical force through the glass.

Yesterday Pill   Iain Benson

The rockets left a scar in the road behind. Debris rained on the roof with booming crashes.

"Wade!" Cassandra's pitch was high.

"Stay down." Unconcerned by the explosion, Anya seemed blasé.

Wade and Cassandra kept low as more bullets rattled across the car. He risked a glance backwards. A dark-haired man with a scarf across his face leaned from the window with an assault rifle.

They headed down a dual carriageway.

Tyres squealed as they bounced over the central reservation, Anya singing along to the last verse of *Jukebox Hero*. Metal scraping added a counterpoint to her words.

A truck sideswiped the Range Rover directly behind them. Anya had ignored the lorry, despite the long low horn that had sounded on their rapid approach. Glass and metal crumpled and cracked as the truck pushed the wreckage dozens of metres down the road. Anya drove in a straight line down the grassy bank towards a playing field. Her angle perfectly aligned with a low fence between the park and a road. The three remaining Range Rovers managed the slope more efficiently, the four-by-fours eating up the distance, closing them down.

The metal railing crashed aside, a front headlight extinguished, but they were back on the road. Anya took advantage, accelerating hard enough to throw them back into their seats. Suburban houses, lights leaking around the curtains, flashed by. Wade felt anxiety at Anya's speed through an area where there would be more pedestrians. Onlookers were the least of their problems as bullets raked the roof with the sound of clattering metal. Wade glanced up, seeing the helicopter gunships keeping pace with their crazy speed through a housing estate.

Anya ignored them. More intent on grappling with the wheel as she pushed the Volvo past the limits of its engineering. They flashed under an underpass, the dual carriageway above them, heading into the city centre with its cramped together high-rises. Wade realised her plan. She would lose the helicopters amid the taller buildings. If the gunships could see the

Volvo, they could tell the pursuers in the Range Rovers their position.

It worked. Wade watched the helicopters peel up and away as the office blocks rapidly gained height. Their route created an additional problem. Traffic became Anya's major obstacle. Wade still did not know why their attackers had targeted them, nor why Anya felt she had to risk her own life to protect them. As Anya pulled the Volvo around a tight bend, avoiding a taxi by inches, Wade thought it was an inappropriate time to get answers. There were more pressing issues.

Different music came from the car speakers, with Anya now singing along to Bon Jovi.

Anya sped at high speed through red traffic lights. On both sides, the screech of brakes echoed off the buildings. Wade briefly heard crunching as vehicles piled into one another, but Anya left them behind, heading under a railway bridge. Bullets blew out the windscreen of a car coming the other way, sending it crashing into a department store. Pedestrians, watching wide-eyed in horror as the vehicles hurtled past. Wade knew how they felt. Inside his head, thousands of thoughts collided like the vehicles at the junctions they crossed. Anya clipped a bus with the back end of her Volvo, spinning them around. The glass from the passenger window by Wade smashed down in glistening diamond raindrops.

He kept his grip on the door handle as Anya hurtled down a side street. He vaguely recognised the area they flashed past. At this speed, they would leave the city high-rises in seconds.

A juxtaposition of fear and self-congratulation half-formed as they emerged from the offices. High-rise apartments still provided some cover. Ahead lay a sprawling supermarket.

Anya bumped through the exit to the supermarket carpark. Sparks flew from the undercarriage as they grated over a speed bump. The Range Rovers instantly gained ground. She sped past parked cars, cutting through gaps in the parking bays. Wade watched as their pursuers careered off parked cars with crunching, ripping metal. Anya exited through the fuel court, suspension howling with a hard turn through the carwash and out

Yesterday Pill   Iain Benson

onto the road.

The leading Range Rover crashed into the mechanism inside, blocking the exit, forcing the remaining two to veer away.

"Who are you?" Wade asked.

"Not yet," Anya replied. "We'll get to all that soon."

Townhouses replaced the high-rise blocks.

Anya surprised Wade yet again by pulling into a garage under a three-storey yellow brick house. She killed the lights.

"Are we here?" Cassandra looked pale in the little light filtering in through the shattered rear window.

"No," Anya said. "Stay in the car."

A Range Rover drove past. Anya started counting.

"What are you waiting for?" Wade was confused, scared and curious simultaneously.

Anya counted to fifteen. The Range Rover came back past. "That."

She started counting to fifteen again. Finally, she turned the engine on and pulled back onto the street.

"How did you know they'd turn around?" Wade asked.

"It's a dead-end," she replied, simply.

Up ahead, the Range Rover turned the corner away from them. She drove sensibly and turned the other way onto the end road. After another corner, she floored the accelerator. The car roared down the street, flashing from the estate and back onto the dual carriageway.

"Listen carefully." Anya kept her eyes on the road as they approached the motorway junction. "Cassandra, put the shoes on now. When I stop, leave the car. After you see the blue van, run as fast as you can to the central reservation. Wait for the black car, then run across the motorway."

"Where are you stopping?" Cassandra asked. "What's going on?"

Instead of answering, Anya pulled onto the motorway, taking the Volvo up past a hundred. She wove around the other road users with almost preternatural reactions. Before she could have known, she swerved to avoid a hatchback pulling into her lane without indicating. The motorway curved up and down, underneath a complicated, multilevel junction. Anya cut across the carriageway onto the hard shoulder, skidding to a stop.

"Blue van. Black car. Run" Anya climbed out. She nodded at two vans before sprinting, finding seemingly a clear corridor between the high-speed vehicles.

"What do we do?" Cassandra's voice was breathless as she contorted to put on the training shoes.

"I don't know." Wade sighed to relieve a built-up tension. "I think we should do what she said."

"Run across a motorway?" Cassandra fastened the laces.

"I am curious," Wade admitted. "I have a lot of questions."

"But the cars," she said.

Wade left the vehicle to stand on a chilly hard shoulder. He wished he'd brought his coat. "She said after the blue van."

Cassandra shook her head, looking pale. Wade helped her down.

Light traffic at such a late hour did not make the upcoming task less fraught. Wade felt trepidation in every rapid beat of his pulse. A black BMW hurtled past, close enough to tug their clothes. Noise preceded it, with silence in front of them and a receding scream. Less traffic seemed to increase the speed in the vehicles that remained.

"Is that the van?" Cassandra pointed.

A blue Transit approached. Wade squeezed her hand. "Ready?"

"No," she said. "But yes."

Wind from the van passing almost sucked them onto the road by itself, aided by leaning forward, ready to sprint. Wade made sure he stayed behind Cassandra as they raced to the central reservation. He helped her over the moulded metal crash barrier, her pregnancy hindering her mobility. The weeds and grass intrigued Wade, somehow growing on the motorway surface where a small amount of dust and dirt collected. He pushed the errant thoughts away and swung his legs over the barrier for the other carriageway. Again, he helped Cassandra over, struggling in her

Yesterday Pill   Iain Benson

expensive white dress, the baby bump swelling and stretching the satin. A long smear of black appeared where her leg rubbed the barrier.

Her feet barely touched the tarmac before a black saloon car blasted past with a swirl of air. Holding Cassandra's hand, Wade ran across the three lanes towards a dark blue Range Rover.

Anya had turned the engine on, the rear doors open. With Cassandra safely inside, Wade ran around the car. As he climbed in, Wade looked over the seat into the boot. Three large suitcases filled the space. Wade recognised two as his and Cassandra's. They'd bought them the year before for a holiday to Scotland that never happened. Another puzzle piece in a mounting mountain of them. Anya pulled onto the carriageway before they'd finished fastening their seatbelts.

As they left the flyover's shadow, Wade saw two black helicopter gunships flying low over the motorway, pulling up to go over the bridges.

"How did they know which way you went?" Cassandra twisted her neck to follow them through the back window.

"I'm guessing they checked CCTV or something." Anya sounded relaxed. "There are no cameras for a few miles in either direction of those bridges. They won't realise we've stopped for some time yet. It will keep them off our tail until they can work out where we are. Which they will."

"Aren't these our cases?" Cassandra gestured over her shoulder at the suitcases.

"The top two are," Anya replied. "I've brought as much as I could."

"You're an excellent driver," Wade told Anya, hoping to ingratiate himself with her and find out what was going on.

"Practice," Anya muttered. "An incredible amount of practice."

"Where are we heading?" Cassandra's question, Wade realised, was pertinent.

"We're leaving the country." Anya's tone held a certainty of having weighed all the options and concluded there were no alternatives.

Wade had an instant objection. "I don't have a passport. The government never worked out who I was, so I'm stuck in the UK."

Despite how important Wade considered this, Anya ignored it. "The moment you used a passport with your details on, they would know where you are. I've had counterfeits made."

"Forgeries?" Wade was unsure. He had always believed modern passports were unforgeable.

"They are perfect." Anya's tone was reassuring, but Wade had his doubts.

"I don't want to go to another country," Cassandra said.

Wade had to agree. "We have a life here."

"You had a life," Anya corrected. "Staying here will mean you die. They have found you now and will not stop until you are dead."

"You cannot possibly know that." Cassandra shifted uncomfortably in her seat and looked through the window. Wade knew her signs of suppressed anger.

"I'm sure you could live in a tent in the woods," Anya said. "Drop off the grid. Live your lives growing carrots and catching rabbits. Eventually, you will slip up. They will know where you are."

"Now you're not driving through supermarkets," Wade said, leaning forward. "Who are *they*? Why do they want us dead?"

"They are Paladin," Anya said. "They are a multinational company employed by governments for security and anti-terrorism."

"I'm nobody," Wade told her. He was returning to the opinion that Anya was almost as dangerous as the pursuers.

"Not you." Anya sounded cross. "Cassandra."

"Me?" Cassandra made a scoffing noise. "I'm a lecturer!"

"Yes. In physics." Anya clarified, as though this explained her point.

"Everything I do is academic." Cassandra had stopped watching the scenery. Her face etched with a mix of fear, curiosity, and incomprehension. "I cover atomic forces with bored students."

"All we know is." Anya looked over her shoulder at Wade. "All I know is they are looking for you. I've kept one step ahead, but I always knew that this day would come. Eventually."

"I've not been hiding!" Cassandra sounded confused. "Wade's the one with amnesia, not me!"

But Anya continued, getting more and more irate as she went. "We have one shot of escaping the country while they're scrambling around looking for us. If we wait, you will die. So, if you don't mind, I would appreciate a little fucking gratitude. I have just saved your life. Again."

"We appreciate it," Wade said. "If it's any consolation, I agree. We need to leave the UK and go wherever this Paladin has their headquarters."

"Absolutely," Anya said, surprising him.

"You said they were hunting us," Wade said, the ideas tumbling into place in his head, carrying on his explanation even though she had agreed. "If we find out why, maybe we can get them to stop."

Anya was about to say something, but stopped and stared through the front windscreen for several minutes. Confusion raged through Wade. He could not fathom the evening's events. Paladin had destroyed the restaurant with missiles fired from attack helicopters, whilst Anya had driven them to safety. Her reasons remained a mystery Wade needed time to crack. Cassandra took Wade's hands in hers. He looked into her eyes and saw the questions, but he had no answers.

Anya eventually spoke. "We need to go to Israel. But not for your reasons."

"Why Israel?" Cassandra asked.

"It's their headquarters." Anya sound as though she believed it was common knowledge.

"When we get there, we find out why they want us dead." Wade reiterated his earlier point. "When we know, we can tell them why it's wrong and they'll leave us alone."

"No. We need to find evidence Paladin was behind the attack at the restaurant." Anya's fingers whitened as she tightened the wheel. "People died. We can use proof to keep them at bay."

Wade's brows furrowed. It seemed the more aggressive strategy.

"If you know it's Paladin, just tell the police," Cassandra said.

"They didn't smuggle three gunship helicopters into the country," Cassandra snapped. "Your government already knows Paladin is here and why. Do you think an absence of police is mere coincidence?"

"Will getting proof help?" Cassandra snapped back. "I can't see how."

"Because we'd give the proof to news outlets to put all over the internet. Paladin always avoids the spotlight." As Anya spoke, Wade tried to place her accent but struggled.

"I'd rather they stopped through choice," Wade said. "Desire is more permanent than fear."

"You've always been a dreamer," Anya said.

That puzzled Wade. Did Anya know him before his seizure? "Do we know each other?"

Anya looked in the rear-view mirror. Wade couldn't see her, so she had to be looking at Cassandra, staring at the trees through the window. "You have to remember, this might be the first time you two have met me, but I've known you both for a lot longer."

"That sounds creepy," Wade told her. "Not to mention highly suspicious."

"What can I say?" Anya released the wheel to make an expansive gesture. "I kept Cassandra away from Paladin's attention. I did a damn good job of it until tonight."

Cassandra tutted at hearing her name.

Their abductor seemed unwilling to expand any further. A surly silence enveloped the car's interior.

Wade ran his fingers over his chin, feeling the stubble emerging. He looked out of his window, seeing his reflection more than the countryside beyond, wondering what Anya kept to herself. Wade knew Anya knew more. The longer he spent around her, the more convinced he was that there was a much bigger picture, one she was unwilling to expand on. At least with Cassandra present.

2

Miles passed as the Range Rover thrummed along, silence reigning inside the cab. Wheels on tarmac and the electric engine lulled Wade to the edge of sleep. Heavy breathing from Cassandra told him she'd nodded off. He shook his head, forcing himself awake.

"You must be tired," he said softly to Anya.

"Shattered," she replied. "I've got a cheap hotel booked near the ferry. We'll be there shortly."

"We're not getting straight on the ferry?"

"The earliest ferry I could get was tomorrow at ten," Anya said. "We couldn't make anything earlier."

"We'll have to hope Paladin isn't watching the ports."

Anya shrugged. "They will think of that. I wouldn't put it past them to sink a ferry. I'm hoping we are staying one step ahead, though."

"You're sure about the passports?"

Anya nodded. "They were fifteen grand each. The forger has them on the passport databases with our biometrics."

"I'm not going to ask how you got our biometrics." Wade wondered where the money came from. "It's a lot of money."

Anya shrugged. "Don't worry. We're well funded."

Wade had assumed Anya had stolen the Range Rover and Volvo. He frowned. There was a subtext he could feel in Anya's words. A shadow of a memory of a memory. His thoughts drifted, incoherent.

A change of scenery outside the window jerked Wade back to wakefulness. They came down a slip-road and through a town, shortly reaching the carpark of a redbrick hotel.

"Cass." Wade stroked her arm and woke her.

Anya pulled a small suitcase off the front seat. "Wait here. I need to keep you off camera."

The silent and still night air had a distinct chill, feeling oppressive.

Iain Benson   Yesterday Pill

Wade watched Anya through the large glass doors as she retrieved a key card using her phone from the automated reception.

She returned and hooked the car up to charge. Taken through the entrance, they skirted reception and went up a floor. Their room's only distinguishing feature, the room's number. A generic hotel room, with a double bed.

"One room only," she said. "It's less conspicuous to get a double room. Besides, we won't all be sleeping at the same time."

Wade found the room quite basic, with standardised furniture bolted to the wall and ubiquitous necessities. By the sink, he found a plastic beaker.

"Do either of you want water?"

"Please," Cassandra replied. Wade had a long drink first before refilling the beaker and passing it to Cassandra. Anya tilted her head slightly. Wade assumed she also wanted something and filled the other cup.

Wade sat on the bed. "What is the plan if we're not all sleeping at the same time?"

"We need one person to be awake and keep an eye out for Paladin." Anya stood beside the narrow window. She opened the curtain slightly with a single finger, looking down at the carpark.

"I'll go first," Wade said. "Cass, you're still asleep, and how you have stayed awake this long, Anya, I'll never know."

"Caffeine tablets and energy drinks." Anya kicked off her shoes and lay on the bed. "Wake me in three hours."

"I'm taking the last watch, then?" Cassandra also lay on the bed. "Fine by me."

Wade envied Cassandra's ability to fall asleep anywhere quickly. She referred to it as her superpower. Within moments of kicking off her shoes and lying down, her breathing changed. Sighing, Wade took up the position by the window, slightly parting the curtains. He had an excellent vantage point for the carpark entrance. Tiredness ached into his bones, but standing helped him stay awake.

Yesterday Pill   Iain Benson

"Get a coffee or something." Anya leant back against the padded headboard.

The suggestion gave Wade an immediate purpose. He noticed only two sachets of coffee. Although he could easily have had both, he took one and waited for the kettle to boil, eschewing the plastic pots of milk. He watched the carpark while he waited. The coffee smelled stale as he poured in water, but he took it to the window and resumed his watch. Cassandra's breathing deepened; the slight snore she refused to admit to.

"You know who I am," Wade said, not turning to look at Anya. "Who I was before my seizure."

There was a sigh from Anya. "Do we have to do this now?"

"Unless you can give me an acceptable reason not to."

Anya rubbed her forehead. Her voice dropped to a whisper. "I am exhausted. There's a long day ahead of us tomorrow. Any explanation must happen when Cassandra is not likely to hear."

"She's asleep."

Anya gave a crooked smile Wade found endearing. "Somewhere I'd like to be."

Wade wanted to press but realised the futility. He made a half-hearted gesture.

"Are you sure you want me to wake you in three hours?"

"Yes." She closed her eyes. "Or if you see dark tinted windows driving into the carpark."

Wade nodded. "Good night."

Within a few minutes, both the women on the bed were breathing deeply. Wade sipped coffee and waited by the window, looking into the carpark. His thoughts jumbled, processing what Anya had revealed. She could only explain while Cassandra was absent. It told him she knew more than she'd provided. Wade's imagination went wild with speculation. Conjecture and guesswork could wait. He needed concentration on the task at hand. Not that anyone could work out where they were.

Wade's reflection partially obscured the carpark until he twitched the curtain a little to cut out the air conditioning light. He became hyper-focused on what little movement there was outside. The late-night drunk walker kept him entertained for several minutes with a staggered, jerking walk until they vanished behind a hedge. After checking his watch, he realised it was finally time to wake Anya. The feeling of tiredness had set into his eye sockets. He felt stiff.

Anya awoke with a start, stifling a yawn.

"That was three hours?" She sounded tired. "Did you leave any coffee?"

"I did."

Cassandra stirred, grunting and snuffling. Wade lay next to her, closing his eyes, listening to the kettle boil.

"We have to go." Anya's tone was urgent. "Wake Cassandra up."

Wade knew he hadn't fallen asleep; the kettle was still boiling. "I thought we had time for sleep."

"We did." Anya picked up the bag. "Now we don't."

Wade shook Cassandra awake.

"Is it morning?" she asked, blinking, looking stiff.

"No," Cassandra replied. "We are going. Paladin is coming."

Wade pulled back the curtain. The dark carpark looked the same as when he'd watched. "How do you know?"

"Doesn't matter." Cassandra opened the door, giving them an impatient look. "We need to leave now."

As they headed down the quiet but brightly lit corridor, Anya frantically swiped through her phone, muttering. Wade pushed open the door ahead of them to prevent Anya from walking into it.

"You'll have to drive." Anya barely glanced in Wade's direction. "I'll tell you where to go while I find us a boat."

"I can't drive," Wade replied.

They passed through the reception, the cold pre-dawn air scorching Wade's nostrils as they crossed to the car.

"Yes, you can." Anya broke off from swiping the phone.

Yesterday Pill   Iain Benson

"I may have been able to before my seizure," Wade told her, thinking it was a way to get information from her. "But I can't remember anything from then."

"Muscle memory." Anya opened the doors with her key fob and climbed into the front passenger seat. "I have to get a different ferry to anywhere."

Cassandra paused by the rear door. "Do you think you can drive?"

Wade shrugged. "She seems to think so. I think she knew me before my seizure."

Cassandra rubbed her neck. "When she realises you can't, she'll have to drive."

Wade nodded and closed the door for her when she struggled to reach the handle. He sat behind the wheel, running the plastic under his fingers, seeing if it felt in any way familiar.

"The start button is there." Anya pointed.

Wade pressed the button. He felt he had seen enough television to know the theory: an accelerator and brake. He pushed the button, but nothing happened. "Maybe I don't know what to do."

Anya sighed and knocked the lever on the dash down. "Put it in neutral."

Wade felt she had told him off, but buried the feeling. He pressed the button, watching the dash light up this time. The headlights came on, and the engine made a purring noise. He slightly depressed the accelerator. Somehow, his arms and legs *knew* what to do.

"Don't think about what you're doing," Anya told him. "Just drive. Turn right when you leave the carpark."

Wade felt an exhilaration, a connection to his life before his seizure. The steering wheel slipped with familiarity under his fingers.

"Pull over here," Anya suddenly announced, pointing at a row of shops with parking bays.

Wade wondered if she now wanted to drive. He stopped between a tiny hatchback and a blue van.

"Turn off the lights." Anya turned off her phone.

Wade turned off the engine. "Why?"

Seconds later, five Range Rovers with blacked-out windows, their lights off, swept through the street back the way they had come.

"Do you want to drive or sleep?" Anya asked. "I have us booked onto a boat now. I can drive again. If you like?"

The idea of sleep appealed more than the sensations of recovering a lost skill. Wade knew he'd get another chance. Sleep-deprived eyes scanned his face. "Do you need more sleep?"

"I do." She gave him a faint smile.

"Then I'll drive." Wade started the car up again and continued down the dark street.

Anya nestled her phone into a holder on the dash and connected the charger. "Follow the blue line."

In the rear-view mirror, Wade looked at Cassandra sleeping, her head propped on her folded coat. Anya rolled up her jacket and lay into the door frame.

Bone-aching exhaustion forced Wade to concentrate on driving, but a connection to before allowed a small part to enjoy it. He rolled his shoulders to ease the tension. It became more challenging when they got onto the motorway. A few times, he had to shake his head to keep sleep at bay. He kept his window closed. The noise it would make might disrupt Cassandra's and Anya's sleep. The rumble strip sounded as he looked for the air blower controls, briefly taking his eyes from the road, making him glad the journey was only an hour. Traffic built up as he neared Poole. The dark road coming into the town illuminated by a long stream of cars already leaving. Ahead, he could see brake lights at a roundabout; the sudden change of traffic jerked Wade back to full alertness, slowing and joining a small queue. Wade felt he had passed his first driving test, even if it was a relatively simple turning. His feet knew how to edge forward and swing onto another dark street.

Further roundabouts kept Wade alert. As they emerged from the

Yesterday Pill   Iain Benson

trees along a long straight road, the sky became tinged yellow by an unrisen sun. Tiredness combined with the view unfolding before him. He braked sharply as the car ahead stopped suddenly, combined with his fatigue.

The jerk woke the two women up. Cassandra was groggy, but Anya came instantly alert.

She looked at the phone. "We're nearly there."

Traffic continued to increase as they crossed a metal bridge, the housing replaced with warehousing.

"Big yachts." Cassandra's yawn was contagious.

"Shame we can't steal one." Anya sounded sincere. Wade glanced at her, deciding she was earnest.

"Because Paladin will catch us?" Wade asked.

Anya shook her head. "If Paladin figures it out, they will have zero qualms about sinking us. At least on a ferry, they might think twice and give us a chance to escape."

They reached the boarding queue for the ferry. The sign by a customs booth gave their destination.

"Jersey?" A surprised tone raised Wade's voice an octave.

"From there, we'll get another ferry to France."

Wade didn't care. He felt more tired than he had ever felt before. The ache ran across his shoulders and down his spine; his hips hurt.

"Any chance you could drive us onto the ferry? I'm not that confident."

While they were stationary in the traffic, Wade and Anya swapped places. Wade closed the door, fastened his seatbelt, and closed his eyes. They snapped open at the loud clanking noise as the Range Rover passed over the boarding ramp. Wade checked the time. He'd briefly closed his eyes and slept for an hour. Anya plugged into the ship's charging port and grabbed her bag off the back seat while Wade helped Cassandra down. The deck smelled of seawater, oil and car fumes from those vehicles still running on fossil fuels.

"I've never been on a ferry," Cassandra said.

"I was going to say the same." Wade gave a slight smile. "However, I wouldn't have thought I could drive, so I may well have done. We'll have to ask Anya if I've ever been on a ferry."

"Before today, you have never been on a ferry," Anya said without looking at them.

Wade shrugged as he and Cassandra followed the willow-waisted woman up the narrow steps to the passenger deck. Behind them, Wade heard the car deck closing. He looked back at other people climbing up behind him, feeling a suspicion that any of them could be Paladin. He stepped over a lip onto the passenger deck, onto a short narrow corridor that opened into a cafeteria filled with wooden tables. Anya put her bag down on a table, Cassandra sliding with difficulty into the moulded seat.

"Did you pack a book?" Cassandra asked.

Anya opened her bag. She pulled out a thick historical romance novel.

"Here you are."

When he saw the red leather bookmark jutting from the pages, Wade realised Anya had brought Cassandra's book from her bedside table. Cassandra recognised it as well.

"This is off my bedside table."

"I have your lavender oil as well," Anya said, rummaging. "I think you only had your deodorant on your table, Wade."

"And a light," Wade said.

"How did you get into our house?" Cassandra asked.

Anya reached into her pocket and pulled out a bunch of keys. She put them on the table. "Through the front door."

Wade picked the keys up and flicked through them. He spotted keys for the porch and front doors, the back door, the garage.

He shook his head and skidded them back across the table. "I need a coffee."

"We need to stick together," Anya said.

"We're on a boat," Wade told her. "The café is on the other side of that wall. I need caffeine."

"I don't want you out of my sight," Anya said.

"It's Cass you're protecting." Wade checked his wallet and found some cash. "What would you like?"

Anya looked to be debating with herself. "Large Americano with an extra shot, please."

"Cass?"

"Bump hates caffeine," she said. "But I feel groggy. Coffee."

The queue of people snaked around a partition of vertical wooden slats. He lost sight of Anya as he entered the cafeteria area, a semicircle of chrome serving tables. Around the edge, bright lights reflected off shining lids. The smells of cooking breakfasts swirled around, making Wade's stomach grumble. It reminded him he hadn't finished eating the night before. He joined the food queue, passing by the boxed cereals. As he slid the tray along the metal runners, somebody dropped a plate behind him in the queue. Wade's head snapped around, his focus zeroing in on the smashed crockery.

As his heart returned to normal, anxiety gnawed at his stomach, giving him jitters. Alone in the queue, Paladin could target him. He tried to calm himself, pushing the tray along whilst the couple directly ahead chatted about the exorbitant pricing. On the way around, Wade grabbed three bacon rolls and a variety of condiments. He realised he didn't know if Anya was a vegetarian.

"More for me," he muttered to himself.

Three large mugs took turns under the coffee machine. Two black and a mocha. He paid and returned to the table, precariously balancing the plates and cups on the tray. Every pitch and yaw made by the boat threatened his balance.

"I'm out of cash." He put the tray down. "Luckily, I didn't want anything else."

"You read my mind." Cassandra grabbed a roll. "I'm starving."

"You're not veggie, are you, Anya?"

Anya shook her head and took a roll. "Thanks. I can't remember the last time I ate."

Wade squeezed into the narrow gap. For a moment, he wondered why they had to bolt the tables and chairs down until he remembered he was on a boat. In the corner of his eye, the horizon through the window sat at odds with the ship's interior. He wondered if the anxiety would turn into nausea. With a sniff, the bacon aroma reawakened his hunger. He ate before he could change his mind.

"How did you get our keys?" Wade asked.

"I took them out of Cassandra's handbag on a night out." Her tone made it sound like she found this normal behaviour.

"What?" Cassandra glared at Anya.

"I put them back." Anya shrugged.

"Not the point."

"I needed them to get your stuff." Anya sounded a little contrite. Her tone firmed. "You would wear those clothes forever if I hadn't."

Wade squeezed Cassandra's thigh, getting his hand caressed in return. The moment's serenity jarred with the hectic previous ten hours. Land disappeared from the window, replaced by a choppy sea. The ship's movement left Wade feeling nauseous.

"You need to look at the horizon," Cassandra told him.

Wade nodded and finished his coffee. "I'm going on deck."

"This staying together is not working so well." Anya sounded annoyed.

"I'd quite like to go on deck as well." Cassandra squeezed Wade's hand. "The engine thrumming is making Bump feel sick. I could do with some fresh air."

Anya drained her coffee and slid out from under the table. "Come on, then."

Cassandra's baby bump made sliding through the narrow gap uncomfortable. Wade sympathetically grimaced with each wince on her face. Despite the tray with plates and mugs on the table, new occupants

Yesterday Pill   Iain Benson

immediately slid into their place. Anya glanced at the family, sighed, and crossed the crowded space, heading to the prow. Away from the galley, the corridors narrowed. Wade glanced in on shops as they passed. The largest billed as duty-free.

They accessed the prow through a metal door with a trip hazard lip.

"Not wheelchair friendly." Cassandra pointed at the lip.

Wade breathed in deeply as he stepped onto the green painted deck. Walls painted white and red reached up to chest height. At the front, holes in the hull showed the sea ahead of them. Spray filled the air, coating his skin. It smelled of salt. It reminded him of his only visit to the sea. The only time he could remember seeing the sea, he corrected himself. The tang resuscitated him more than coffee. Cassandra took a seat on a bench by the bulkhead, facing forward. She closed her eyes and tilted her head back, a slight smile creasing the corners of her lips.

Wade took the seat next to her, their fingers entwined. Wind whipping her short hair, Anya leant on a rail. She turned and looked at them.

"I'm going to get some answers," Wade told Cassandra, disentangling his fingers.

With a dismissive glance at Cassandra, Anya shook her head. "I'm not telling you anything."

Wade leaned on the hull and looked out across the choppy sea to the horizon. He fancied he could see land. It was probably cloud. "Why not?"

"You'll tell Cassandra."

Wade considered that. It was probably true. "We don't have any secrets."

"All you need to know is that I protect Cassandra."

"MI5?"

Anya laughed. "No."

Wade thought about the driving and a few statements Anya had made. "But you knew me before my seizure?"

Anya turned and looked out over the sea. "Do you think that's Jersey or cloud?"

"Cloud," Wade replied. They watched for a few moments. Eventually, he unloaded his thoughts. "I have no memory of life before my seizure. Or if my name is Wade. The only possession I had on me when Cassandra found me was my signet ring. Etched inside the word Wade. Is it my name? I've found no connection with my past. And I've looked My first memory was Cassandra bending over me in the street. Can you imagine how that feels?"

Emotion clogged Wade's throat as he poured his past out onto Anya, effectively a stranger. He saw Anya's head turn towards him but forced himself to continue looking forwards. She was biting the corner of her top lip.

She narrowed her eyes. "Your name is Wade."

Wade smiled at her. "That wasn't too difficult, was it?"

She gave her head a barely perceptible shake. "If I told you everything, the repercussions would be huge."

"I'm sure she could handle it," Wade said. "She's a strong woman."

"It's not her I'm worried about," Cassandra whispered. "I cannot tell you anymore without risking everything we've already worked for."

She sounded pensive. Wade wondered just what had her so worried. Just who did Anya think Cassandra was? Wade suddenly wondered who Cassandra was.

"She's a lecturer." Wade's mind was racing. "Is one of her students important? No, you knew me before my seizure, so you've been watching for over five years. One of her research projects?"

"I'm not telling you," Anya reiterated. "I've said too much. No doubt you're already working through every permutation."

She knew him well. "I have so many questions."

She raised her eyebrows at him before returning to looking at the horizon. "I can't answer any of them. If there is any other choice, I cannot risk you telling Cassandra."

Wade looked back at Cassandra. She gave a little wave. Wade returned to sit next to her.

"What did you learn?"

Wade paused before speaking. "She knew me before. Wade is my name."

Cassandra nodded. "Why is she protecting us?"

Wade looked at Anya, staring at them with intensity. "She won't expand. I don't think she wanted to tell me what she did."

"Why?" Cassandra sounded almost as frustrated as Wade.

"She wouldn't say that either." Frustration threatened to boil over inside him.

Cassandra propped her elbow on her knee and leaned her chin on her hand. "She knew you before, but she can't say why she's protecting us?"

Wade shrugged. "I guess you're important enough to somebody. They're just not letting us know why."

Cassandra did her hip wiggle to get off the low bench and strode over to Anya. Wade had a sinking feeling and followed.

"Who the hell are you? Why are you protecting me?" Cassandra's pitch was almost a shriek.

Anya spread her hands and shrugged. "As I told Wade, I can't say."

"What would you do if I climbed over the edge of this boat and jumped into the sea?"

"I'd ask you not to," Anya replied, checking her watch. "I can't stop you from doing that, but I'd prefer it if you didn't."

Cassandra placed both her hands on the metal hull. Wade could almost believe she would jump, just to test Anya's resolve. "Cass!"

She took her hands off. "I wasn't going to."

"There is another deck down there, anyway," Anya said. "About three metres down. You'd survive, but your baby might not."

Cassandra's hands automatically went to her bump. She had the good grace to look a little abashed. Wade saw the move as a cynical

Iain Benson   Yesterday Pill

controlling move from Anya.

"A little uncalled for, Anya," Wade told her.

She shot him a stern glance. "We can't all be improvisers. Some of us have to plan what happens."

Anya glanced at her watch again.

"Do you have to be somewhere?" Cassandra asked with a touch of acid in her tone.

"We do." Anya brushed past them. "Try to keep up."

Cassandra shared a confused glance with Wade before following Anya. He shrugged and followed them both back into the interior. Anya was already heading into a chemist and a beauty shop. She seemed to know exactly where she was going, taking a pair of sunglasses and a bottle of nail polish remover to the counter, leaving the exact cash. In under two minutes, Anya returned.

"Let's keep going." Anya led by example, turning, heading past the cabins. Wade watched as she slipped past a cleaner who had opened a room.

"Sorry," Anya said to the cleaner, lifting a security pass from the cleaner's pocket. As she squeezed past the cart, she lifted out a white bottle with a trigger spray.

Every seat in the cafeteria had occupants. Families, couples, and singles, reading, chatting, or playing video consoles for the last half an hour onboard. Cassandra and Wade struggled to keep up with Anya as she took a curving path through the seating. Wade felt he could almost predict the scene as it unfolded: The woman with the pram; the man with a tray, hurrying back to his table; the ship's motion. It all combined. The tray flew as both the man and woman tumbled to the ground, scattering belongings around table legs. Passengers tried to help, scrabbling around to help retrieve the fallen items.

Anya's timing was impeccable. She reached the carnage a second after it began and helped pick up some items. It allowed Wade to catch up. He passed a child's counting toy to the woman with the pram.

Yesterday Pill   Iain Benson

Wade pointed under a table. "I think there's a book under the table."

A young girl at that table slithered underneath and passed the book out. Wade handed it up to the mother.

"Is he okay?" Looking into the pram, a soft smile lit up Cassandra's face.

The mother looked to the heavens. "At the moment. When are you due?"

"February." Cassandra rubbed her bump, still smiling. "He's lovely."

"You wouldn't say that if you're in the car with him." The woman shook her head. "Nothing but tears the entire way here. The moment the boat sets off: pow, asleep."

Cassandra chuckled.

Anya had her hands on her hips. "Cassandra. We must go. Now."

Cassandra gave an apologetic shrug at the mother and ran the back of her fingers across the baby's sleeping cheek.

Wade caught Anya's sleeve. "What's going on?"

"They're waiting at the port." Anya did not need to specify who was waiting at the port.

Wade nodded. Holding Cassandra's hand, he followed Anya back down a corridor to the door they had come up through. A security access pad prevented the door from being opened. Anya used the stolen cleaner's card to access the door.

Anya impatiently gestured. "We can't leave it open. It'll alert the crew."

Wade clattered down the metal steps first, with Cassandra close behind. The light dimmed as the door closed behind him as Wade emerged onto the car deck, the vehicles all closely packed and fastened in place. Over the far side by the hanging cargo nets, deckhands in luminous orange vests unfastening the straps, ready for disembarking. Wade returned to their car.

"Take all our bags out," Anya said over her shoulder. "I've unlocked it."

Wade formed a question, but Anya was already off. Instead of heading for their vehicle, she'd gone to a white Mazda four by four. Lifting the boot, she pulled out three bags and carried them over to where Wade had removed their suitcases and bags.

"What are you doing?" Cassandra reading Wade's mind.

"They'll be looking for our car." Anya lifted the last bag out.

Wade realised she took the keys during the collision in the cafeteria.

"We can't take their car!" Wade said. "They're a family."

"We're going to leave it in a prominent place on the island." Anya brought the bags over to their Range Rover. "We will need to change the car quickly anyway and do the same again when we get to France. We will change cars frequently. Get used to it. If it is a choice between inconveniencing somebody for a few hours or watching you die, I choose inconvenience."

"Which family was it?" Cassandra desperately wanted to know. "The man or the woman?"

"The man." Anya loaded the Range Rover with the suitcases from the Mazda. Between the three of them, they loaded the Mazda up with their cases and bags. Anya grabbed a games console off the back seat and took it to the Range Rover.

Moments after she'd closed the door, the deckhands reached the Range Rover's section. Anya returned. "We need to wait by the door, or they'll see us."

Wade concluded Anya received information from somewhere to give her an edge. While they waited in the shadows, watching the dockhands remove fasteners, Wade tried glancing into Anya's ears, but he could not see past her hair. She glared at him, sensing him looking.

Through his feet, Wade felt the engines revving up. The deep throbbing sound reverberated through his whole body. His sense of balance told him the ship's final manoeuvring had begun. The moment the deckhands passed the Mazda, Anya returned to it. They were now close to the ferry exit and would be almost the first to leave.

"Get in the back, stay down." Anya held the door open.

"Where are you going?" Wade asked, realising she wasn't getting in.

"I need to slow down the car's owner." She held up the vodka, nail polish and spray bottle.

"Are you getting him drunk?" Cassandra's tone dripped with sarcasm.

Anya held up the spray bottle. "This is bleach. Mix it with nail polish remover and vodka to get a chloroform gas. Nobody will come through that stairwell."

Wade watched her go, stepping over the door lip. "I think she's getting information from somewhere." Wade realised he had no reason to whisper, but did, anyway.

Cassandra nodded. "From what she said, she knows Paladin is waiting on Jersey for us. And they know our car."

"Plus, she knew when they were coming to the hotel last night."

"Do you think she's fed information?" Cassandra sounded as though she'd come to that conclusion as well.

"I tried to look to see if she had an earpiece," Wade told her. "But her hair was in the way. Next time she sleeps, either you or I look."

Cassandra gave a terse nod. "She's coming back."

Anya pulled down a scarf from over her face as she climbed into the car. Wade had no recollection of her wearing it when she left. Wade peered through the front window when he heard a grinding noise. The massive door descended, revealing bright sunlight beyond. Throughout the deck, people returned to their cars. The entrance to their section remained empty.

Anya impatiently tapped her fingers on the wheel. She rechecked her watch. "Come on."

Finally, deckhands waved them forward. Anya made a grunting sound. "Stay down."

The Mazda clanked across the ramp. Wade's curiosity got the better of him; he peeked over the window lip. As they disembarked, he saw two men and a woman wearing black standing by a helicopter gunship on the quayside. They watched every car leaving the ship. Anya slipped on a pair of sunglasses and ignored the operatives on the dock. Traffic moved slowly away from the ferry; eventually, they were away from the port. Anya drove around the block and headed past some grey and blue flats towards a diner.

"Can we sit up yet?" Cassandra looked uncomfortable.

"Yes. It's safe," Anya replied.

Cassandra saw their surroundings and looked puzzled. "Are we eating?"

Anya shook her head and exited the vehicle. "I'll be four minutes."

Wade watched as she walked up to the counter and ordered coffee. While waiting, Anya slipped her hand into a handbag belonging to the woman beside her at the counter. Just over four minutes later, Anya returned to the car.

"You stole that woman's keys." Wade did not hide his distaste.

"She's about to go on holiday." Anya looked unconcerned. "We need a car that nobody will miss for a few days."

Cassandra gripped the seatbacks and leaned forward. "How do you know?"

"Know what?"

Cassandra's face set in a hard stare. "Don't play innocent. How do you know that woman is about to go on holiday?"

"She has a suitcase. Her family has suitcases. They are acting excited. You don't act excited upon your return."

Wade had to concede this was a reasonable explanation. What caused his suspicion to return was her unerringly driving. The large, impressive buildings at the seafront rapidly changed into housing. The tourists and travellers became suburbanites. Anya did not have a satnav, but found her way to a semi-detached house a couple of miles inland from the port. Wade could see nothing to distinguish this house from any other on the street as they drove past. White render on the walls and relatively new-looking brown window frames repeated endlessly.

They parked up beside a set of black wrought-iron gates and a box hedge. Anya used the keys to go inside.

"Do we wait here?" Wade asked.

"I need the toilet." Cassandra headed after Anya without waiting for Wade. Wade debated with himself and followed.

He met Anya by the threshold. She had the garage clicker and car key fob.

A low hum signalled the garage door rolling up and back into the roof. Inside, a pale blue Mercedes crossover surprised Wade.

"We got lucky," Wade said. "That's a nice car."

"Yeah, lucky." Anya rolled her eyes.

Anya slipped behind the wheel and pulled it onto the drive. She popped the boot. Wade didn't need telling, transferring luggage as the car stopped rolling. Anya watched as he carried the bags to the Mercedes.

Cassandra emerged from the inside. "Are we putting the Mazda in the garage?"

Anya shook her head. "Wade will drive it into town and leave it for the owners to find."

"Where?" Wade asked.

Anya shrugged. "Somewhere near the port. By now, they will have worked out which car we took."

"It's only been half an hour," Cassandra said.

"These people are experts in information." Anya threw the last bag into the Mercedes's boot. "Once they've got a scent, getting them to lose it again will be hard."

Anya's reasoning dawned on Wade. "And if the Mazda owners find their car, they won't go looking for it elsewhere."

Anya nodded. "Drive it back to the diner. Walk to the port entry. We'll meet you there."

Exhilarated about driving again, Wade got behind the wheel. He'd always had an excellent memory, but he surprised himself by reversing the route they had taken in, returning to the diner. He wondered if he needed to rub the wheel and hard surfaces down to remove fingerprints. Paladin already knew the car they'd taken and who they were. It would be pointless. He put the keys behind the sun visor and walked away, hands in his pockets, attempting to look casual.

Wade used the high bushes to conceal himself from the road as he walked back to the port. Even knowing the danger he was in, he felt a sense of freedom. Possibly for the first time since his seizure. He'd never felt trapped with Cassandra, but Anya gave him a connection to his past. He'd given up on finding who he was a long time ago. She had yet to provide solid details, but Wade could work on that. If he could find more about his life before his seizure, it would help him recover lost memories. Wade smiled as he reached the high metal fence that surrounded the ferry port.

At the corner, he saw a Range Rover sweep from the exit onto the road. It reminded him to be a little more careful. He took the pedestrian entrance, looking at a colossal ferry visible above the port buildings. Where would Cassandra and Anya meet him? He found a small circular garden. Beside the ticket office, he saw metal mesh benches and sat on one. Lunchtime arrived; a few individuals arrived with pre-packed sandwiches, chattering, and laughing among themselves. The sun warmed his face, making him feel sleepy, but Wade kept alert.

He saw the black helicopter from earlier taking off and heading inland. No doubt they'd be chasing down a lead. He heard two men and a woman talking in Hebrew. Surprising himself, he understood them.

"There's been a sighting at Mont Mado," one said. "It's not conclusive. It could just be any white Mazda."

"Get Kobe to check it out," the woman replied.

Wade exited the garden, heading for the ticket office. Hunger and thirst drove him from hiding. He used the reflections in the ferry building to examine the trio. All three had dark hair. Sunglasses, black jackets, and white shirts with black trousers formed an almost uniform. They paid him scant attention, though he kept his back to them. It was a risk, Wade knew, but he felt walking away from them was safer than staying in the garden where they could look at any moment. Next to the ticket office, Wade found a busy pharmacy and sandwich shop. He checked his wallet and sighed at the lack of money. Putting his hand in his pocket, Wade extracted his loose change. A quick count revealed he had a choice between coffee or a sandwich. He opted for the coffee.

His cards looked at him from his wallet.

A quick tap: he could have anything in the shop.

It would also tell his pursuers exactly where he was and when.

"What can I get you, love?" asked the woman behind the counter.

"Americano, please," he said, passing over the last of his coins.

Anya had said she had a source of funding. He'd have to make sure that he and Cassandra could tap into that if they needed. Wade hated the feeling of deciding between drink and food. Sipping from the cup, he headed for the exit. The three operatives remained by the road, presumably watching all the vehicles coming into the terminal. Wade lifted the coffee beaker to his lips as he walked past, naturally obscuring his face. As he walked, he watched for the pale blue Mercedes.

At the roundabout, a large office block with a portico provided a good view. He could see the roundabout and all four feeder roads. Though he knew which road they had taken leaving, he felt Anya would be a little more cautious on her return, so he needed to see all the routes in. A low wall became a seat, sipping from the cup and watching the road. Even paying attention, he nearly missed the Mercedes, coming from his left up the dual carriageway. Wade leapt up and crossed the road, arriving at the zebra crossing at the same time as Anya.

She saw him, pausing long enough for him to get in the passenger seat.

"Drive straight on." Wade pointed at the roundabout. "They're checking all the people driving in."

Anya nodded and took the Mercedes across the roundabout and into the carpark for the swimming pool. As they drove, Wade told her what he'd seen and overheard.

Anya pulled into a parking space and turned to face Wade. "I have bought tickets for a ferry that is embarking in twenty minutes."

Wade had a thought. "Won't they be looking for the people on the previous ferry who owned the Range Rover?"

"I burned those identities," Anya said. "We're on our next set now. French nationals. You are Jean and Marci Dubois."

"Married?" Cassandra sounded amused.

Anya looked confused. "Is that a problem? With you being pregnant, it is more likely you'd be married."

"It's not a problem." Cassandra gave a half-smile. "It is something we'd been discussing."

"Consider this a practice run." There was a tone of suppressed indifference in her words. "Wade, you are in the back. You'll both have to duck down."

Sunglasses back on, she added a red-peaked baseball hat and tucked her hair up inside it. She headed back to the port, keeping her speed steady, avoiding glancing over at the agents. They joined the queue of cars already formed, other cars pulling up behind them, blocking them in.

Anya spotted more Paladin agents. "Keep down."

"I hope we can get up soon." From her tone, Wade decided Cassandra was uncomfortable. He reached over and held her hand as they knelt in the rear footwells. Wade could feel every stop-start and bump in the road as the car edged forward.

"We're approaching the customs booth," Anya said, looking forward. "You'll need to be in your seats for that."

Wade unkinked his legs, manoeuvring into the seat and helping Cassandra into a sitting position. Anya had joined the shorter queue for the customs booth. Anya reached and extracted three passports and brought up their tickets on her phone. She passed the documents over. Wade watched as the young woman in the booth scanned them under a laser, glancing at both him and Cassandra before handing them back. Wade watched a man in a woollen hat and Hi-Viz jacket wave them to a lane painted on the tarmac. He felt slightly optimistic.

Tiredness returned in stages. Apart from a few dozes, since waking thirty-six hours earlier, Wade had been awake. He wondered how long since Anya had slept. He knew she'd had three hours of sleep, but the planning that had gone into rescuing them from the restaurant and onto a ship was immense. She had done it without putting a foot wrong.

Anya slammed on the brakes to avoid crashing into the car ahead of them in the queue. "Bad timing," she muttered.

They edged forward.

"They will have agents on board," Anya said as the Mercedes clanked up the ramp onto the boat.

"Do they know where we are?" Cassandra asked.

Anya shook her head. "In their position, I'd put operatives on every ferry leaving the island."

"They must want us dead badly," Wade said.

"They devote a lot of resources to finding Cassandra," Anya replied. She applied the handbrake and turned off the car. "So yes. They want Cassandra dead more than anything. You and I, Wade, we're collateral."

"Do we have to stay in the car?" Cassandra asked.

Anya shook her head. "There is a cabin with this ticket. We're only on board for an hour and a half. We'll get you to the cabin, stay there for the duration, and then get off again."

"You make it sound so simple," Cassandra said.

"It's all about timing." Anya flashed a smile.

She took the carryall from the passenger footwell and led them to the nearest steps up to the deck. As they emerged onto the blue carpeted corridor, she turned left without hesitation. Wade looked along a cross-corridor. He saw a lithe-looking man casually leaning on the wall, occasionally glancing down at a tablet. They switched from port to starboard down another corridor. Cassandra and Wade followed like baby ducklings. They swapped back again. Paranoia told Wade she avoided actual Paladin operatives. Rational thoughts told him she exercised extreme caution.

"We're here." Anya used her phone ticket to open the door on the scanner.

Cassandra went in first. A sink between two beds formed the room's only furniture. Wade closed his eyes; his tiredness combined with the ship's rocking in the claustrophobic cabin made him feel nauseous.

"Lie down," Cassandra told him, sensing his disquiet.

Wade discovered his feet touched one wall while his head touched the other. "I am going to close my eyes for ten minutes."

"That sounds like a plan." Cassandra took the other bunk.

From the door, Anya glanced at both beds before sighing and closing the door. She leaned against it. Wade was about to be chivalrous.

"Don't you dare offer your bunk." She'd narrowed her eyes.

"The thought never crossed my mind," Wade lied.

"Yes. It did."

Wade made an embarrassed shrug. "It did."

"Go to sleep. We'll need to rest before getting off again."

Wade closed his eyes, thinking he wouldn't fall asleep. Too much had happened in the past twenty-four hours, scrambling in his head. However, he must have slept as he jerked awake to Anya's alarm.

He woke effortlessly, glancing across at Cassandra before looking at Anya. She also roused to her alarm. In one hand, she clutched the locket on her necklace. Wade looked more closely. He'd previously seen the chain, but she kept the locket tucked away. Anya pushed the locket back down beneath her shirt. She glanced up with almost a guilty expression. Wade stretched and slid off the bed, yawning. He didn't mention the locket, but it was another puzzling puzzle piece in his connection to Anya. Curiosity burned inside him. Questions like this were for another time.

"I need the toilet." Cassandra imperceptibly winced, getting to her feet.

Anya nodded. "I'll come with you."

Checking both ways onto the corridor, Anya led Cassandra through the ship. Wade brought up the rear, checking over his shoulder. Queues formed, getting ready for disembarking. Wade could not explain who he searched for, but he decided that checking for anybody examining the passengers was helpful. While the two women were in the toilet, Wade leaned against the wall, wishing they'd changed clothes.

"I could do with a shower," he told Cassandra as she emerged behind Anya.

"You and me both," she said, squeezing his arm. "I also need to get out of this dress."

The public address system instructed everybody to return to their cars. They slotted into a queue of people shuffling towards the nearest door.

Moving his head around to get a better look down the corridor, Wade spotted somebody he recognised. "One of those guys is by the door. He's checking everybody leaving."

Anya compressed her lips. It was the first time he'd seen her think. Until now, she'd operated on blind luck or exquisite planning.

She left the queue to take a cross-corridor. Wade used his slight height advantage to look down toward the exit. His sightlines had passenger's heads in the way, but it looked clear.

"They must only have one person on the boat," Wade said.

Anya shook her head. "There are three."

Frown lines creased Wade's forehead. Anya had been with them the entire time they were on the boat. He'd only seen one. "How can you know that?"

"They always work in threes."

Wade thought back to the port; he had seen three. It made sense.

"They needed six on the boat," Wade said. "There are six doors. They can't watch them all."

"It benefits us," Anya told him. "I'm not complaining."

They descended to the car deck, joining the hordes in leaving the ship. Wade felt safer in the crowds. Disembarking, he and Cassandra did not need telling to duck down; Anya had put on her red cap and sunglasses. In under twenty-four hours, Anya had earned his trust. Wade already felt as though he'd known her for much longer. It was her easy familiarity with him. Her keeping them alive played a large part in their trust.

Saint-Malo's subtly different architecture flashed by the windows. Wade's thoughts returned to mulling over how Anya received her information about Paladin's procedures. Wade had a sudden insight that she was a former operative herself. Having decided this, he had a corollary thought: perhaps he'd also worked for them. It was enough to rouse him. He realised he'd been falling asleep again.

"Where are we heading?"

"Eventually, Tel Aviv." Anya tossed her hat onto the passenger seat but kept on her sunglasses with the low sun directly ahead. "We don't have the charge to get there in one go, so we'll be stopping."

"Would you like me to drive for a while?"

"It would be helpful. I could do with something to eat."

"We're approaching Rennes." Cassandra displayed her knowledge from her student days of backpacking through France.

"Have you been?" Wade asked.

Cassandra nodded. "A road trip to Saint-Malo while we were in Paris."

"Have I been?" Wade asked, leaning forward to Anya.

Anya shrugged. "No idea."

"I discovered I speak Hebrew," Wade said. "Any other languages?"

Anya took her eyes off the road for a moment to give him a long steady stare, before returning to look forwards. She didn't answer.

Instead, she returned to the subject of food. "We'll get something in Rennes and swap over driving. I'll try to find somewhere to sleep and charge the car."

"Le Mans will have plenty of hotels and car charging points," Cassandra told them.

Puzzled, Wade twisted in his seat to look at Cassandra. "Why?"

Cassandra laughed. "It's a major racing town. Lots of people visit for car racing."

"Is it on route to Milan?" Anya asked.

Cassandra looked like she was reading an atlas in her mind and nodded. "Yes."

"I plan to cut across the top of Italy, scoot around through Turkey and head down to Israel that way. We may get help in Turkey. I know some people."

"It'd be quicker to fly," Wade said.

Anya gave him a sad shake of her head. "The second we step foot in an airport, they'll have us. So many cameras and scanners."

Wade had to admit she was right and lapsed into thoughtful silence.

3

He realised he'd dropped off when he awoke to a different vista. They drove through vast, flat fields, the horizon darkening. Anya pulled into the emergency lane. "Wade? Can you drive? I am desperately tired."

Dark rings below Anya's eyes sent a pang of guilt through Wade. He nodded, getting behind the wheel. Anya had set the satnav to take them to a motel on the outskirts of Le Mans.

"Just follow this?" Wade pointed at the display.

Anya gave a sharp nod. "There's a contactless card there for the toll booths."

Wade located the card next to the phone. He slipped the wheel through his fingers a few times, the feeling of control returning. He checked over his shoulder as he pressed the accelerator, getting up to speed. A large truck rocked their car, but the gap behind it was large enough. Driving on the right felt more natural than his previous stint behind the wheel in the UK. As the kilometres rolled under them, his thoughts drifted into who he'd been. Not long after his seizure, he'd been quite introspective into trying to work out who he was. He had, with Cassandra's help, moved forward. Anya's sudden eruption into their life had brought it all back.

As his driving became automatic, Wade looked out over the scenery. The landscape felt different to the UK. He had no memory of anything else, making France feel exotic. He could see for miles, with no signs of civilization. When Wade pulled up at the tollbooth, it felt out of place: an oasis of humanity in a sea of nature. He pressed the contactless card against the pad on the tollbooth. After a worrying moment, the barrier lifted. Beyond that, he was the only car on the road.

Civilisation returned in an instant. Fields replaced by housing the roads busier, like a flipped switch at the town boundary. Opposite a low grey and black office block, Wade found the sprawling three-storeys tall white motel and restaurant. Ivy crawled up the walls, making it feel

Yesterday Pill Iain Benson

established.

The two women awoke as the car's movement stopped.

"Do we have a booking?" Cassandra asked.

Anya shook her head. "I picked a random motel with a restaurant that had vacancies for both."

Cassandra looked down at her dress. "Hopefully, we'll get to change and have a shower." Wade took Anya's bag from the passenger seat. Anya hooked the car up to a charging point.

Wade looked at the three suitcases. "Do we need all three?"

Anya turned, shaking her head. "Leave one of yours, if you want."

After the car's warmth, the air had a chill. It stung the inside of Wade's nose, leaving a metallic taste on his tongue. The slight breeze carried away the sound of his shoes crunching on gravel. Anya and Cassandra flanked him. Only two dozen cars occupied a large carpark, explaining why they had vacancies. A short path between low box hedges led to automatic glass doors. Warmth from a spacious reception area erased the chill. Off to the right, people already half-filled a doglegged restaurant, eating in the dimmed lighting.

They approached the angular white reception desk, a large stack of local attractions at one end.

"Do you speak English?" Anya asked the receptionist.

"A little," the young woman in a blue suit jacket and white blouse replied.

"I've got this," Cassandra said. "One night?"

Anya nodded.

Cassandra turned to the reception with a broad smile. "Bonjour."

It was as much as Wade could pick out. He lowered his voice. "I don't know French."

"You surprise me," Anya replied, sardonic.

"Could you pay?" Cassandra said, turning to Anya. "We have two adjacent rooms for one night and a meal in the restaurant."

Anya had the grace to flash a thank-you smile to Cassandra. She stepped forward and paid on her card, receiving two room keys in return.

The receptionist directed them to the left and up a flight of steps. Wade liked the decoration. The deep brown carpet felt luxurious, and he found the white colour scheme with occasional colour splashes helped with navigation. Their room pleasantly surprised Wade. A wide bed with a padded headboard and a low desk holding the television and kettle.

"I am next door," Anya reminded them. "If anything happens, come straight to me."

"We will," Wade promised.

Cassandra looked at Anya before she could vanish into her room. "Our reservations are in an hour."

Anya nodded.

Wade found stifling his yawn impossible. He dropped their bags on the bed and investigated the small shower room. "Do you want to shower first?"

Cassandra nodded and slipped out of her clothes. Stained and ripped, grubby from their travels. "It's hard to believe that yesterday, we were in a different restaurant."

While waiting for Cassandra, Wade found some new clothes and toiletries while the shower thrummed. Steam seeped under the door, bringing a waft of scented soap. He looked through the draped net curtains onto a large empty field. A slight smile forced its way onto his lips. A wanderlust he'd suppressed returned now he'd gone abroad. Something he'd wanted to do for a long time.

Cassandra finally emerged, her hair bandaged up in a towel, a second one wrapped around her. Wade gave her a passing peck on the lips before stripping and joyfully standing under the hot water. Cassandra had left enough in the soap bottles. He used them all. He felt like the previous twenty-four hours had lasted weeks. The water washed away the aches in his lower back. Eventually, he knew he had to stop. Cassandra had dressed by the time he returned. Her choice of a pale grey jumper with a star motif and black leggings with flat pumps looked more suitable for being on the

Yesterday Pill   Iain Benson

run.

"Have you seen the pendant on Anya's necklace?" Wade asked while he dressed.

She shook her head. "I've seen the chain."

"You know my ring?"

She looked thoughtful. "The signet ring with *Wade* etched inside?"

"That's the one." Wade used the towel on his hair. It was only short and was already almost dry. "The shield and swords emblem on the ring is the same as the one on her pendant."

"That cannot be a coincidence."

Wade shook his head. "She knows so much about Paladin's methods that I think we both worked for them."

"That's an enormous leap," Cassandra said. "Though it sounds like you both have a connection."

"But not the link to Paladin?"

Cassandra shook her head. "I'm sure most security services would know their modus operandi."

Wade shrugged and put on his shoes. He wondered if he had time for a coffee. He was still dog-tired. "I could do with finding out where that symbol is from."

"We looked." Cassandra came over and rested a hand on his arm.

"I wonder if she found my ring," Wade suddenly said. "It was in my bedside table drawer."

Cassandra made a face. "I'm pretty sure she did. She knows so much about us. I keep wondering what might have been if we'd not gone with her."

Wade rested his hand on hers. "We'd have died."

"If I am honest, it was only that gun that made me go."

Wade nodded. "Threat is an effective mechanism."

Anya had also showered and changed into a pair of black leggings and calf-high boots with a dark blue tee-shirt; she had kept her denim jacket.

By the entrance to the restaurant, they had to pause by a small bar with another dark-haired young woman behind it.

She took their details and asked something else.

"Anybody want a drink?" Cassandra translated.

"Absolutely," Wade said.

"I'll just be having coffee," Anya replied.

Cassandra translated, requesting water for herself.

After eating, Wade looked up at the ceiling. Lights danced, reflections from the pool outside the window. The bacon rolls on the ferry felt a long time ago; he welcomed the food. Wade dragged his attention back to the two women chatting about Cassandra's trip to France. As he watched, Anya froze. It was only momentary. She looked distant, her eyes perfectly still, the coffee cup halfway to her lips. She put the cup down and winced. Anya took a strip of paracetamol from her jacket pocket and took two caplets with a glug of coffee.

Animated again, she looked at them both. "We'll need to change cars tomorrow."

"I thought we'd have longer," Cassandra said. "That was why we took this car."

Anya nodded and looked serious. "As did I."

"Have they tracked us?" Wade wondered if she'd received some information by an earbud. With a surreptitious movement, he felt around his ear, seeing if he had implanted tech.

Wade frowned, castigating himself. He'd had so many MRI scans that any kind of implanted technology would have shown up.

"They're probably following up every car that bought a ticket today." Anya sounded thoughtful, as though planning their next move. "They won't be sure we were on that ferry. Necessity will have split their resources."

"Have we time to sleep?" Wade asked. He needed sleep.

Anya nodded. "We all need time in a proper bed. They won't know where we are just yet. But tomorrow, we must start early."

Yesterday Pill   Iain Benson

Even a company with massive resources would surely struggle to find them at a random hotel. Using forged identities in a country the size of France should make them invisible. They could be anywhere. "Surely, we have time. There will have been loads of vehicles leaving Jersey."

"Rural France has almost zero traffic CCTV," Anya admitted. "Paladin will find us if we stay still. They'll have their AIs combing the footage for any trace. By my estimation, we have until lunchtime tomorrow."

Cassandra looked a little sad. "They're never going to give up, are they?"

Anya was blunt: "No."

"What have I done to them?" Cassandra's tone was plaintive, pleading with uncaring heavens.

"Yes?" Wade asked pointedly. "What has she done to them?"

Anya held Wade's gaze. "That's what you're going to find out at their headquarters, isn't it?"

Wade blinked first. "Yes."

"I just hope it's worth it." Anya finally looked away. "I'm still going to collect evidence on their attack in the UK."

"Both will give us the most leverage." Cassandra played the mediator.

"I'm going to bed," Anya announced, standing up. "Enjoy your desserts. Here's the card for paying. The pin is twenty thirty-six."

Dessert sounded good. "You not stopping for one?"

Anya shook her head. "I'm going to have to get up early. I have an unpleasant combination of tiredness and headache."

"It's not quite what I'd envisaged our anniversary to be," Cassandra said, with a lopsided smile after Anya had gone.

"We are in France," Wade replied, intertwining his fingers with hers. He felt the familiar warmth of love between them.

"True. Mon amour."

Several hours of uninterrupted sleep lured them both back to their room. As Wade closed his eyes, he half expected Anya to burst in and prevent them from sleeping. Instead, the alarm he'd set woke him from his unconsciousness. Already up, Cassandra had located their toothbrushes, brushing her teeth in the small ensuite. Wade joined her, their closeness a reassurance, her familiarity a warmth.

Cassandra found a note pushed under the door as they were about to head down for breakfast. "Two croissants, butter, raspberry jam, orange juice and a large pot of coffee. I'll meet you at breakfast at about ten."

"I think it's Anya's breakfast order."

Cassandra nodded with a smile. Wade realised he'd spoken the obvious.

Wade got Anya's order before he got another plate for himself. He worried people would think he was greedy, but surreptitious glances around suggested nobody looked or cared. Intense sunlight flooded the restaurant, in complete contrast to the night before. The heptagonal swimming pool outside created a rippled effect in the light, creating an illusion of liquidity to the air.

Cassandra found a table, farther along than the previous night, looking out over the rear carpark and endless fields beyond.

The restaurant had nearly emptied by the time Anya arrived. She looked flustered, wearing black jeggings, a black blouse, and her denim jacket.

"Early morning run?" Wade asked, watching her drain the orange juice.

Anya demolished her food and coffee. She paused and gave Wade a sarcastic look. "I was securing us a new car."

"How long have you been up?" Cassandra sounded more sympathetically.

"I got up at seven," Anya replied, brushing crumbs from her clothing.

An answer to a different question. "Three hours?"

"Something like that," Anya replied. "We need to get moving.

Yesterday Pill   Iain Benson

Paladin will be here before noon."

Back in their room, Anya collected her bags and spread out a map of Le Mans on the bed in Wade's room.

"Did you pick this up this morning?" Wade asked.

"We haven't got long." Anya pointed at the map, picking out a bridge. "This is Pont des Vendéens. Be at these shops in three hours."

"Where are you going?" Wade asked.

Anya handed him the Mercedes key fob. "In about three hours, we will be at that bridge in a white Jeep."

Wade accepted the key fob. "And I'm hiding the Mercedes?"

Anya nodded. "Make it hard to find, but not impossible."

He held up two fingers. "Two things I'll need: cash and the map."

Anya nodded and passed the map with thirty euros. Wade slid both into his back pocket. He had some ideas on how to make the car hard to find without being impossible. He drove into the centre of Le Mans, down the open streets towards the cathedral. As he neared, the sun vanished behind cramped together tall housing. Wade noted wide pavements with shrubbery and trees for the pedestrians. It surprised him a little, with Cassandra telling him it was a car city. He drove the Mercedes onto a wide plaza dominated by an impressive gothic sandstone cathedral. He allowed his muscle memory to assist him around a tricky roundabout and down a tree-lined drive into a municipal carpark.

After checking he had taken everything of theirs, he opened the boot, locked the car, and dropped the keys in the boot before closing it. Although his French was poor, he saw the sign asking if he'd paid for parking. He shook his head at the sign.

When he reached the plaza, planning his route in his head, Wade paused, admiring the Cathedral. He found it magnificent architecturally, tempting him to go inside. The stained glass would look impressive in the strong sunlight. His early calculation of a half-hour walk meant he had no time for sightseeing. A woman walking a yapping dog had to pull it back at the road as a white van took the corner sharply. She shouted something in

French after the driver. Around the Cathedral, modern glass and concrete buildings gave a stark dichotomy to the ancient structure at his back. He strolled down the wide pavement, under sweet-smelling trees. Wade had to step aside as two youths weaved amid the pedestrians on skateboards. A yell attracted his attention: their friend riding his bike down the road. He had a glance at the map, hoping it was up to date and he'd find a café where it said.

At a junction, he found a bank, a mini-mart, and a bistro. As well as buying coffee, Wade used the toilets before returning to the road. He blew into the hole in the cup, feeling content if not happy.

A dark blue van mounted the kerb, screeching to a stop. Wade joined the other pedestrians to watch it, wondering if they would witness a bank robbery. Dozens of camera phones focused on the unfolding events as the side doors to the van slid open. Two men leapt out, clad in black jumpers and balaclavas.

Before Wade could think that they were a little stereotypical, they grabbed him and pulled a hood over his face. His coffee cup went spilling away as they dragged him towards their vehicle.

He squirmed, trying to go floppy, dropping to the floor. His heart raced. Breathing with shallow breaths. The black hood's musty smell filled his nostrils. The two men had a good grip on his arms, not letting go even as he tried to drop and twist. He tried to force calmness into his mind, but tumultuous thoughts prevented him. Wade pushed forward with his feet, trying to break the grip. He thought he'd succeeded as the assailant momentarily released his left arm. A backhand smashed into his mouth, leaving him tasting copper. Pain shot through his shins as they threw him in the van. Metallic echoes thudded back at him, his hip sending a scream up his throat as he twisted awkwardly, crashing into the side.

The door sliding shut echoed loudly. Acceleration flung Wade backwards, the van shooting off with a squeal of tyres and a smell of diesel. Before he could remove the hood, they bound Wade's hands with a zip tie. Wade rolled away as they tore around a corner, his face smashing into the wall. He could feel blood trickling down his top lip. His brain felt foggy. He somersaulted around the floor as the van twisted and turned, his shoulder twisting under him, sending waves of agony down his arm.

A crunch of metal heralded Wade lurching across the van, the corrugated flooring catching his knee. He heard car horns as the Renault restarted, making several sharp turns at speed.

The grumbling engine altered. Wade knew he needed to keep track of how many turns and where the sound changed, but the pains in his shoulder and face caused him to lose focus.

With an abrupt stop, the van came to rest. Wade heard the door open.

He wanted to resist. Battered and bruised, he struggled to put up a fight as they dragged him from the van by his armpits. Fire coursed through his shoulder. He felt the skin come off his knee as he landed on a rough concrete floor, the smell of grease and dust making its way through the hood. They roughly pulled him to his feet and hurled him into a chair. It creaked and rocked alarmingly. A bright light made Wade wince as they pulled the hood off, allowing it to shine in his eyes.

At the edge of vision, a roller door closed. A hotel across the road vanishing as the sunlight disappeared. Wade turned his head away from the spotlight blinding him. He could see a car lift. He knew he was in a garage.

A gloved hand smelling of leather pulled his face back into the light.

"What do you want?" His voice cracked.

"Where is Cassandra Roberts?" The accent was slight. Wade placed it as possibly Russian.

Trying to keep his head straight, Wade winced toward the voice. "Who?"

The gloved fist smashed into his cheek, sending two teeth out of their sockets. Blood gushed over his tongue and his ears rung. A cut had opened above his eye, blood dripping down and blinding him on one side.

"Cassandra Roberts!"

Wade shook his head, trying to clear it. "I don't know her!"

He tensed, expecting another punch. Instead, he heard the Russian talking to a woman in Arabic. With half a thought, Wade realised he understood Arabic.

"He matches the description," the man whispered.

"Wrong clothes." The woman's accent sounded American.

Wade could feel consciousness slipping away. A slap across his face, causing his eye to swell, brought him back.

"Who are you?"

The only person Wade could think of was his neurologist. "Michael. Michael Dodgson."

"Why are you here?"

"You brought me here!"

There was muttering. "Why are you in France?"

Wade's faculties were in overdrive. "I'm on a stag do! We're going to do the Le Mans twenty-four-hour challenge."

More muttering came from the shadows. A silhouette partly blocked out the bright light. The slim man stepped forward and drove a fist into Wade's midriff. Blood sprayed from his mouth. He rolled off the chair onto the floor. His cheek lay on the concrete only for a moment as the man and woman lifted him back into the chair. They tied his arms into an unnatural position against the chair back. He felt the ligaments in his left shoulder pop with a spasm of pain that had him gasp out involuntarily.

"If you do not know Cassandra Roberts, we will have to kill you."

The only part of Wade's body that was pain free was his right leg. He wanted to live. He brought his right foot back under the chair and pushed forward. Both he and the chair came up, driving into the silhouette's stomach with his shoulder. Waves of pain washed down from his shoulder.

The two crashed backwards into the light, falling over. The bulb exploded, shrapnel flying from the shattered bulb, gouging out a chunk of Wade's cheek. He rolled to the side onto his back, smashing the chair and pulled his legs through his hands. Using his knee, he snapped the zip tie and

Yesterday Pill   Iain Benson

got to his feet. His left knee was threatening to give out under him.

The broad assailant with a scruffy beard came from the side. Wade discovered a fighting spirit as he drove his hand up; the heel of his hand met his attacker's chin with a crunch, lifting him off his feet. Wade felt the impact in every joint. He staggered to the side as the woman caught him on the side of his head. The Russian who had been questioning him grabbed him from behind. Wade shoved his head backwards. A satisfying connection of soft nose accompanied with a Russian profanity, telling Wade he knew Russian. Wade shoved the man back into the car lift, the metal hard enough to free him, albeit only for a moment.

The gunshot in such a confined space deafened Wade. If they had hit him, he couldn't feel it, although he could feel wetness around his stomach. He staggered backwards, feeling for the dampness. He looked down; his hands were bright red. His vision blurred at the edges. He could smell ice. Wade looked up at the woman, pointing a gun at him. Wade staggered slightly, unable to make out her features.

A resounding crash signalled the rollaway door, ripping aside as a white Renault crashed through it.

The woman with the gun bounced off the bonnet, sending a spidery crack across the window. With a crunch, the car came to a stop on the broken spotlight.

Anya leaned across and pushed the door open. "Get in."

Wade collapsed into the passenger seat. Anya reversed back onto the street, a metal tearing sound as they left the passenger door behind.

"Jesus Wade, you're a mess." Her tone was worried and tender.

Anya whipped the wheel around and careered up the road, narrowly avoiding a parked car. Wade nearly fell out.

"How did you find me?" Wade was struggling to get the words out.

"It took a while," Anya admitted. "A bit of social media and news reports of a dead body, mainly."

Wade's consciousness faded.

Anya stopped the car and turned Wade over. Dull pain

accompanied her lifting his shirt and swearing.

"You're not going to make it," she said.

Anya took out her locket and manipulated it. A white disc, the size of a breath mint, appeared in her hand. It swam in and out of focus. "Don't you dare die on me. Again. I can't go back further."

She muttered something, stroking Wade's cheek.

"What?" Wade said, double vision swimming, a buzzing filling his ears.

"Do it better this time."

She pressed the mint to his lips. Wade tasted marshmallow and fog dissipating on his tongue as it dissolved.

The world stretched out ahead of Wade, the car's interior becoming a two-dimensional scene before vanishing to a point in the distance. Pain became a memory as the world snapped back into focus.

Le Mans Cathedral filled his view.

Wade's brow furrowed together. He remembered the pain, but as he moved his shoulders and touched his stomach, he felt fine. Confusion befuddled him for a moment. He scratched the back of his head. Had he imagined all that he had just endured?

A yap from a dog as a white van cut the corner caught Wade's attention. The woman yelled after the driver. Wade's puzzlement grew. He turned and started walking down the road towards the bridge where he was meeting Cassandra and Anya. Two youths on skateboards wove around him while a lad on a bike yelled from the road.

"Not possible," he muttered.

He was an hour into a past he had already experienced. Wade realised he walked down to where the Renault had taken him. He got to the coffee shop and went inside. It was impossible to travel through time. There had to be another explanation. A severe case of déjà vu.

He remembered every blow and Anya crashing through the door. The gunshot echoed in his memory. Consciousness fading and the pain clear as a genuine memory. Did déjà vu allow him to predict the future? Anya

Yesterday Pill   Iain Benson

gave him something. Her words echoed in his mind: do it better.

"Désirez?" asked the woman behind the counter, in precisely the same bored tone he remembered from his déjà vu.

It had felt solid; it had to be more than a memory.

"Deux cafes," he replied, holding up two fingers. He needed to do something different to shake away the discombobulation.

He passed over notes and left the bistro. Exactly as before, the blue van mounted the kerb. Around Wade, once more, his fellow pedestrians were recording the expected bank robbery on their phones. Wade expected the balaclava-wearing men as they burst out. He watched it in a dream-like state.

Wade used his thumb to flick the lid off the coffee in his right hand as they got close. The contents went straight into the man's face.

His potential assailant stumbled to the side, grasping at his eyes. Wade drove his fingers, knife-like, into the other assailant's throat. The broad-shouldered man crumpled and fell against the van, his hands to his throat. Spinning, Wade drove his foot into the Russian's midriff. Both collapsed.

Wade could see the woman, the driver, in the wing mirror. The van set off in a squeal of tyres, leaving the two on the pavement beside the road.

Wade set off down the road, taking the first corner and ducking into a doorway. He leaned against it, sipping his coffee, able to see the main road from the shadows. The blue van crawled past. Wade waited for a few more moments and then set off down the street, away from the main road. He reviewed the map, finding an alternative route down to the bridge. Each time Wade heard the rumble of a diesel engine, he hid and checked the vehicle to which it belonged. Wade hugged the wall and holed up in doorways. He moved down the back streets, using the pavement on the side with parked cars. Houses crammed in all around.

Exposed, Wade had to cross tram tracks along the main road. He took what cover he could get from the trees flanking the street, constantly alert for dark blue Renaults. Even after crossing the street and reaching the riverbank, Wade felt unsafe. Every jogger and dog walker loomed in his vision.

He crossed using a footbridge, the river rushing over a weir masking the sound of other pedestrians. Wade left the path, scrambling between tall apartment blocks. He emerged at the shops, grateful to see Anya leaning against a white Jeep. She had a takeaway coffee. Cassandra already had the back seat.

Anya didn't bother with greetings. "I'd given up hope."

"Something extraordinary happened." Wade wondered what to tell her. Unsure himself what had happened, nerves jittery.

"Tell me about it while we're moving."

With considerable relief, Wade took the passenger seat, feeling Cassandra's hand squeeze his shoulder. Anya put her cup in a cupholder and set off into traffic.

"What charge do we have?" Wade asked.

Anya glanced down. "Five hundred, if I'm cautious."

"Paladin tried to take me from the street."

Anya glanced over. Cassandra made a concerned noise from the back.

Anya clicked her tongue. "What happened?"

Wade took a deep breath. "I appear to know how to fight. I threw coffee at one and hit the other in the throat."

"They could have followed you." Anya sounded annoyed.

"I took the back streets."

Anya's eyes narrowed as she looked down the long road hemmed in by the high apartment blocks. Wade was expecting her to explain about her dramatic rescue of him from the garage.

She gave no sign she knew what happened. With a slow nod, she softened towards Wade. "That was quick thinking with the coffee."

Wade looked at her. "You didn't know where I was?"

She made a noncommittal face. "None."

Wade's eyebrows went up. "You didn't come looking for me?"

"I told you where we would be," she told him. "We were there."

"I don't know how you did that," Cassandra said.

"It felt natural." Wade turned and gave a tight smile.

"It would," Anya said with a touch of acid.

"Are you admitting I've had fighting training?" Wade made a questioning face.

Anya sighed as though cross with having said as much as she did.

Wade lapsed into silence as the car left the buildings behind when they crossed a major road. Farmland returned as far as they could see. Anya opened the car up and engaged cruise control. Wade looked out at the countryside, wondering how Anya did not know what had happened. If he'd had déjà vu, surely that would mean she knew something. There was no way Wade imagined all those details. He didn't understand but couldn't reconcile the two series of events, nor put the discordance into words. He struggled to keep them straight in his mind; forming the words to convey that morning's events seemed impossible.

4

They stopped at the services about sixty kilometres from Lyon, the car's charge running dangerously low as they rolled into the charging bay.

Wade looked out across the carpark towards a stone and wooden shed. It felt more like a picnic spot than a service station.

"That's a toilet," Cassandra said. "I'll be right back."

"It's not much of a service station," Wade said.

Anya watched the stone block where Cassandra headed. She looked anxious. "Needs must."

"I suppose." Wade came and leaned against the car beside Anya. "Were we close?"

Anya took her eyes from the toilet black to gaze with surprise at Wade. "Why do you ask?"

"I get a sense from you that there was more to us."

Anya shrugged and made a noncommittal noise. "It was years ago. Even if we had been close, time passes."

"That is not a 'no'."

"It's not a 'yes' either."

Wade shrugged. "Why are you protecting Cass?"

"If she dies, there's a chance that the world will end."

"If she's that important, tell her." Wade looked over to the block where Cassandra emerged into the weak sunlight.

"If she finds out too soon, it could also cause the world to end."

Wade shook his head. "Do you realise how dramatic that sounds? How completely implausible?"

Anya nodded. "You used to understand."

"Make me understand again."

Anya shook her head. "You have no secrets from her."

"Not if it's that important." Wade made a cross-his-heart sign on his chest.

Yesterday Pill   Iain Benson

"There's no more time." Anya gave him a sunny smile as Cassandra emerged. "I'm going to the toilet. Try not to get abducted. I'll only be a few minutes."

Cassandra stood toe to toe with Wade and wrapped her hands around his neck. "What did you two talk about while I was gone?"

"You." Wade wrapped his hands around her waist. "Something strange happened this morning."

"You said." Cassandra gave him a swift kiss. "You were very brave."

"I didn't say it all." Wade checked Anya had gone into the stone block. "The first time they took me from the street, they beat me and shot me in the stomach. I nearly died."

"Are you okay? What do you mean, the first time?"

"Anya rescued me," Wade said. "Suddenly, I was back an hour earlier."

"Time travel?"

Wade kept coming back to time travel. It explained everything. He nodded. "I went through it again, only this time I bought two coffees and used one to throw at the people who took me."

"How were your injuries?"

"They'd never happened."

"Not possible," Cassandra said, gazing into his eyes.

"I thought you'd told me time travel *was* possible."

Cassandra gave that smile that Wade loved. "Theoretically, yes, it is. There is nothing to prevent it, but it would require some exceptional equipment that you're not going to find on the street in Le Mans."

Almost unreal, the incident formed a hazy memory. Fog. There had been a taste of fog. He shook his head. "She had something."

"The size of a building?"

Wade shook his head. "No. It tasted of fog."

Cassandra shrugged. "Memory is a weird thing. Imagination can feel real. Perhaps you reconstructed it all after the event."

Wade sighed. "Perhaps."

It was a more straightforward explanation.

It was more likely, more plausible.

But felt wrong.

Wade also visited the toilets, an acrid smell stinging his nostrils long after he'd left and returned to the car. Cassandra handed him a coffee while they waited for the car to charge.

Wade cupped the beaker and blew on the hot liquid. "Do we stop for the night or push on?"

Anya looked at the sky as though determining which direction the wind was blowing. "We could push onto Italy. I think we have enough charge. You'll have to share the driving, though."

"I'm fine with that." Wade went to the driver's side.

"I'll get some food." Anya headed for the burger van.

Cassandra took the front seat. "I'm fed up with being in the back."

"Fine," Anya sounded anything other than fine. "I can stretch out and sleep."

They ate in the car while the charging station finished topping up the car's battery. As soon as the light changed to green, Anya jumped out and disconnected them from the station. Light mid-afternoon traffic allowed their boxy Jeep to make good time. After an hour, the landscape changed, becoming hillier as the road wound around. Enjoyment tingled Wade's fingertips, though he had to concentrate as the landscape morphed from hilly to rocky. Huge promontories of rock crowded them as they edged closer to Italy.

"We need to swap places." Anya leant between the seats, startling Wade.

They passed a green sign telling them there was a tunnel in a kilometre.

Wade shrugged. "We're nearly at the tunnel."

"Paladin is coming up fast behind us."

"I'll cope. I'm a quick study."

"Wade, I'm serious!" Anya thumped the seat back.

Yesterday Pill　　　　　　　　　　　　　　　　Iain Benson

Wade glanced over his shoulder. She looked furious. "So am I."

Anya swore and buckled her seat belt. "I could do with Cassandra being in the back."

"Well! I'm not crawling between the seats," Cassandra said.

An almost physical itch told Wade that Anya's glared at him. He pressed the accelerator further down, taking his speed past a hundred and fifty kilometres an hour. He could see the Alps rising above the road, a white-topped barricade between France and Italy.

"It won't be like back in England," Wade told Anya over his shoulder. "There's only one road."

Customs and toll booths forced Wade to slow.

Anya sounded insistent. "Please, Wade."

Wade gripped the steering wheel. He looked at Cassandra. "Who do you want to drive?"

"Sorry to break it to you, Wade." Cassandra gave a slight smile. "But Anya is probably better at this. She remembers her training. You don't."

"Okay." Wade surrendered.

Anya squeezed Cassandra's shoulder. "Thanks."

As Wade brought the car to a stop behind a queue of four cars, he and Cassandra got out, letting Anya into the driving seat. At the border control booth, the guard barely glanced at their passports, waving them through.

Anya's acceleration threw them backwards in their seats, overtaking two cars before tucking back into the lane. She flew through the tunnel. Barely a kilometre in, Wade heard approaching vehicles. He glanced backwards. Emerging from the two white walls that rapidly vanished into perspective, he saw the motorbike headlights like dots in the distance. They quickly expanded into the bikes themselves. Anya started flicking through the radio stations, overtaking cars as she found a station playing music.

They hurtled through the tunnel, catching snippets of *Purple Rain*, *Changes* and a dance track Wade didn't recognise.

"What's wrong with those?" Wade couldn't fathom what she was

Iain Benson Yesterday Pill

doing.

She carried on searching. "They are too repetitive."

She stopped on a hip-hop station playing *The Message* and began singing. Wade didn't think she looked like the sort of person who listened to classic rap songs. Anya kept her speed high, overtaking and sweeping back between trucks and cars. Despite her speed, the bikes closed with each passing second. When Anya reached a clear stretch, she floored the Jeep up to its maximum speed. The motorbikes were faster. Wade glanced back, seeing the lead bike reach them and pull out a machine pistol. The rider had only one hand on his handlebars. As she sang to *The Message,* she twitched the Jeep's steering wheel. Their tyres squealed with an echoing scream off the tunnel walls. The motorbike flipped and somersaulted behind them as the rear of their car touched it. The rider thudded into the wall, his bike leaving a trail of sparks on the tarmac. Anya slammed her brakes. The second bike hitting the car made Wade wince.

A fast-moving truck slid and jack-knifed on seeing the accident. Anya ignored it, leaving the blockage in the tunnel behind them, and caught up to an articulated refrigeration lorry. She pulled in behind it. Close enough for Wade to read the small print on the truck doors.

Low, shafting sunlight illuminated the tunnel's end. The Jeep popped out, tailgating the truck. Waiting in a side parking bay opposite the customs and toll booths were more motorbikes and black Range Rovers.

Anya swerved around the truck and accelerated. Squeezed through the narrowest of gaps, they got ahead as the Paladin pursuit set off, caught unawares, struggling to catch up. Anya used the truck as a blockade in the constricted section, allowing Anya to put a little distance between them. A brief hard shoulder allowed the motorbikes to swerve around the truck. Wade looked down at a small town nestled in the foothills. They were high above the red-roofed buildings.

"This is going to be a straight drag race," Anya said.

Fortunately, very little traffic came down the road in the early evening, allowing Anya to hit the Jeep's top speed.

Yesterday Pill   Iain Benson

"Shame you didn't steal a Lamborghini," Wade replied.

"No back seat," Anya answered, as though giving a valid reason for dismissing that car.

Anya again twitched the wheel, sending a motorcycle over the crash barrier. The engine screamed as it fell the long way down to the conifer trees below. Wade felt as though the road perched on the side of a sheer drop, with a steep forested hill on one side and a precipitous drop on the other. Anya hurtled along at over a hundred kilometres an hour, singing *The Message* whilst avoiding slower vehicles and bullets from the pursuers. Wade heard a *whomp* noise and glanced over as a black helicopter rose level with the road. A Paladin operative opened a door in the side and pointed a rifle in their direction.

A muttered line from Anya under her breath, she twitched the wheel. They crashed through road cones placed across a gap in the central reservation. Three chasing cars and a motorbike carried on down the road, but two motorbikes and a Range Rover made it through. Anya calmly flicked between the carriageway and the hard shoulder. Wade heard Cassandra squeak. He squeezed her hand. Out of her window, the retaining wall flashed by centimetres from the wing mirror, the individual blocks of stone a blur. Trucks and other vehicles broke the eye line with the helicopter.

Although she had slowed, any collision with the oncoming traffic would be fatal. As a motorcyclist found out, suddenly vanishing from Wade's window. Wade suspected a connection between his repetition and Anya's ease behind the wheel in extreme stress. Possible. This could be the hundredth time Anya had performed this manoeuvre.

Anya muttered lyrics and pulled hard on the wheel at "panhandlers", hitting the brakes and taking a dirt track into the trees through a drainage gap. Wade lost the helicopter among the branches.

Both chasing vehicles shot past, lost in the traffic. Anya banked to the right down a fork. She followed a muddy track downhill passing under the motorway. Wade looked up at the feet of engineering that held the roadway onto the mountainside. As she sang along to the final chorus, Anya emerged from the trees in a blast of gravel and shot across a road and rail track down towards a small town.

To Wade, the buildings looked like holiday homes, wooden cladding and verandas looking onto the mountains. Anya slowed and investigated the houses. She curved around the back of a red van and into a darkened chasm of a garage. Rising above them, Wade saw a three-storey holiday home.

Wade jumped out, back onto the road, checking for pursuit. The sky had darkened. He could see the helicopter in the distance above the trees, a spear of light sweeping across the ground. The town's silence allowed him to hear the distance faded rotors. The only light came from a weak streetlamp and a sliver of light from a window across the street as a winter chill seeped through his light clothing.

"What can you see?" Anya asked from the cavern-like garage.

"Nothing."

"Good." Anya came out.

"How many times did you do that?" Wade decided it was a good time to let Anya know she'd given the game away.

She looked up at him. "Do what?"

Wade shook his head. "How many times did you have to jump back to get through that chase?"

"Has your memory returned?" Anya sounded hopeful.

"No. It's true, though. Are you jumping back an hour each time you fail? Is that why you play a song? It helps you remember where to do things."

"That was your idea." Anya's smile faded; she looked down to the side away from his face. Wade felt a knot of guilt for dashing her hopes.

She hadn't denied the time travel, but Wade stopped his line of questions as Cassandra emerged.

"Where are we?"

"Somebody's holiday house." Anya looked up. "They're not home."

"I take it we're staying here?" Cassandra looked up at the house.

Yesterday Pill Iain Benson

The house looked magnificent, even in shadow. "The last thing anybody would expect would be for us to stay here." Wad's breath condensed in the air. "They will look further in the direction we were originally heading."

"That is true." Anya looked like she weighed it up. "I guess we can stay here."

Wade took a few steps up the drive onto the road. To his right, a closed-up shop. Just on the edge of perception, he heard the thrum from the motorway they'd left. The air smelled of pine and cold, the bitter air pricking his skin. With the sun now set, the chill increased. He gave an involuntary shiver. tone steps led up to the front door. Cupping his hands on the glass, Wade peered into the interior. He could see nothing, the shuttered windows blocking every vestige of light.

He returned to the garage. "It's all locked up."

Anya hooked the car up to the charging port.

"There's a key safe here." Cassandra's voice came from a recess under the stairs.

"I suppose we could work out the combination," Anya said.

"Do you have a torch?" Wade asked.

Anya rummaged into her carryall. "Ah, here."

Wade shone the light around the box. "Do you have a screwdriver as well?"

Further rummaging produced a red-handled flathead screwdriver.

Holding the torch in his teeth, Wade slipped the tip into the narrowest of cracks. He used the heel of his hand as a hammer, cracking open the safe.

He extracted a chunky key.

The house smelled closed with a cold, musty odour as Wade pushed open the door. Anya brushed past him to the alarm box. She punched in a code, halting the beeping.

"Zero one eight four," she said.

Wade raised an eyebrow. "I bet that took a while."

Anya flashed a wry smile. "Just once. I could keep trying after the alarm went off."

Cassandra came through the door, closing it behind her. "This is nice."

Elongated light patterns on the marble floor vanished as Cassandra flicked on a light switch. Glaring white light reflected off the floor. Wade walked through to the kitchen at the back. He switched on the light. His reflection in the double doors momentarily startled him. He found an expensive-looking kitchen with pale wooden surfaces.

Wade rasped his beard growth, wondering if the cupboards held food.

"This place is lovely," Cassandra said, coming in and linking his arm. "There are two living rooms. One has an enormous television."

In the corner, a large American-style fridge with double doors. He opened it, allowing a draught of cold air, smelling of ice, to wash out. Bottles of wine clanked together in the door, but otherwise, it contained nothing to eat. Wade tried the freezer and found some freezer-burned boxed leftovers. He quickly checked cupboards: dried pasta and tinned tomatoes. It seemed unlikely he could rustle up a feast from the contents of this kitchen.

Anya leaned against the doorframe. "There are five bedrooms. Do you want a view over the mountains behind the house or the ones to the side?"

"What about the mountains to the front?" Cassandra asked.

"I'm taking that bedroom." Anya waved toward the front door. "I can watch the road."

"We'll look out onto the back." Cassandra headed to the door. "I'm going up. Are you coming?"

Wade collected their suitcase from the hall and followed her up to the back bedroom. Once he'd opened the shutters, he could see darkness beyond. He closed the curtains as Cassandra turned on the light. They remedied the unmade bed after Cassandra found sheets in an ottoman.

Yesterday Pill   Iain Benson

Cassandra plumped a pillow and lay down, her hands across her swollen baby bump.

"I might just stay here," she said after a moment. "It's late enough."

"I need a drink of water." Wade headed for the door.

"Can you bring me one, too, please?" she asked.

Wade nodded and returned down to the kitchen. Anya had half the cupboards open. He could see the glasses glistening slightly in the lights. Wade took two out. Anya looked over.

"That's a good idea. Could you get me one?"

Wade grabbed a third glass. He opened the cold tap and let it run for a little while before filling the glasses. Listening, Wade decided Cassandra was unlikely to come down.

"I got taken off the street and beaten." Wade didn't turn to see if Anya was listening. "They shot me. Then you arrived, crashing through the door. I nearly died, but you gave me something. Suddenly, I was back where I'd started an hour before."

Anya remained silent for a moment. Wade turned and gave her a glass of water, sparkling in the ceiling spotlights. She spoke. "That surprises me."

"Why?"

"If necessary, I'd have jumped back a day for you. I must have already jumped."

"It was real then?" Wade asked.

Anya nodded. "Yes."

"I only went back an hour. Not a day."

"You had one dose."

Perplexed, Wade had questions. "Dose? How does it work?"

Anya shrugged. "No idea. You always wondered that. You had so many theories. Have you told Cass?"

Wade shrugged. "I did, but she didn't believe me. Why can't she know?"

"There was a warning when we started: if she knows, it will cause the end of time and space. You used to think that she had something to do with creating the pills. That perhaps she invents them, so if she knew, she wouldn't create them. Somebody we once knew said it was important that she didn't know." Anya gave a faint smile, a memory of something momentarily lighting up her face, before returning to shadow. "He used to say it could end the universe and unravel spacetime."

"Dose? Pills?" Wade remembered Anya touching her necklace. "Your pendant. It has a symbol on it, like my ring."

Anya extracted her pendant and looked at it. "We used to work for the same organisation."

"Did you bring it?" Wade suddenly had a fear that the ring was still in a drawer in his bedside cabinet at home.

"Your ring?" Anya asked. "Of course."

Anya unzipped the side pocket of her bag and fished around inside. She produced the signet ring. Wade twirled it in his fingers, looking closely at it. It was his only possession from before his seizure. He knew it intimately, the faded red stone inset with a shield and sword symbol. The gold band had his name etched on the inside. Wade smiled and handed it back.

"If I wear it, Cass will know something is going on."

"Are you telling her about the time-shifting?"

Wade thought about it. "No."

Anya's left eyebrow arched. "I didn't expect that."

"I'm full of surprises," Wade said.

Anya shook her head. "Believe it or not, you're more like you were than you know."

Wade didn't know how to take that. He knew he had to get some sleep, though. He picked up the two glasses. "I have so many questions. We'll have to continue this another time."

As Wade climbed the stairs, his mind whirled with questions he hoped he could now get out of a more amenable Anya. Interspersed with the questions, a realisation he had travelled through time!

Yesterday Pill   Iain Benson

He found Cassandra sitting up in bed. Their nightwear currently occupied a suitcase in the jeep, so she wore a strappy vest.

She looked up from her book. "You took your time."

Wade placed the glasses on the bedside tables. "I was trying to get something out of Anya."

"Did you manage anything?"

Wade gave the briefest of a head shake as he hunted through the open suitcase for his nightshirt. He wasn't going to lie to her, but nor did he want the universe to end.

"She knows something. Getting what that could be is hard."

Cassandra nodded. "Wear her down."

Wade eventually found a tee-shirt. He slipped it on, the lure of sleep pulling the tension from his spine. The sheets smelled a little musty, but even that did not prevent sleep from overcoming him.

He'd often envied Cassandra's ability to sleep easily. Tired as Wade was, he matched her. Unaware he'd fallen asleep until the sun shafted through the slightest gap in the curtains. Prisms of light reflected off a mirror and bathed his face. He came awake instantly, a disturbing dream scattering as his eyes adjusted to the light. He opened the curtains, still unable to see the mountains as low clouds obscured the distance.

Soft snowflakes fell, lightly dusting the bushes and fence post finials.

"Mm," Cassandra murmured, stretching. "I could stay here forever."

Wade found himself some clothes to wear. The suitcase lid rested against a slightly ajar wardrobe. It had been the mirror on that door that had reflected the morning light into his eyes. He nudged it closed with a touch of morning irritation. It pushed open again with enough rebound energy to shut the suitcase. Wade opened the wardrobe, checking they had not broken it. He intended to leave the house with the chalet's owners unaware there had been a break-in.

Highly padded ski suits in a variety of colours gave Wade pause.

"I don't think we can stay here another night." Wade dressed quickly. "I suggest you get dressed. We'll be leaving soon."

While Cassandra dressed, he knocked on Anya's room. The heavy door swung open. He caught the long handle before it could crash into the wall beyond. Anya's bedroom looked unused. Wade padded down the steps. The granite slabs looked oily in the morning light, as though his socked feet were stepping into a void.

He found Anya in the kitchen. She'd found coffee. "Want one? It'll have to be unsweetened and black."

"I'd mainline granules at the moment," Wade admitted.

"It is ground coffee." Anya waggled a silver tin at him and pointed at an espresso machine. "We're in Italy. I think there's a law against granules."

"We'll need to leave soon." Wade examined the mechanism for the espresso machine. He emptied the filter holder into the waste disposal and refilled it from the tin Anya had found. It wafted chocolate smells as he spooned it into the stainless-steel filter, making his mouth water and his stomach growl.

Anya watched him over the rim of her cup. "I was planning on leaving early. Why the hurry? It's quite nice here."

Wade found cups in a cupboard above the machine and put an oversized mug under the spigot. The coffee burbled and growled as coffee poured in a frothing stream. The steam hissed out, odours of warming coffee twining around it.

"I found ski suits."

"So?" she asked.

Wade took the cup and repeated his actions to make a drink for Cassandra. "We're in the mountains. It's snowing. We are in a ski lodge."

Anya winced. "Probably accurate."

Wade had an idea and opened the large cupboard under the stairs. It slid out on well-oiled hinges, revealing a rack of skis. "Accurate."

"We'll make sure the place is clean and leave this morning."

Cassandra, up and dressed, folded sheets as Wade brought her coffee. He placed it on the nightstand next to the two empty glasses.

Yesterday Pill   Iain Benson

"That smells divine." Cassandra came over and gave Wade a lingering kiss. "Mm. Tastes good too."

"You haven't drunk any yet."

"No, but you have."

They expunged any trace of their night they could find. Wade heard Anya gathering her belongings down the corridor.

After a final toilet break, Wade searched through the kitchen drawers until he found some glue. Anya turned the alarm back on and locked the door. Their last act was to repair the broken safe with the key back inside.

Wade rattled it; happy the owners would never know. "It's like we were never here."

"How did you know the alarm code?" Cassandra asked, suddenly puzzled.

Anya looked startled, but Wade answered for her. "They wrote it inside the key safe."

Cassandra nodded. "Oh. Right. I guess that makes sense."

They left the village at a sedate pace. More comfortable than the bumping arrival. The mountaintops remained out of sight, now lost in swirling snow. Insufficient snow had fallen yet for them to leave telltale marks on the drive. Heavier snow came as they drove. Soon they were leaving tracks. They passed under a railway bridge and left the village.

"Are we not using the motorway?" Cassandra asked.

The motorway's pale grey stanchions formed a smear in the dark green forest. "There will be a lot of cameras there."

"Paladin has to be tracking us somehow," Anya confirmed.

"We need a new car." Wade wished they could keep the Jeep. He liked it.

"It's getting one that nobody will miss," Anya said. "Anything that somebody reports stolen is a red flag to the Paladin search algorithms."

Cassandra sounded excited. "How about a licence plate?"

Anya shook her head. "It might take longer to realise it, but eventually, the car owner will report it stolen."

"There was a wreck in a field back there." Cassandra twisted in her seat to point back down the road.

Anya slowed and swung the car around, driving back carefully.

Wade smiled and nodded. "It's a good idea."

In a farm field, opposite a track down to a farmhouse, they saw a faded red Citroen. Anya parked by the roadside and climbed out. Snow quickly coated her hair. Wade joined her, the air feeling much colder than the warmth inside the car. They climbed over a rickety fence. The creaking gave Wade feelings of trepidation, but it held. They waded through waist-high grass that quickly soaked through Wade's jeans. The Citroen looked a considerable margin from roadworthy, missing glass and wheels. The bodywork twisted and dented, long gashes of rust on the door.

"It has licence plates." Anya pointed with her screwdriver.

Wade checked and found the plate's twin.

Getting them off was a different matter. Wade could barely feel his fingers by the time they'd removed them. Uncontrollable shivers wracked him as they replaced the plates on the Jeep.

Wade blew into his cupped hands and gratefully got back into the car.

"You're frozen!" Cassandra said. "Both of you!"

Anya nodded, turning the heater up to full despite what it would do to their battery. Once they'd recovered enough, she turned the car around and searched for a way back onto the motorway.

Wade sat on his hands and leaned forward. "Hopefully, they will only read the plates and not the make, model, and colour."

"We'll soon find out," Anya replied.

Wade ducked his head slightly to look at the wooded slopes past Cassandra. Kilometres of forest undulating with the crumpled rock under their roots. It would be possible to lose themselves amid the pines for years. Paladin would know their position the moment they needed to get back on the grid. Should Cassandra go into labour, or a supermarket surveillance

Yesterday Pill   Iain Benson

camera catch a glimpse.

They skirted past Turin. The mountains disappeared into the distance behind them, with the snow turning to drizzle.

"Why has it taken them so long to find me?" Cassandra asked after a couple of hours of silence. "I've never really hid."

"Paladin has been looking for you for about fifteen years," Anya replied over her shoulder. Wade guessed Anya's following words had nothing time travel related. "Wade is right. We knew each other before his seizure. We used to head off any ripple you would make in the electronic ocean."

Cassandra looked a little affronted and glared at Wade as though he was personally responsible for ruining her life. It softened as she looked at him.

"Ripples? Like what?

Anya gave a single shoulder shrug. "What's your name on your tax forms?"

Cassandra's brows furrowed. "That's always annoyed me. I'm down as Sandra Roberts. That name has dogged me for ages. Even if I spell it out, I couldn't renew my passport because they struggled to match my records together."

"That's Wade's fault." The chortle was audible in her tone. "He used to change your details. He'd hack systems and change them back to Sandra."

"Oh!" Cassandra gave Wade another glare, more puzzled than angry.

"I don't remember," Wade admitted.

"You are good with computers," Cassandra said, slowly, as though thinking. "That's why I got you the job at the university's IT department."

"I wonder what changed?" Wade asked. "Paladin found you."

Anya shrugged. "You weren't amending Cass's data anymore."

"And I corrected my details at the hospital when I had my first scan," Anya said, shaking her head.

"They found you because I couldn't remember. I needed to change your name, and I didn't." Wade suddenly felt to blame. He'd not been there to protect Cassandra.

Cassandra must have sensed his inner turmoil. She took his hand and smiled. "You couldn't have known."

Wade squeezed her fingers. He had a question about their rescue from the restaurant. At first, he felt it was a question that would have to wait until Cassandra had left Wade and Anya alone until Wade realised he could ask it if he phrased it correctly.

"You knew about the attack at the restaurant," he said, speaking slowly and thinking through where he was heading. "Why not stop us going? Ring up and cancel our reservations or something?"

Anya gave another half shrug and looked at Wade in the mirror. Her eyes narrowed slightly. "They weren't attacking the restaurant. They were attacking you. It wouldn't have mattered where you were. They'd located you."

Wade nodded. He felt that there was more to it than that. Asking any more would reveal too much to Cassandra. He felt duplicitous for keeping it from her, but the unravelling of spacetime would be detrimental and best avoided.

"I'm getting hungry," Cassandra said. "This 'drink a coffee in the morning' diet is great for losing weight, but Bump is kicking me for dinner."

"If we stop and charge the car, we can probably push on to Croatia this evening." Anya bit her bottom lip. Wade could almost see her planning a route out in her head.

A green signpost with *Verona Sud* approached at speed. Anya slipped over into the exit lane and joined the early afternoon traffic curving back over the motorway and into a city. The city had been hiding behind a row of trees. Now Wade saw offices, hotels and apartment blocks rising around them. Anya slowed into the toll booths. To get ahead of a slow-moving truck, she accelerated hard. The road narrowed into two lanes, hemmed in on either side by corrugated concrete walls.

"I've always wanted to see Verona," Cassandra said. "It's where Shakespeare set *Romeo and Juliet*."

Wade looked at the wide streets and modern buildings they passed through. "He might have chosen somewhere else had he seen it now."

Anya turned off the main road. "If we survive this, perhaps we can come back this way. I'm not sure we have an option for sightseeing until we neutralise Paladin."

"Makes sense, unfortunately," Cassandra said, looking out of her window with longing.

5

Anya had to have been following signs as she found a Moto-Stop, a combined charging station with an attached restaurant. "I want to avoid places that might have cameras."

Wade ducked his head to look around outside the car. "You think they're using facial recognition?"

Anya nodded. "If I wanted to find us, that's what I'd do."

"It looks pretty safe here," Cassandra said, unfastening her seatbelt.

Wade agreed. It felt good to stretch out. Wade reached for the sky, going up onto tiptoes. The air smelled of lavender from the planters around the carpark's edge. The air held a threat of winter, but felt pleasant enough.

Anya connected the car up. "I'll go in and check if they have cameras, and if they do, we can go somewhere else."

A current of warm garlic swept past them as Anya went inside. Wade's stomach responded. He could see Anya through the glass, wearing her baseball cap and oversized sunglasses. Cassandra came to stand by his side and twined her fingers through his. Her skin felt silky. He lifted her hand and kissed her knuckles. Anya gesticulated as she spoke to the Moto-Stop employee. After a few moments, she looked at Wade and waved him to come inside.

The air inside cuddled Wade with warmth, taking the chill from his skin. He breathed the smells in deeply, relishing them.

"Follow me, please?" The server spoke German. Wade added it to his list of languages.

She led them to a table at the back, placing menus on the table.

Wade watched her leave. "What did you say to her?"

Anya gave a short, barked laugh. "I told her you were a German TV star having an affair, and that I was your manager. She's turned the cameras off for you, so the press won't get any photos."

Her ingenuity impressed Wade. "I thought I'm the improviser?"

Yesterday Pill   Iain Benson

Cassandra got back out of her chair. "Arrabbiata for me. Where are the toilets?"

"Over there." Anya pointed to the opposite corner.

The moment she was away from the table, Wade lowered his voice. "You said you could go back a day, so I'm assuming that's how you set everything up for our rescue from the restaurant?"

"I had to redo that day quite a few times, but mostly I got by in a single hour. I try to avoid day jumps."

"Why?" IT puzzled Wade why trying to cram everything into an hour would be preferable.

Anya glanced towards the toilets. "First off, there are the headaches. The way we learned about it, as we age, our consciousness changes. Over an hour, that's small. Over a day, though it's still small, it's large enough for a perception shift that leaves you with a headache."

Wade understood that. It sounded how he'd explain something complicated. "You said 'first off'? Is there another reason?"

Anya nodded. "Our minds aren't the only thing that changes. You once said 'you can never see the same river twice' because things change. Over an hour, they rarely accrue into anything meaningful, but over a day, they can sometimes add up."

Wade scratched his chin with his thumbnail. "I guess minor changes could mount up. Somebody stops to wipe a surface in a kitchen, and it changes the time they leave the house."

"Only by a second," Anya agreed. "It barely changes their day."

"But it could be big." Wade's mind was racing. "They miss a change in the lights, and a truck crashes into the back of them."

"I've never seen a change that big." Anya shrugged. "It's possible, though."

"Quantum fluctuations. Cass would know more about that." Wade nodded, remembering conversations he and Cassandra had had. "Can you go back further than a day?"

"If you take three doses, it sends you back a week, but that's the last resort. There are too many changes, including your own mind."

"Four doses?"

Anya shook her head. "We only have three doses."

"Shame," Wade said. "If we could go back to when Cass corrected her name, we could put it back again."

Anya nodded.

Wade saw Cassandra coming through the swing door back into the restaurant. He held up a surreptitious finger.

"Has the waitress been?" she asked, squeezing back around the potted fern into her seat.

Wade shook his head. "Not yet."

The waitress had to have been waiting for Cassandra to return as she chose that moment to appear.

"Are you ready to order?" She sounded offhand.

"Three penne arrabbiata, please." Anya handed back the menus. "And can we have a bottle of sparkling water?"

"That was easy," Wade said.

The server nodded and retreated to the bar to fetch them a bottle of water and glasses.

"Your water," she said, the bottle top popping as she flicked the mechanism.

The food, when it arrived, was pleasant enough, but Wade barely tasted it, his mind back to mulling over time travel. There were so many possibilities. He understood now why Anya had said they had funding. A lottery jackpot could be lucrative, especially weekly.

"Bump approves," Cassandra said as she finished a portion of ice cream.

"We need to get moving." Anya raised her hand and called the waitress over to pay. "Although I could quite happily have a snooze after that tiramisu."

"It looked good," Wade admitted. "It'll probably put you over the limit."

Anya switched to German when the server came over with the card machine. "Danke."

"What's the food like in Croatia?" Cassandra asked, musing aloud.

"I've never been." Anya pushed through the glass door.

A waterfall-like crescendo drowned out any other thoughts. The glass door became millions of diamond-sharp shards cascading down in an ice-blue avalanche. The shot's crack came afterwards.

Wade didn't pause, acting on automatic.

The world went into slow-motion.

He turned and pulled Cassandra back into the restaurant.

She staggered back into the shadowed interior. Wade half-supporting, half-dragging her towards the bar. Cassandra's mouth was open as she pointed back towards the door.

Wade looked over his shoulder. Anya was in a puddle, a rapidly expanding pool of red encircling her dark hair.

He had no time to process that scene as he pushed Cassandra behind the bar. Too many other thoughts cried for his attention.

"Anya!" Cassandra was mouthing, over and over.

The girl who had served them had a hand over her mouth, the card machine dangling from one hand.

With Cassandra as safe as he could get her in the immediate now, Wade turned his attention back to Anya. Keeping low, he headed for the door, looking through the large glass windows. Across the road in a blocky orange three-storey house, Wade saw the black barrel of a rifle against white shutters. He pulled his head back as the window exploded inwards, showing him in glass fragments. He grabbed a table and knocked it over to use as cover to get to Anya.

A fist-sized hole punched into the table, wooden splinters scoring marks across Wade's face.

Wade felt nothing.

An entire section of Anya's forehead was missing, blood still slowly seeping from the wound. He felt horror rise inside him.

An ice-cold determination descended as another hole smashed through the table.

Wade noted the thud in his shoulder, but it seemed insignificant.

He grabbed Anya's necklace, snapping the chain.

Pulling himself back into the interior, he joined Cassandra behind the bar.

"You're shot!" Cassandra went to touch Wade's shoulder but pulled back.

"You!" Wade rounded on the server and almost spat German at her. "What did you do? Who did you tell?"

She was hesitant in her reply. "I asked *Knot* if any of my followers knew who you were."

Wade swore. Social media had caused this. "You photographed us?"

She nodded.

Wade glanced back up over the bar. He saw a blacked-out Range Rover pull up.

"We're going to die." Cassandra's voice was toneless.

Wade looked at the necklace's pendant. The hazy memory of what Anya had done to get a dose from it played in his mind like watching a tiny television screen at a distance through a fog.

Wade heard an authoritative voice call out from the carpark. "Fan out. Kill everybody."

Wade quietened the world and closed his eyes. His fingers caressed the pendant. Muscle memory took over, pressing, twisting, and squeezing the charm between his fingers. He had no actual memory of how to use the necklace; he hoped his fingers knew.

Bullets thudded into the bar, shattering bottles and sprinkling them with wine and spirits. Wade paid it no attention, serenity falling on him. The pendant deformed. He looked down as the waitress spun around and fell onto his legs. The necklace had a single circle of white.

It appeared to be two dimensional and of infinite depth. The edges looked and felt fuzzy, like a distant cloud held on Wade's fingers.

Yesterday Pill   Iain Benson

"Say goodbye," said a Russian accented voice from somewhere above him.

Wade pressed the pill to his lips, tasting the fog.

The world flattened; a bullet froze, exploding from the end of a barrel.

Wade's perception of it made it look like a painting.

With a surge, the picture raced away into the distance, streaks of colour and texture swirling around him.

Impression snapped back into focus.

"Are you okay, Wade?" Cassandra asked. "You blanked out for a moment."

Wade looked in at Anya, talking to the waitress. She waved to them, gesturing for them to come in.

Prepared, Wade smiled at Cassandra. "I'm fine."

While Cassandra and Anya took their seats, Wade turned and caught the waitress's arm as she walked away.

"I know you're thinking of putting a picture on social media."

She looked guilty. "I would never."

Wade fixed her gaze. "Yes, you would. If there is any hint of us being here on your social media, you will never work again."

She switched to Italian. "I understand."

Wade held her gaze, searching to see if she understood him.

He supposed he would find out when they left if she truly understood. "We would like some sparkling water, please."

Wade took his seat.

"What was that about?" Cassandra asked.

"I was making sure she didn't take any photos and put them on social media."

Anya looked a little affronted. "I had that covered with a story of you being a German TV star having an affair. I said I was your manager. She turned the cameras off."

Wade shook his head. "That wouldn't have stopped her putting the pictures on social media and having Paladin finding us that way."

Cassandra got to her feet. "Well, it certainly seems safe enough. I need to go to the toilet. I'll have arrabbiata."

The moment Cassandra was out of earshot, Wade filled Anya in on the previous iteration.

"And to think, Cassandra and I thought you were getting secret messages from somebody in Paladin when the truth is far stranger."

Surprised, Anya's eyebrows rose. "You worked out the locket?"

"I don't think I could do it now," Wade admitted. "It was quite high pressure. I let my fingers remember."

Anya reached into her bag and took out his ring.

"Watch. Always squeeze where the sword handles are."

She pushed the emblem down with her index finger, squeezed the top and bottom, and gave a forty-five degrees twist to the left. She released and twisted it back to the top before depressing it in again and rotating ninety degrees to the right.

"This is important," she said. "Ninety degrees to the right is one dose, one-eighty is two, and two-seventy is three. Three-sixty will cancel the dose."

"You can never get over three doses." Wade nodded to show he understood.

"One dose will send you back an hour," Anya said.

Wade interrupted her. "You gave me the times and why you cannot go back further already. You can never see the same river twice."

Anya gave a smile that lit up her face. It was the first time Wade had seen genuine joy from her. "You always used to say that."

Wade let her keep the joy by withholding that she had been the one to tell him. "Cass is back."

The waitress came over with their water and glasses. She glanced nervously at Wade.

"Your water," she said, popping the lid.

"Three penne arrabbiata." Anya handed the menus back.

"Make that two. I'll have the carbonara," Wade said. He hadn't been impressed by the arrabbiata on his first iteration.

The signet ring went into his trouser pocket. He could feel the weight of it. He knew he should tell Cassandra everything, but it felt like a secret he kept for all the right reasons.

The carbonara turned out to be better than the arrabbiata.

"Bump approves." Cassandra rubbed her distended tummy.

"We need to get moving." Anya raised her hand, attracting the waitress. "Although I could quite happily have a snooze after that tiramisu."

"I'll drive." Wade held out his hand. "It smelled like there was enough alcohol in that tiramisu to put you over the limit."

Anya wordlessly handed the car key fob over.

"What's the food like in Croatia?" Cassandra's words put Wade into a hyper-alert mode.

"I've never been." Anya was right behind Wade at the door.

Cassandra scowled at him. "Are you going to open the door with your hands or try to use your mind?"

Wade checked for snipers in the orange building. He had difficulty seeing it, making it an ideal sniping location.

He opened the door, pushing it with one hand and tossing the car key fob up and down, nonchalant. As he stepped out, he missed the key fob and had to bend to pick it off the floor. He was hoping the movement looked natural.

Nothing. No gunshot. With a smile, Wade scooped up the fob and strode forward.

"Smooth," Anya said.

"Clumsy more like!" Cassandra laughed.

Wade took the wheel and checked their charge. "The charge is nearly full."

"Next stop Croatia." Anya climbed in the back. "I am having a snooze. I've earned it."

Cassandra settled into the front passenger seat, wriggling down into it with a contented sound. "The back seat is comfortable enough, but this now feels like a luxury."

"The satnav is saying nine hours to Belgrade," Wade said.

"We'll have to stop before then," Cassandra said. "Especially if Bump kicks my bladder."

After an hour, they passed a sign for Venice. The temptation to turn off so they could visit felt almost vital to Wade. He sighed and carried on past the junction. He continued along the motorway, the miles passing under the hissing tyres.

"I'd hoped to see the sea," he told Cassandra. "According to the satnav, it's on the other side of that fence."

The sky had the peculiar paleness he associated with the sea.

"They put that fence there, so the sea doesn't distract drivers," Cassandra theorised.

"Killjoys."

They sailed through the border with Slovenia. Wade only realised they had changed countries when diacritics other than acute accents appeared on the street signs. Wade finally got to see the Adriatic as they swept down from the mountains that formed the border between Slovenia and Croatia. There had been a little more security at the border crossing, with Anya having to find their passports at a checkpoint. Wade had been glad they were not in a truck. He crept past a long line of stationary trucks off to one side, waiting to pass through customs. As it was, a bored-looking man in a pale green shirt waved them through after a cursory glance at their documentation.

The late afternoon sun slanted down onto the sea, creating a dizzying diamond reflection off the dark blue water. A flash of memory, seeing Anya fall amid broken glass, rose unbidden. A touch of haze hung over an island in the bay. With effort, Wade pushed the memory away. It had never happened.

Cassandra pointed at some approaching services. "We need a break."

Yesterday Pill　　　　　　　　　　　　　　Iain Benson

Wade nodded and left the motorway onto a utilitarian carpark. Anya accompanied Cassandra to the toilet block. Wade parked, looking out across some low bushes that rolled down to the Adriatic beyond. He could almost forget they were running, trying to stay one step ahead of a group that wanted them dead. Despite the thrum of cars sweeping past on the motorway, it felt peaceful.

The two women returned, and Wade went himself.

Anya took the driver's seat. "I'll drive for a while."

"I don't need to worry about a car chase?" Wade asked, trying to keep his tone light for Cassandra.

Anya shook her head.

The food and drink amenities were on the other side, across a metal bridge over the motorway. Wade did not want a highway between them and their car. After using the facilities, he used Anya's card to get coffee from a vending machine.

Anya had linked her phone to the car's entertainment system, throwing the news onto the car's console screen.

Cassandra pointed at the screen. "Wade, you need to see this."

Wade sat in the back and looked between the seats. He passed out coffee and watched the British news report about the attack on the restaurant.

Anya pressed a button on her phone. "I'll restart it."

An elegantly dressed news anchor had a small screen beside his right ear. They could see the restaurant explosion where the missiles had struck. They couldn't see the helicopters.

"What you are about to see may be distressing," the anchor was saying. The footage moved to fill the screen. "Police are still searching for the terrorists they believe are behind the explosion at a popular restaurant in Coventry. A group of three fled the scene in a white Volvo shortly before the explosion."

A shaky, blurred CCTV image showing the car appeared. The mushrooming orange scene of destruction was conspicuous by its absence.

"They abandoned the Volvo under a bridge on the M6, near the M42 junction. Police are looking for any information from witnesses in the area late on Friday night."

The serious-sounding anchor gave out further information. Wade couldn't understand how the report omitted helicopter gunships or the car chase through the town centre.

Anya tutted. "It won't be long before Paladin gives the news outlets our pictures."

"That will let work know where I am," Cassandra said. "I was thinking of ringing in sick tomorrow."

"No chance." Anya shook her head. "That would immediately pinpoint our exact location. I think they roughly know where we are as it is."

Cassandra rolled her eyes. "I wasn't serious."

Anya ignored the eye roll. "I was serious."

"Why was the news article wrong?" Wade wondered aloud. "Where were the helicopters?"

Anya shrugged. "I told you. Paladin doesn't want the spotlight. Somewhere at their headquarters, there'll be proof of what they did and why."

"Surely there were hundreds of witnesses?" Wade persisted.

It was Anya's turn to roll her eyes. "There were hundreds of witnesses. They will fill social media with what they saw. Nobody will believe them."

"But the news..."

Anya's eyebrows went up a little. "Those in charge can manipulate the news. It becomes the nation's truth. We won't be saying what we saw. We will put on the internet evidence and proof."

Worry made Wade change the subject. "We could do with getting another set of number plates. The farther we get from Italy, the more suspicious they'll become."

"I'll keep an eye out," Cassandra said.

Anya disconnected her phone and restored the satnav. "It's saying

Yesterday Pill　　　　　　　　　　　　　Iain Benson

midnight by the time we reach Belgrade."

"What charge do we have?" Wade imagined their current position near the Mediterranean, trying to work out a route they could take. He wished they had the World Atlas from home to choose the ideal course.

"We're back up to four-fifths." Anya read the charge. "Are you thinking of pushing on?"

Wade nodded. "If I have some sleep, I can take over. That way, we can get as far as possible."

Anya flicked around on her phone. "I was already planning that in, with a couple of loo breaks. We'll need to park up somewhere and top up the battery for a few hours."

"Can we sleep in a bed?" Cassandra let out an audible sigh.

"You slept in a bed last night," Wade reminded her. A thought struck him: "And the night before, and every night forever before that."

Cassandra laughed. "When you're sitting down all day, a bed seems like a wonderful dream."

Anya rapidly got up to speed and headed off down the motorway. The surrounding landscape changed from rocky scrubland to wide open spaces with mountains on the horizon. They got some food and charged the car at a diner. It had been further from the motorway than they'd expected. The restaurant barely seemed to be on the electricity grid, lessening their fear of cameras.

6

Darkness had fallen as they skirted Zagreb, the city's lights twinkling off to the left, soon behind them. Wade took the wheel for the last stretch. He tried to stay awake during a four-hour slog through dark farmland, with the only illumination coming from the occasional towns. Light returned as a dome of light, delineating the border with Serbia.

"We went through an entire country without issue," Wade said as people in army uniforms stopped them.

"I think you've jinxed it." Cassandra glanced around at the several armed guards watching them.

"It doesn't help that we're the only car." Wade reached into the glove compartment and pulled out the passports.

A soldier in a peaked cap waved them forward. Wade decided he was in charge, as the other soldiers sported berets.

"Papers," the soldier said in English.

Given the passports' nationality, Wade adopted a blank expression. "Parles Français?"

"Non." The soldier took their passports and opened them. "Deutsch?"

"Ja." Fluent German replaced Wade's limited French.

The soldier sniffed as he looked through the passports, closely looking at the pictures and bending down to look through the windows. He walked around to Cassandra and Anya's side, looking in again.

"Please wait here." The soldier had reasonable German.

Wade's anxiety levels rose as the soldier took the passports into a border booth. He tried to maintain a calm expression, keeping both hands visible on the wheel. The other soldiers appeared jittery. Their automatic rifles levelled at them. He attempted to appear as little a threat as possible.

"The passports are perfect," Anya hissed from the back seat.

After a lifetime of seconds, the soldier returned, holding three

Yesterday Pill   Iain Benson

sheets of paper. Wade had a sinking feeling they were not visa forms. The soldier held the paper out and had a good look at each of them. He came to the window.

He paused before speaking, translating into German what he wanted to say. "Is this you?"

Wade looked closely at the sheet of paper, but the letters were incompressible. He could make out the Union Jack and his face.

"I don't think so." Wade looked up at the soldier. "It's a poor photo."

"It is. Please exit the vehicle."

"I have a bad feeling about this," Anya said.

Wade rummaged in his pocket and slipped his ring on as he climbed from the car. "I agree."

Behind him, he heard Anya and Cassandra exit.

"We are looking for these people." The soldier brandished the sheaves.

"Does it say my wife is pregnant?" Wade gestured to Cassandra. It felt good to say wife, bringing out an involuntary smile.

The soldier looked at the sheet for Cassandra. "It does not."

"Then it cannot be us." Wade slipped into improvisation mode.

"It is not." The soldier appeared humourless, maintaining a severe disposition.

Wade glanced at Anya as she gave out a little gasp. With a slight nod of her head, she pointed across the border. Four blacked-out Range Rovers rolled to a silent stop.

Black-clad soldiers in body armour disembarked their vehicles, creating up a defensive position. From the fourth car, two men and a woman appeared. Wade clasped his hands behind his back and manipulated his ring. It was back-to-front, but his fingers knew the pattern.

He felt the pill pop into his fingers.

Anya moved to stand between the approaching Paladin operatives and Cassandra.

"Very noble, Anya." Wade identified the speaker as a lithe, dark-haired man. He spoke Arabic with a Russian accent. Wade realised this was the man who had been in the restaurant after Anya's assassination, but the wrong shape for the one from the garage in Le Mans. He had to park the questions on how he got around so quickly and how many people worked for Paladin to focus on the immediate issue.

"She's pregnant, Adrian." Anya confirmed Wade's suspicions that once Anya, and possibly himself, had worked for Paladin.

Adrian looked over at Wade with eyes so dark they almost bordered on black. "I know you will go to extraordinary lengths to protect her, Wade, but this is the next level."

"When it's important, you do what you can." Wade thought on his feet. He wanted a reply that sounded inherently defiant but had no meaning.

Still looking at Wade, Adrian brought a gun up and pointed it at Anya.

That was enough for Wade. He brought his hand up to his mouth as though the gun shocked him.

The world froze.

The bright lights that bathed the border crossing grew in brightness on a flat, two-dimensional shadow of reality.

With a snap, it shrank away, replaced with a long straight motorway.

It took Wade vital seconds to regain his composure, even though he'd prepared for it.

"Are you okay?" Cassandra asked, jerking awake.

"Micro-snooze," Wade lied.

Wade's mind raced. The scene at the border occupied his mind, but he needed an acceptable alternative that Cassandra might believe.

"Do we need to stop?" Anya asked from the back seat.

"Yes."

"Pull in at the next services," Anya instructed.

Yesterday Pill   Iain Benson

"Yes, miss," Wade replied.

Although he could have carried on driving, tiredness provided an excellent excuse for stopping and talking to Anya. As the dark kilometres zipped past the windows, Wade tried to work his way through several methods for getting past the border. Most he discarded immediately. A high-speed smash through the barriers would have their car riddled with bullets. His best idea centred on waiting until a busier time and hoping overloaded guards had less time to check every passenger.

The oasis of light in the absolute dark revealed the services before they reached the sign identifying it.

The carpark only contained one other car and a tractor. Wade would have preferred totally unoccupied services. They rolled into a charging bay outside the slope-roofed building that housed the toilets, shop, and restaurant.

"What's our range?" Anya asked as they climbed out and stretched.

Wade's breath misted as he replied. "Two fifty kilometres."

Anya checked her phone. "It's about two hundred to Belgrade. We might as well charge and go to the loo, get a coffee and a sandwich."

Cassandra pre-empted the suggestion, already heading up the path to the porticoed entrance. "I'm one step ahead of you."

Anya tapped on her phone. "I'll be right there."

"We had a problem at the border," Wade said.

"Which is about forty-five minutes from here." Anya nodded, obviously realising the micro-sleep had been a return to this time. "You handled the landing well, considering we were probably doing a hundred kph at the time."

"I figure if we wait here and try to get through when it's busy, we might stand a chance. The border guards had our pictures. They were looking for us."

Anya shook her head as she finished setting up the car charge. "We could try that unless I can figure something more likely to work."

Wade followed her up the path. "Harsh."

"How so?" Anya glanced up at him.

"You essentially dismissed my plan."

Anya stopped, looking a little puzzled. "Not dismissed. If they're checking pictures on passports, they will do it, even if it's rush hour. It might be a Serbian thing because they're not in the EU. We might not have this problem getting into Bulgaria, or indeed again in any country."

She pushed through the bright orange painted door. Wade followed her into an interior that smelled heavily of polished pine. Wade digested what she'd told him. Perhaps they could take a path through different countries.

Though the restaurant had a rope barrier preventing access, the shops and toilets remained open. Wade went looking for an atlas amid shelving crammed with music and books. He found a rotating display unit stuffed with paper maps. He unfolded a Baltic States map, tracing a route down past the Adriatic through Montenegro and Albania into Greece. From there, they could cut across to Turkey, or Hungary, Romania, and Bulgaria. It would add hundreds of kilometres to their journey. Wade refolded the map and returned it to the stand.

With Cassandra still in the toilets, Wade visited an antiseptic smelling bathroom with orange tiles. A broken hand-dryer left him with damp hands. He emerged back into the lobby, drying his hands on the seat of his pants.

Cassandra and Anya were by the fridge on the back wall. Wade joined them. He glanced over at the sleepy-looking youth behind the till. His fingers twined into dark curly hair to prop up his head. Anya took out her phone.

"I need to take this, Cass, one minute. Find a sandwich or something."

She left the shop standing by the closed restaurant. Wade joined Cassandra, slipping his arm around her waist as they tried to guess the sandwiches by looking through a small plastic window.

"I think this is some kind of cheese and bacon." Cassandra showed

Yesterday Pill   Iain Benson

Wade the green packaging. The lettering was Cyrillic, lending no clues as to the content.

Wade looked closely. "Bacon and brie, I think."

Anya returned. She grabbed a wire basket from beside the till and started collecting items from the shelves.

"What's she doing?" Cassandra asked.

Wade shrugged. "Her shopping list appears to have increased."

Anya grabbed a map off the spinning rack and returned to the sandwiches. "Might be worth grabbing a couple each."

"What's going on?" Wade asked.

"I'll explain in a minute."

Cassandra looked concerned. "I don't know what any of these sandwiches are."

Anya nodded. "What do you want to avoid?"

"Soft cheeses."

Anya approached the youth behind the counter. After a brief exchange, she identified English as their shared language. He came over.

He took sandwiches off the shelf. "Werst and tomato, or ham and mayonnaise."

Cassandra looked relieved. She took two sausage and tomato sandwiches. Wade grabbed the bacon and brie rather than look through or wait for the laconic translations.

Anya grabbed a compass, paracetamol, and a rucksack before they returned to the car as a final purchase.

She leaned against the passenger door, taking two paracetamol caplets with a swig of water from a bottle. "Paladin knows we're in the country. Our pictures are at every border crossing. Including those with Bosnia and Herzegovina."

"What does this mean?" Wade asked.

"It means I'm going to drive through the border on my own." Anya opened the Jeep's boot, rummaging through the suitcases. She located their coats.

"And us?" Cassandra asked.

Anya passed them their coats. "You're walking."

Wade shook his head. "I'll walk, but you take Cassandra."

Anya gave Wade a long stare. "Even with two women in the car, they'll check, they'll notice."

Wade thought of his plan. "What's wrong with waiting until tomorrow?"

Anya sighed. "Even if we wait until their busiest time and go to a different crossing, they *would* notice us."

Wade understood. Anya must have tried various approaches and had come back a day.

"We walk," Wade conceded. "Bump and all."

Anya got the map out and folded it into position. "There's a villa here."

Wade looked. In a dark green patch of forest, he saw the path and villa. "Must be big."

"It used to belong to the president of Yugoslavia," Anya said, handing over the map. "I'll meet you there."

"Are we walking from here?" Cassandra asked.

"No." Anya disconnected the charger and opened the doors. "I'll drop you at the last turn before the border."

Half an hour later, Anya followed a sign directing drivers to Lipovac but pulled over by the road sign pointing back towards the motorway. Wade grabbed his coat and the backpack off the back seat as Cassandra exited the car on the other side.

"It's about five miles." Wade checked the map in the light from the car. "It'll probably take two to three hours, depending on what the terrain is like."

Anya gave a sharp nod. "Good luck. If I'm not there, give it an hour, then carry on without me."

Wade had one hand on the door. "You'll get through."

"This is my first attempt with you walking," she replied with a half-

Yesterday Pill   Iain Benson

smile.

Before he closed the door, Wade leaned in. "When they caught us on the border, Paladin came. Somebody called Adrian arrived. He knew us."

Anya cursed under her breath. "Good to know. I'll keep my wits about me."

Wade closed the door and watched the taillights get swallowed by the dark. Wade shuddered, feeling stranded beside a wide, dusty field. An icy wind carried a smell of recent rain. Heavy clouds obscured the moon, leaving them in a pool of light from a nearby streetlamp. The illumination puddles punctuated the dark in three directions. The fourth held only blackness.

Wade pulled his coat together and zipped it up. "It's this way."

Cassandra gave a heavy sigh. "How does she know?"

Wade maintained the fiction, though the knot in his midriff tightened. "She took a phone call at the services."

Cassandra nodded. "Somebody must be feeding her information."

"I am more and more convinced she used to work for Paladin. She said something about them working in threes. Perhaps her source is the third."

Cassandra looked puzzled. "Who's the second?"

"Me." Wade gave a slight shrug. "Come on."

The uneven ground kept turning Wade's ankle, but Cassandra didn't complain, so he kept quiet. Wade thanked his foresight for putting jeans on that morning. The ankle-high grass scratched against the denim. At the field edge, they scrambled down a steep-sided ditch filled with scrubby bushes. Getting down was the straightforward part. A gash opened on the back of his hand as he reached back to help Cassandra struggle up. In the dancing light from the torch, he saw the hawthorn responsible. Wade felt they had been scrambling across the fields for a long time, but the lights from the road still appeared reasonably close.

Although uneven, they made good progress across the field to the line of trees. If Wade's calculations had been correct, they would cross the border while in the forest. A forest Wade hoped would hide them as it hid the dome of light over the customs station. The little beacon of torchlight swallowed by the greater darkness around them.

Trees cut off the wind's chill, allowing Wade to feel a little warmth from their exertions. He helped Cassandra through some thickets. "How are you doing?"

Cassandra's expression was impossible to see. "I'm fine."

Two metres into the forest, the darkness became absolute. Wade knew it would be easy to get lost.

A hundred metres in, and Wade almost fell into the border.

A concrete ditch, two metres deep with an electrified fence running in it, blocked their path.

The tree canopy above them was continuous. At nine weeks off Cassandra's due date, her tree-climbing days were on hold.

Cassandra played the torch down the border in both directions. Wade had no concerns about the soldiers seeing it; they were over two kilometres from the customs station.

"That's a flimsy border," Cassandra said. "But effective."

"You head that way. I'll go this way." Wade wondered what he would do for light. "Go for half an hour and come back. I'll do the same."

"What are we looking for?"

"A path across."

Wade slid down into the ditch. The fence loomed three metres over him, but the concrete floor allowed for easier walking. He glanced back, seeing the little bobbing light heading in the opposite direction. He concentrated on where he was going, wondering if he'd reach the border crossing before his half an hour was up.

After half an hour, he turned around and headed back.

He'd found a few dead animals, plenty of tree litter and branches, but nothing that would allow them to get across. No holes in the fence, no trees crashed down over it. The light from Cassandra's torch warmed his heart.

"There's a tree over the fence." Cassandra pointed with the torch. "About ten minutes that way. I'm cold."

Wade nodded. He took the ring out of his pocket. "We'll save some time in that case."

"Is that your ring?"

Wade nodded and manipulated the stone back and forth. The pill popped out. "The reason Anya knows what's happening is she's already been through it once. Sometimes more than once."

"I'm not following."

It felt good to tell her. "I have this ring. She has a locket. When we twist and press them in the right way, these pills pop out. We can travel back along our timeline for either an hour, a day, or a week."

"Time travel?" Cassandra sounded amazed.

"Yes." Wade smiled in the darkness.

"But only back into wherever you were? How does it work?"

Wade shrugged. "No idea."

"Could be information only that's travelling." She sounded like she was working through the permutations. "Maybe a quantum connection between two points in time."

Wade ended her musings before she ended the universe. He took the pill. The transition was his weirdest yet, with darkness replaced by darkness.

Wade stumbled as they entered the forest.

"Are you okay?" Cassandra asked.

"I'm fine," Wade replied.

Wade stopped Cassandra from stepping into the border.

"That's quite a flimsy border." Cassandra flashed the torch down on it. "But effective."

"We'll have to find a way across," Wade said.

"Which way?"

Wade made a show of looking in both directions. "Away from the border crossing."

They slid into the trough and set off. Ten minutes down, they found the tree that had taken out a section of fencing.

"I told you it was flimsy," Cassandra said triumphantly.

Wade checked the compass to orientate himself while Cassandra scrambled across the rough bark. As soon as she was safe, Wade followed.

The forest floor formed an additional, treacherous natural barrier. The torch illuminated only a few metres at a time, with every sightline obscured by trunks. Monitoring the compass, they stumbled nearly a kilometre before emerging into a clearing. After the absolute dark, the clearing felt almost bright.

Rather than race onto the easier footing, Wade briefly extinguished the torch, looking around and checking for any sign of border guards. He could see a plinth with a statue. A paved teardrop-shape path looped around it and headed into the forest. The track made walking more accessible, and they caught up some time.

Using the map, Wade worked out which paths to follow.

"Someone maintains these paths," Cassandra said.

Wade had to agree. The sun rose unseen behind clouds as they passed a low building with stables. From what he could see, the house held no life. It had an air of abandonment. The windows were curtainless, with one papered over. Wade could make out the shape of a tractor in the farmhouse courtyard, grass growing up past the punctured tyres.

"It's not the villa," Wade said. "That's up ahead."

Trees closed back around them as they walked up the path towards another clearing. Two properties, separated by a carpark. A two-storey log cabin and a building shaped like a black ramp with a white house slotted underneath. Anya's jeep had been left by the ramp-shaped building.

"Where is she?" Cassandra asked, peering into the morning gloom for any sign of Anya.

Wade had a bad feeling. "Wait here. Better yet, go back to that other house and hide in the stables. I will come and get you if it's safe."

Cassandra's eyes widened, but there was no argument. Wade

Yesterday Pill — Iain Benson

slipped his ring onto his finger and twisted the logo into position for an hour's dose.

At the door, he leaned against the wall, pushing it fully open with the flat of his hand. He listened. The building creaked as it expanded and contracted; breathing, as he called it. There had been many a morning when he lay there, back when he was in Cassandra's spare room, listening to the way the building moved. He had always felt reassured, knowing that something as solid as a house flexed with the changing environment.

Other than the faint creaks and groans, Wade heard nothing. The silence had an ominous quality. Moving as quietly as possible, he glanced around the door, looking across the highly polished marble floor to the staircase. Dark wooden doors flanked the expansive hall. The marquetry flooring had liquid splashes from the light seeping through the narrow windows to his left. Wade slipped inside, his shoes making the slightest of squeaks on the slippery wood. Heavy wooden tables lay between him and the staircase. He wondered if it was a hotel. The staircase zigzagged up to a landing before vanishing into the second floor.

With no idea where Anya would be, Wade headed to the nearest door. It opened onto a suite. He could see a low green sofa, an arch through to a bedroom with a double bed and a dressing table. It had to be a hotel. Checking up the staircase as he crossed the hall, he glanced in the other room, similarly laid out, but with a chequered sofa in browns and oranges.

"I preferred the other suite." His whisper echoed in the stillness.

The only other door led into another hall, with a quartet of blue sofas, a wall-sized television screen and double doors onto the garden. A second dark-brown stained staircase switched back and forth to the upper storey. Wade rested his hands on the bannisters and placed a foot on the bottom step. Slowly, he let it take his weight, fully expecting a squeak that never came. He took the first few steps equally carefully, but this was a lavishly made staircase and creaky steps an anathema to the artisan that had built it.

Instead of holding the bannisters as he took the switchback, he pressed his back to the wall. Seeing a loveseat on the mezzanine, Wade wondered how many chairs one house needed. A shadowy landing led to other rooms. Wade inched along the wall and peered around the corner. He had a choice of three doors. Slowly, he pushed open the first door. A large double bed dominated the room, but Anya tied to a chair in the corner drew his attention. Her head lolled down, her chin almost to her chest. Her pale green shirt ripped and bloodstained.

Wade knew he had made no sound; the waft of a draught from the door had to have told her she had company. Her head lifted; the defiance in her eyes softened when she saw him. She had a gag tightly into her mouth, pulling her cheeks taut enough to make them bleed. Checking quickly over his shoulder, Wade stepped into the room. Heavy drapes kept the light out, the only illumination coming through the door.

Anya's eyes widened, the whites visible in the small amount of light. She jerked her chin and made a strangled sound.

Wade felt the presence by the movement of air. He turned, leaning backwards as a fist swung, holding a blackjack. Wade had no time to take in his assailant. He disengaged his brain and let his body handle the situation. At some point, Wade now knew Paladin had trained him. He stepped forward, planting his back foot onto the floorboard behind him, driving the heel of his hand into the man's midriff. As the wind left him, Wade followed it up, raising his elbow into the descending chin, snapping the man's head backwards and lifting him clean off his feet.

Now his brain took in the man's details, greying hair at the temple, a large, hooked nose and black clothing. He wore gloves; the truncheon fastened to his wrist by a loop. He didn't look like any of his attackers in Le Mans. Two others came from the room across the landing; Wade recognised Adrian, the other a woman with long black wavy hair Wade recognised as Adrian's companion at the border. Adrian saw Wade, his face set into grim continence. Wade took the scene in instantly, the holstered pistol, Adrian's hand reaching for it. Wade stepped back and kicked the door closed, falling backward as the gun made a loud retort. The wood in

Yesterday Pill   Iain Benson

the door splintered at head height; Wade rolled to his feet.

"Do it differently." He scrambled over the bed towards the chair, hoping an hour was sufficient for her to escape.

He depressed his ring. With the pill in his hand, he heard the door smash open.

There was no time to pull the gag down and give the pill to Anya. Mouthing an apology he knew she would never hear, Wade hurtled back an hour.

Although he was out of danger, Wade felt irked that he had to hike back through the dark forest again. Cassandra, slightly ahead, played the torchlight across the clearest path available.

"There should be a clearing up ahead," he said, realising where they were.

They reached the plinth; Wade kept the map in his back pocket as he knew the way. As they passed the abandoned house with stables, Wade planned their next actions. He opened a stable door and looked inside to find a spacious building with individual stables all the way along. A faint whiff of horses hung in the air, ingrained in the stones that formed the partitions, walls and wood.

Cassandra craned her neck towards the buildings. "Is this the villa?"

Wade "The villa is along this path."

She gave a tight smile. "I didn't think this looked like a villa. Any horses?"

"All gone," Wade replied.

Knowing Adrian and his two associates were inside the villa, Wade could see what had made him suspicious about his first iteration. Additional tyre tracks led back to the chalet-style restaurant across the clearing. He could see a Range Rover's bonnet, peeking from behind the restaurant.

"Where is she?" Cassandra said.

"Paladin are here." Wade pointed at the mostly hidden Range Rover. "Go back to the stables and wait."

He surreptitiously checked the Jeep's door. It was open, the key fob sitting in the central cup holder where Anya dropped it while driving. Wade turned the engine on, the electric engine making no noise. He put the car in reverse and pulled away slowly, pointing the car back the way he'd come.

"I hope this works," he muttered.

He floored the accelerator, spinning off down the road back towards the stables, knowing he'd made a lot of noise. He skidded to a stop by Cassandra.

"Get in," he said.

She complied. Wade reached the stables, pulling the car around in a tight circle into the dark stable's interior.

He got out. "Stay here."

"Where are you going? Where's Anya?"

"I think this was a trap." Wade leaned in to talk to her. "I'll check she's alive. If she is, try to rescue her."

"Be careful."

Wade nodded with a smile. He wanted to portray a confidence, belying his fear.

He kept to the road's edge, hoping Adrian and his cohorts had left the compound. The Range Rover had gone, but he knew it was unlikely all three had left unless Anya was dead. An involuntary sigh escaped at that thought. He could always go around again.

Now he knew her precise location, Wade moved unerringly through the building.

Anya was alive.

He held his finger to his lips. Wade padded across the corridor to where he'd seen Adrian and the woman. He opened the door. They weren't there. Instead, they came up the stairs seconds before they saw him. Wade dived back into the bedroom as the gunshot hit the doorframe.

"Third time lucky." Wade took a pill.

"Are you okay?" Cassandra called back over her shoulder.

"What do you mean?"

"You sighed."

"I'm bored clambering through this forest," Wade said with feeling.

"There's a clearing." Cassandra turned off the torch.

Wade emerged from the trees beside her and looked at the path. "It's this way."

"Somebody maintains these paths," Cassandra said.

"The villa is probably a hotel by now." Wade tried to sound spontaneous but felt a tinge of boredom creeping into his tone.

Wade set up the stables, ready for the car.

Cassandra came in, wrinkling her nose. "Any horses still here? It certainly smells like it."

"No. We need to go further on to the villa." Wade knew his memories were real and not déjà vu, but the repetitive nature gave him a disorientated feeling.

They made the short walk up the tree-covered road. The temptation to pre-empt Cassandra's comment almost made Wade giggle.

As Wade knew she would, Cassandra looked around. "Where is she?"

Wade pointed at the Range Rover peeking from the chalet. "Paladin are here."

"Anya?" Cassandra sounded worried.

Wade started the Jeep. "Get in."

Looking confused, Cassandra got in. "Are we leaving Anya?"

"No." Wade rolled silently backwards and shot off towards the stables as loudly as he'd managed the first time.

When he reached the stable, he squeezed Cassandra's hand. "I'm going to see if Anya is still alive. If she is, I'll rescue her."

"I'll wait here."

Wade smiled at her.

At the corner, Wade got to see the Range Rover pull away this time. Wade slipped through and up to Anya's prison.

Wade held his finger up to his lips as he entered, tiptoeing. He knew the two Paladin agents were downstairs. He untied her and removed the gag.

She massaged her wrists and grabbed her pendant. Wade shook his head. He knew jumping back wasn't the answer. If that worked, he wouldn't be here now.

"Jumping back isn't working for you. We should only jump if this rescue fails."

Wade grabbed the curtain and pulled it off the runner to the tune of pinging plastic fasteners. With quick motions, he took the rope that had bound Anya and slipped out. Wade moved into the shadows on the landing as he heard Adrian and the woman coming up the stairs.

The woman was speaking. "She's not going to give us anything."

"That's a shame," Adrian replied. "We were both in the same division back when we started."

"Doesn't matter. Kobe will catch up with them, and this is all over."

Wade stepped out; the curtain raised. He dropped it over Adrian, kicking out at the woman, sending her tumbling back down the stairs. Off-balance, Adrian lashed out, trapped in the curtain, becoming more entangled. Wade looped the rope around Adrian's ankles with efficient movements, pulling it tight with the curtain forming a bag. He had no compunction in yanking the cord. Adrian crashed down with a painful sounding crack. With Adrian out of action, Wade turned his attention to the woman. She was by the loveseat on the mezzanine. Even without medical knowledge, he could tell she was unconscious with a broken arm.

A gunshot from behind him reminded him that Adrian had a gun.

Wade returned to the supine bundle on the landing. He could see a black hole, smoke curling out of it, the gun's barrel forming a blocky shape against the fabric. Wade stayed away from the firing line and bent beside Adrian, grabbing the gun, twisting it. He heard a crack, presumably a finger. He stood up and kicked down on Adrian's hand.

Adrian grunted. It wasn't the cry Wade had hoped for, but it gave him a little satisfaction. Given he hadn't recognised him, it may have been somebody else with a Russian accent back in France who had beaten him.

Yesterday Pill   Iain Benson

They were different heads from the same body. And, Wade reminded himself, even if it had been Adrian, it had never actually happened.

Anya emerged. She looked in pain, wincing. Her sweeping glance took in the scene before returning to Wade. She raised her eyebrows and looked like she was about to speak. Wade shook his head and held out his hand. She took it, using his support to get to the steps.

Once they were outside, Anya looked about. "Where's the car?"

"In a stable."

"Of course." Anya let go of Wade's hand. His hand had recognised her touch. He missed the fit in his. "It's toast. We need a new car."

"We do." Wade led her down the tree-lined path. He felt it looked artistic, with the sunrise casting long shadows. "Or at least a new plate. Are you okay?"

"Not really." She sounded like she meant it.

"How long had you been there?"

"About two hours," she replied.

"In one rescue attempt, I was going to send you back an hour. It wouldn't have helped."

"I would have got to have them break my rib again. I might have to go back to yesterday."

Wade shook his head. "Something is going on here. I don't think it matters now, even if you were to go back over it another dozen times. Adrian has information that's keeping him ahead of us."

"He doesn't know about the pills." She sounded sure of that.

"It's not part of Paladin's arsenal?" Surprised, Wade had assumed Paladin used something similar to the pills to keep finding them.

"When we learned about Cassandra, we also learned about the pills." She looked wistful. "You won't remember Craig. He built Paladin. It was him that uncovered the plot to kill Cassandra, and him that found the event that unravels time."

"Where is he?" Wade wondered who Craig was. It made sense he existed. Perhaps he was their third.

"He died."

"Oh!" Wade's core held a pang of sadness for a man he had known but of whom he had no memory.

"You thought he'd taken four pills." She shrugged and lifted her chin. "It's cold."

Wade felt stupid for not thinking about that. He took his coat off and slipped it over her shoulder. She gave him a small smile, pulling the jacket tight.

At the stable, Wade hugged Cassandra. She shrugged him off and took Anya's hands in hers. "You're hurt!"

"I'll heal."

They got her into the backseat.

"Sleep," Wade instructed.

"We can't take this car." Anya's tone was insistent.

"I've got it covered." Wade collected the screwdriver from Anya's bag and took it to the tractor. The licence on the back was rusty, but that didn't matter. Both plates came off effortlessly, with no need for the screwdriver. The holes were too large to screw onto the Jeep, but duct tape secured them in place.

"Let's go." Wade got in. Despite having been awake for a long time, his adrenalin had wired him into fight and flight.

"Leah will unfasten Adrian soon," Anya told them as she made herself comfortable, lying down on the back seat.

"I don't know." The memory of Leah's arm made Wade think otherwise. "When she fell, I think it broke her arm."

Wade looked at Anya. She touched the red swelling under her eye. "And I'm down at least one rib and a cheekbone."

Cassandra turned in her chair to look at the damage. "I'm not sure what we can do. I think hospitals let them heal on their own."

Anya nodded, wincing. "They do. That doesn't stop it from hurting."

Wade concentrated on putting distance between him and the former president of Yugoslavia's villa. He ate a sandwich as they cruised

Yesterday Pill   Iain Benson

down the motorway towards Belgrade. Wade knew it was a risk, but it was the quickest way to the capital. The alternate of single-track roads through towns and cities held no appeal.

Rush hour eased as they reached Belgrade. High-rises gave him something to look at in the slow traffic. Especially a distinctive double high-rise connected by a peculiar circular construction on the top few floors.

Cassandra peered up at the odd-looking building. "The concrete is brown."

"It's old." Anya sat up to see.

"I meant to ask," Wade said. "Having no memory, I've never heard of Yugoslavia. Aren't we in Serbia?"

"It was a Communist bloc," Cassandra answered. "We learned about it at school when we covered the cold war. At least that explains the architecture."

As the motorway crossed the river, traffic slowed to a crawl, giving them a touristy view over the brown-green water, turgidly moving through the old city. The heavy traffic's source became apparent.

Cassandra hissed. "Paladin."

Wade looked at the roadblock of Range Rovers and an armoured vehicle. He could make out dozens of armed guards. Even at this distance, he could see white slings on two of them. Adrian and Leah.

Wade tutted. "They're checking the cars."

"How did they get here so fast?" Cassandra sounded incredulous.

Anya sighed. "They have a helicopter."

Wade had to acknowledge the foresight. "It's a great place to look for us. I wonder if they're on every bridge."

"Only one way to find out," Anya said pointedly from the back seat.

Wade admitted to himself she was correct. He rummaged in his pocket and removed the signet ring.

"Oh!" Cassandra looked over. "You brought your ring."

Wade twisted and pressed, producing a pill. "Anya? Would you like our resident physicist to have a go at working out how this time travel works?"

"What's the point?" Anya shrugged. "I won't remember it."

"Time travel?" Cassandra's brows knitted together.

Wade nodded and took the pill.

He was ready for the transition to an hour previously. If his calculations were correct, they would be approaching Belgrade. As the two-dimensional image snapped away, replaced by the rapidly approaching motorway. Wade gave a small smile; he'd judged correctly. He could eat his sandwich again.

"The concrete is brown," Cassandra once again craned her neck to look up at Geneks Tower.

"They built it while Belgrade was part of former Communist Yugoslavia," Wade said.

As they approached the bridge, Wade took a turn off.

His manoeuvre perked Anya's interest. "Are we avoiding the main bridge?"

"It's an obvious route across the river," Wade replied over his shoulder. "If I were to put a blockade somewhere, it would be there. Once you're on the bridge, you're trapped."

Anya sat back with a smile. She knew.

However, Cassandra frowned. "How do you know Belgrade so well? Is your memory returning?"

Wade shook his head. "I'm trying to plan the safest route."

Parallel to the river, they passed modern buildings; the glass reflecting the river. Paladin had blocked every bridge. Halfway down the three-lane road, the traffic changed from rush-hour to stationary, a pair of black Range Rovers corralling the vehicles.

"I think they must have every bridge blocked."

Cassandra peered ahead. Only one car at a time got through. "What can we do? If we turn around, they'll see us."

"I think we try to avoid the centre of Belgrade." Wade checked through the satnav and found an alternative to the south of Belgrade.

Yesterday Pill　　　　　　　　　　　Iain Benson

"We're already here."

Wade nodded, taking out his ring. "I'm going to do it again."

"Is that your ring?" Cassandra asked as he twisted the motif.

"Yes." Wade popped the pill. "Third time lucky."

"Third time lucky?" Her sentence hung in the frozen, two-dimensional universe surrounding Wade before being whipped away.

He'd finished his sandwich this time, giving him an unreasonably glum feeling. Before they reached the airport for Belgrade, Wade turned off, heading away from the city.

"Are we not going to Belgrade?" Cassandra asked.

"The bridges over the river are a choke point." Wade gestured at the satnav. "If Paladin has put any blockade in place, it will be there."

"I was kind of looking forward to seeing it." Cassandra sounded a little upset, but understanding. "We learned about it in school history when we covered the Cold War."

Anya gave Wade a knowing look. "We can add it to the list of places to visit on the way back."

They drove through farmland the entire way to the bridge over the River Sana. Only the occasional flash of housing relieved the monotony. The traffic flowed freely; Wade knew he had selected the correct route. Across the river, they discovered more industry. After a few more kilometres, Wade saw the first hill for over a hundred kilometres, with the road going under it in a short tunnel. The terrain became a little more varied on the far side. Wade relaxed. They had left Paladin's operatives in Belgrade.

Whatever they knew, they had to be unaware of their destination.

Wade took advantage of this. He planned to push on to Sofia with a brief toilet break, picking up medical supplies and food. They would have to cross the Serbia Bulgaria border. Cassandra treated Anya's swollen eye socket with cream and applied a bandage to her ribcage, whilst Wade charged the car and examined a map.

"Do you have a plan to cross the border?" Anya asked, between gasps and winces. "I have no wish to add to my scars."

"I do." Wade hoped he had read the map correctly. "It might even work."

They had an uneventful journey until about three kilometres from the customs point.

Wade recalled the map. "If Paladin monitors anywhere, it'll be here. Only two other roads cross the border."

"Borders are a corral," Anya admitted. "Perfect places to look for us."

They crept along with the other traffic until he saw the sign for the small town of Dimitrovgrad. Grateful to be moving at a reasonable speed again, Wade pulled off the main road onto a single track. He headed up into the hills, glad that they had kept the Jeep. Scrubby mountains gave them a good view over the valley, where the motorway continued to the border crossing.

Wade had to fight the wheel over potholes, slowing them down. The road, now just dirt, pockmarked from years of neglect, constantly jolted and bumped the car. Nobody noted road conditions on maps, despite how useful it would be.

"Any alternatives if this doesn't work?" Anya had both hands on the roof to cope with the jolting.

"Only one. There's a mountain pass that might have no border guards. It's hundreds of miles out of our way in the southwest."

"Is it a proper road?" Cassandra asked, clutching her seatbelt strap.

Wade managed a chuckle. "I thought this one was."

A narrow bridge, barely wide enough for the Jeep, crossed a small river. It was a cue for Wade, letting him know he was nearly there. Trees crowded around the track, now little more than a tractor route to farm fields. Occasionally, he glimpsed the border crossing station. The path bore off to the right, but a pair of ridged tyre tracks drove into a field. Wade paused and took out his map, looking closely, estimating their exact position.

He made a satisfied noise and followed the tyre tracks.

Yesterday Pill   Iain Benson

"Weird," Cassandra said, "this feels like a satnav journey. Where you take a crazy route."

"Except this time," Wade replied as they reached a fence, "We're choosing the route."

"Exactly." Cassandra gave a little laugh.

Leaving the two women in the Jeep, Wade walked down to a fence. From here, he could see down a slight incline to a rail track. The border crossing's concrete flanks were just about visible on the hill opposite. Wade lay his map out on the fence as a last check. Bulgaria appeared in a sliver on the map, showing the rail line and woodland.

Wade looked at the woodland. No doubt there was a fence along the border there. Otherwise, it would have been his preferred route. Examining reality and comparing it to the map, a few concerns crept into his mind.

"I wish I knew when the trains were," he muttered. His concerns were becoming fear of failure.

Reminding himself he had a fallback plan of reliving the previous day, Wade removed the crossbeams on a section of fence and returned to the car.

He turned to look at the two women. "If you thought the road was bumpy, the next bit will be worse."

Wade drove down the slight incline onto the track, pointing the wheels towards Bulgaria. The border was mere metres away, but where he could get off the track was another matter.

The Jeep felt as though it would shake to pieces. He had one pair of wheels bumping over the sleepers, the other in the gravel beside the track, driving as fast as he felt he could. He looked at the speedometer; It read the heady velocity of twenty kilometres an hour.

Anya sounded hurt. "Is it too late to head for the alternative route?"

"We're in Bulgaria." The tracks remained resolutely wooded, with added fencing to prevent access. The rails split into two, one side entering a small station. A Jeep driving through a station would be suspicious and best avoided. He chose the other route.

They heard the train before they could see it. The rails hummed and sang with the train's approach. Anya twisted in her seat. "That's a big train."

The rear-view mirror confirmed Anya's warning. Wade pressed the accelerator, twisting the wheel. The Jeep complained, squealing, lights flashing all over the dash, but it got up the embankment towards the fence, wheels spinning in the mud. Sparks flew as the Jeep ran into the wire mesh. Behind them, the train rocketed past, rocking the Jeep. Wade's heart pounded. He realised he was holding his breath. The train felt long, rushing past for an age, the repeated thrumming reverberating through the car.

The Jeep rested against a fencepost. When his mind had calmed, Wade saw they had considerably bent the post. He again put the accelerator to the floor, collapsing an entire section of fencing with a pleasing, waterfall-like sound. Gratefully leaving the danger behind, he drove into a farmer's field. The earth was brown, uncovered, looking ready for planting. Wade kept to the edge where tractor tyres had already forged a path, eventually making it onto a more defined track with gates across between fields.

"If possible, I would rather we did not do that again." Cassandra sounded quite firm. Wade had to agree. Had they stolen a longer car, or one that could not climb the embankment, the train would have hit them.

Yesterday Pill — Iain Benson

7

Darkness descended as they left the rutted dirt and found a tarmac road. Wade patted the wheel, rewarding the Jeep as though it were a horse. The satnav could finally provide them with a route, having had them in a blank void since they had left the road in Serbia.

Decrepit concrete buildings, seemingly without purpose, lined the street. Wade decided they were ex-military.

Apart from the occasional pool of street lighting, their headlights provided the only illumination. Concrete walls and telegraph poles on twisting roads forced Wade to keep his speed down. The road held sudden turns around rocky bluffs. After half an hour, they reached a bridge carrying the motorway. He turned up a dirt track that barely seemed legitimate. Cars and trucks thundered past in the dark, their headlights forming streaks. Eventually, Wade saw a gap large enough and took a sizeable chunk of their charge to get up to speed.

The charge warning light came on, this journey refusing him time to relax. He checked the satnav. He had seventy kilometres left in the battery with fifty to Sofia. Any hopes of pushing past Sofia gleamed in soft amber on his dash. The recent exertions from the car had used the power up more quickly than he'd expected.

"We'll be in Sofia in half an hour," he told Anya over his shoulder. "We're going to need a charging point and somewhere to lie low."

"On it." Anya took out her phone and started searching.

By the time they reached Sofia, Anya had located a suitable location. She sent the destination to the satnav. Wade happily followed it.

Sofia looked much like any other city. A main road surrounded by offices, car showrooms, businesses, and the occasional residential block. A late-night tram trundled past, heading in the opposite direction.

Across from a concrete edifice with a colonnaded top floor, they drove into a multistorey carpark. Wade found a booth and connected the charger, imagining the Jeep making gulping sounds as it recharged.

"I suggest we find a new car." Anya patted the Jeep's roof. "This one has done well, but it's battered and obvious."

Wade caressed the scratches, damaged front bumper, and dents in the sides. A broken taillight and over a dozen bullet holes above the rear passenger-side wheel and along the boot would draw suspicion.

He had to agree. "Maybe in Istanbul?"

"New continent, new car?" Cassandra asked. "Any chance we could find somewhere to sleep, preferably with food, drink and a toilet?"

"There are several restaurants and hotels in this area," Anya replied.

"Perfect." Wade stretched out his back. He felt old. How long had they been travelling? Wade tried counting beds. That list was easier to maintain; each one felt like a treasured memory. He decided this had to be the fourth bed if he included the brief snooze on the ferry.

The main street was still busy, despite the hour. Anya led them to a pedestrian area. The restaurants were closed, but a pizzeria remained open, serving the late-night revellers. They walked as they ate, passing a mix of run-down and occupied premises.

"We're here." Anya stopped opposite a building across the road. She ate her pizza.

Wade liked the hotel's white marble façade. He missed the CCTV, but Anya spotted the black dome of a camera hanging outside the hotel entrance. Heads down, in a tight group, they entered the hotel. Risky, but any hotel would be the same.

The hotel was a little flashy for Wade's liking, clad with intricately carved cream marble. Anya left them by a mahogany circular table to get some rooms.

"I've had to get a family room." She looked unconcerned. "It should be big enough."

Cassandra gasped when she saw the sumptuous room. "It certainly is large enough."

Yesterday Pill   Iain Benson

Wade walked into the blue-tinted room, his reflection coming back to him from several mirrors and highly polished surfaces. A king-sized double bed could have taken all three of them, but with two twin beds on the other side of a central partition, they could have a bed each. Wade lay on the double.

Cassandra lay next to him, lying on her side. "Are you bothering with getting undressed?"

Wade felt the tiredness through his bones. A week ago, he had no memory of driving. He let the weariness consume him and drag him under, only to be awakened by Cassandra gently shaking him.

"Anya's already gone down."

Wade came instantly alert. "Did I sleep?"

"It's morning, love."

Wade felt a little more alert and a lot stiffer. "Really?"

He rolled off the bed and opened the curtains to look out onto a domed church. Wade used the bathroom, the grey marble far too opulent for his taste. He looked at his haggard face in the octagonal mirror to wash and shave. Wade sighed and patted his face dry on a dark grey towel.

It was time to leave. It was always time to leave.

As he closed the door, he looked at the splendid suite. "Not bad for bed four."

Cassandra looked at him. "Bed four?"

"I have completely lost track of days." He gave a self-deprecating laugh. "I'm measuring time in the beds I have slept in."

"Four?"

Wade ticked them off on his fingers. "Portsmouth, the ferry, that ski lodge, and this one."

"You didn't sleep in Portsmouth, though, did you?"

Wade shook his head. "I did briefly lie down. It's no surprise I'm tired."

"I think driving across the whole of Serbia, and a bit of Bulgaria, would do that."

Iain Benson   **Yesterday Pill**

Wade headed to the reception desk, where a diminutive, dark-haired woman wearing a smart navy-blue suit and pale blue shirt gave him a sunny smile.

He smiled back and chose Arabic as his language. "Do you have a map of Bulgaria? A paper one?"

She spoke flawless Arabic. "I'm afraid we don't. However, there is a bookshop by the Roman ruins. They will have one."

"Where are they?"

She pointed at the front door. "You leave the hotel, down the steps, and they're on the right. The bookshop is past them, on the left."

He thanked her and headed for the dining room, Cassandra linking her arm through his.

"I'm pretending this is a grand tour," she said with a sunny smile. "I'm ignoring the reason we're here. How else could we stay somewhere like this on our salaries?"

Anya had all the options in the continental breakfast on her plate when Wade and Cassandra joined her.

Between mouthfuls and looking at her phone, she glanced up at them. "I don't want to stay still longer than necessary. Grab food. We need to go."

Cassandra picked up the plate. "I was thinking. Don't Paladin know the identities we were using?"

"They knew mine." Anya tilted her head. "No matter, I've abandoned those identities. When we booked in here, it was as two sisters and a brother. We're on our Israeli passports now. We only have one other set left."

"Who are we now?" Wade asked.

"Adam and Hanna." Anya pointed at them with her fork. "I'm Sarah. We're the Cohens."

As they exited the hotel, Anya turned left.

Wade stopped her. "Before we go anywhere. I need a map."

He led them to a collection of shops in the pedestrian zone. As the

Yesterday Pill   Iain Benson

hotel receptionist had said, they passed ruins. According to an information board, the workers had uncovered them when resurfacing the main road. Wade located a small group of shops in glass cubicles near the steps back up to the road. The first one was a bookshop with limited stock.

On a stool at the shop's rear, reading a graphic novel, the bookseller barely acknowledged their entrance. Wade glanced over the packed shelves, locating a decent map. He unfolded it and checked it over. It had sufficient detail to show the border with Turkey.

"You want that one?" Anya asked.

Wade nodded.

Outside, Wade unfolded the map and covered an information board describing a pile of sandstone blocks as the remains of a Roman fort. He traced his finger along the border.

"Is that a road running along the border?" Cassandra asked, looking over his shoulder.

"It looks like it."

Anya also looked. "Good. No train tracks."

Despite her injuries, Anya insisted on taking over driving. Wade took the passenger seat, scrutinising the map, looking for anywhere they could cross without going through the border crossing.

Instead of taking the direct route to Turkey, they turned off onto a single carriageway road. Sun blasted, barely undulating, farmland stretched as far as they could see. A slight traffic build-up crossing a bridge worried Wade momentarily, but it was a broken-down vehicle. Two hours after leaving Sofia, the countryside became scrubby hills.

As they descended into an arid landscape, Wade leaned forward. "Take the next left."

Opposite a Portakabin café, the left did not appear to lead anywhere. In all directions, featureless scrub was all Wade could see. With every turn, the vista grew more forlorn. They reached a small knot of lonely, widely spaced buildings far from anywhere.

"This one." Wade pointed to a dirt track that led down across the hill, past stumpy gorse, and hawthorn trees.

"Are you sure?" Anya sounded unsure, pausing before taking the turn.

Wade double-checked, tracing the path with his finger. "Positive."

With a shrug, she followed the path. Barely more than a deer run through the trees. Taller trees hemmed in the track, narrowing it, making Wade unsure of his earlier positivity.

They emerged onto a paved road running alongside a fence.

"Smart." Anya looked through the windscreen. "It took us more than an hour to get here."

A substantial fence blocked the route. Wade checked the time. "It'll be my first day back."

"Take paracetamol." Anya looked at the fence as though wondering if the Jeep could go through it.

"What are you talking about?" Cassandra looked at the two of them suspiciously.

Wade twisted to look at Cassandra. "The time to get here."

She sat back.

Anya gave Wade an amused look. "Shall we go left, or right? We might as well make use of how long it took to get here by seeing if there are any gaps."

Wade shrugged. "Right?"

"Right."

Anya turned the wheel and joined the tarmac road.

Cassandra looked at the kilometres of stout metal fencing. "Remember when we had that quote to replace the fence behind the house?"

Wade nodded. "It was more expensive than I thought it would be."

"How much did this cost?" Cassandra gestured.

"They have to maintain it, too," Anya said.

"I wonder who has responsibility?" Wade said. "Bulgaria or Turkey?"

Yesterday Pill   Iain Benson

"It's the animals I feel for," Cassandra added. "They cannot cross either."

As they travelled, Wade looked for an alternative. They passed the occasional watchtower and what appeared to be Second World War gun emplacements. In random sections, the fence became a wall. As the sun set, they reached the customs border.

"Do you have a better idea?" Anya asked.

"There's a crossing in the mountains on a minor road." Wade showed her the map. "It's about fifty kilometres from here. It's a long way around from Sofia, though."

"Sounds good." Anya turned the engine off.

"Do we have the charge for that?" Cassandra asked.

Wade checked the time. "See you yesterday."

"Wade?" Cassandra asked as Wade dialled two doses.

Oly a single pill popped out, surprising Wade. "It's just one."

"Yes, it's always one," Anya said. "It's something to do with them not being here."

"Are you ignoring me?" Cassandra sounded quite angry.

Wade smiled at her. "It's okay. You won't remember."

He took the pill.

"There are several restaurants and hotels in this area," Anya said to Cassandra.

Wade winced. The flattening effect had been the same, but the snapback had a wavering edge, making him stagger slightly on arrival. Anya had been underestimating the headache. It made him wonder about his seizure. Perhaps he did not have the right brain for a jump of a week. He stored that thought away to check with Anya when he could next talk to her.

Cassandra touched Wade's arm. "Are you okay, Wade?"

Wade rubbed his temples. "I'm exhausted."

"That is understandable. You've driven across two countries and haven't driven for years."

"That'll be it," Wade said. "Does anybody have any paracetamol?"

Anya passed a small blue packet over. "Anything to be concerned with?"

Wade shook his head. "I don't think I'm about to have a seizure. Just a funny turn."

Anya seemed to understand. "I'm starving. Oh! Look! Pizza."

They again got a pizza, eating it as they headed to the hotel. This time, Wade pointed out the CCTV by the hotel door. While Anya booked them in, Cassandra rubbed his temples for him.

"Are you sure you are all right?"

Wade nodded. "Honestly. It's nothing a good night's sleep won't solve."

She lightly kissed him, making Wade feel guilty for treating her like she was unimportant before he'd jumped back. He resolved never to repeat that.

"I've had to get a family room," Anya said. "It'll be big enough."

Anya led them up a lift and down a marble-clad corridor, opening a plain wooden door with a manual key.

"It certainly is large enough," Cassandra said with a gasp.

Wade made straight for the bed.

Cassandra lay next to him, lying on her side, and stroked his temple. "Are you bothering with getting undressed?"

"Nope."

Again, it felt like he'd barely glanced off the envelope of sleep before Cassandra woke him with a gentle shake.

"Anya's already gone down. How are you feeling?"

Wade was glad the headache had eased to a vague memory of one. "Like I barely slept."

She lingered a kiss on his lips and slid off the bed. "Come on."

In the lobby, as they headed for the dining room, Cassandra slipped her arm through his, smiling. "I'm pretending this is a grand tour. I'm ignoring the reason we're here. How else could we stay somewhere like this

Yesterday Pill   Iain Benson

on our salaries?"

Anya loaded her fork with sliced meat.

"I don't want to stay still longer than necessary. Grab food. We need to go."

Cassandra picked up the plate. "I was thinking. Don't Paladin know the identities we were using?"

"They knew mine. No matter, I've abandoned those identities. When we booked in here, it was as two sisters and a brother. We're on our Israeli passports now. We only have one other set left."

"Remind me," Wade said.

"Adam and Hanna." Anya pointed at them with her fork. "I'm Sarah. We're the Cohens."

At the car, Anya held out her hand. "I'll drive. You navigate."

Wade passed the key fob over.

Anya started the Jeep. "Where are we heading?"

Wade made a show of looking at Anya's phone. "East."

"I thought we needed to go south?" Cassandra asked.

"We will eventually," Wade replied. "We need a crossing that's going to be safe for us."

"No train tracks this time, please," Anya said. "That train was about ten centimetres from the Jeep."

"Take the A1, heading for Plovdiv."

Anya nodded and navigated the city streets as the morning rush hour eased.

After two hours of driving, Anya yawned. "I am going to put this road down in my top ten most boring roads in the world."

Flat plains of farmland stretched to the horizon.

"Designed by a firm with too many rulers." Wade checked their position on the satnav. "We're probably pushing the battery."

"This kind of driving is light on the battery," Anya said.

Wade turned to look at Cassandra. She'd fallen asleep; her cheek squished up against the glass. He held off the conversations about the pills, his past, and Paladin. However much the need to ask burned on his tongue.

Cassandra woke up needing food and the toilet. They had fish and chips sitting on a wall looking out over the Black Sea. The English owned café had a prime position near the beach.

Wade felt more comfortable about their range as he took the wheel for the next leg.

The road south took them over a peninsula and into a much more varied countryside. The Jeep wound over hills, through woods and picturesque villages.

Wade glanced at the back seat where Anya read her phone. "This road is anything but boring."

Wade saw touches of snow hanging in the shadowed hollows and overhangs as they got higher. The trees were bare, with sparse evergreens providing the only colour. The first sign of life for half an hour was a fuel stop and a small knot of temporary-looking houses making a small community near the customs point.

Cassandra twisted as much as Bump allowed. "The customs check is up ahead. Do you have our Cohen passports?"

Anya nodded, rummaging through her bag. Wade slowed as he approached, wondering why the red and white barrier was up. Anya passed through the passports, but Wade waved them away. Through the small glass window, he could see a gaunt-looking soldier reading an eBook. With a gesture, he sent Wade into Turkey.

Cassandra punched Wade on the arm. "Now, wasn't that easier than crushing us all with a train?"

They dropped from the creased looking mountains down onto a featureless plain. Wade ended the silence that had been running for over an hour. "We're running out of charge."

"We need a break, anyway," Anya said. They passed a road sign. "I'm sure we'll find something in that town."

Stress levels increased for Wade as they hunted for a charging station. He knew they had low charge; the alarm beeping added pressure he

Yesterday Pill   Iain Benson

didn't need.

Eventually, with the range in single figures, they found a charge point.

"I didn't realise Turkey was still using fossil fuels," Anya admitted. "It's been a few years since I've been here."

Sitting in a bistro-like café across the road from the refuelling station, Wade used Anya's phone while she accompanied Cassandra to the toilet.

Before they even sat down, Wade gave them his results. "It's about two hundred kilometres to Istanbul."

"About four hours' charge." Anya looked thoughtful. "We could stay here for that long."

"We'll need at least another coffee." Wade gave a wide smile.

"I meant in Kirklareli." The way Anya pronounced the town name told Wade she might be Turkish herself.

"It'll be dark when we reach Istanbul," Cassandra said, doing the calculations.

Wade nodded. "I still think we need to dump the car when we get there."

"At least if we pick up a diesel, we can keep moving," Anya agreed. "Every time we stop, it gives Paladin a chance to narrow down where we are."

"If they work out where we are going," Cassandra said, with a slight fear trembling in her voice, "they'll be able to get us at the Bosporus."

"Only if we drive over the bridge or use the tunnel." Wade's grin grew as his idea formed.

Cassandra gave him a puzzled look. "Are you suggesting swimming?"

"Stealing a boat." Anya looked thoughtful. "They're normally tracked."

"I was thinking of getting a taxi."

Anya's grin also grew. "That's brilliant."

Anya located a hotel in Istanbul while they had another coffee. As it came time to go, Cassandra disappeared off, unaccompanied by Anya. Wade took his chance.

"I have a question," he asked.

Anya glanced at the swing door to the corridor where the toilets were. "You've probably got a few minutes."

"Could the pills have caused my seizure?"

Anya shook her head. "You'd made plenty of jumps. Even made a few week-long ones. Lots of headaches. No deaths."

"There was Craig," Wade pointed out. "How did he get four pills?"

"He built the locket and ring. Maybe he'd added it to his. We've been over this."

Wade shook his head. "You've been over it. I'm coming at this fresh."

She acknowledged that with a tilt of her head. "My personal theory was that he misjudged the timing back to where he was and crashed his car."

Wade had no recollection. He had to rely on Anya's memory of that period of his life. "What would happen if you took three doses straight after emerging from a three-dose jump?"

"Nothing." Anya shrugged. "It'd be the same as taking an hour pill straight after an hour jump. Nothing happens. You must wait until that hour is up before you can go back again."

"If you get in trouble during that time, you stay in trouble?"

Anya touched her eyebrow with a grimace. "That's how Adrian caught me. I couldn't jump. I mistimed my route through the border."

Cassandra returned. Her cheeks flushed with a rosy glow. "Ready?"

Anya took the wheel, despite Wade's protests. Wade noticed she had turned off the satnav, and yet she found Istanbul without it.

Istanbul's red roofs spread out for miles as they drove on the motorway that bisected the city centre. A tall hotel cast a long shadow across the neighbouring buildings. A block of grey and white with a glass

Yesterday Pill   Iain Benson

front, much more modern than the surroundings.

"Are we staying here?" Cassandra asked as they took the suitcases from the Jeep. "I thought we wanted to get moving as quickly as possible?"

Anya nodded and tossed Wade the key fob. "It is far less suspicious to be waiting at a hotel with suitcases to get into a taxi."

"What shall I do with the car?" Wade swapped sides to the driver's side.

"Lose it." Anya gestured back the way they had come. "This city has some fantastic spots for losing cars. I think the best place would be a district called Listros. Down there and take a right. Keep the motorway on your right until you get to the hospital, then find a suitable street."

"Do you know the city?" Wade thought he already knew the answer.

"I grew up here." She smiled at him. "Technically, across the river. Though I spent a lot of time around here."

Wade returned the smile. He drove past a goods yard, and over the motorway that flowed through the city like a river. Negotiating Istanbul, Wade had several hairy moments from other drivers. Eventually, though, he turned back over the thoroughfare and into a warren of densely packed housing crammed into every space. He knew he was in a more impoverished area by the faded paint and crumbling render on the houses. Although he deliberately twisted and turned farther into the warren, Wade memorised the route for retracing.

Among mainly four-storey tall buildings, he found the perfect place for losing a car. He left the Jeep with both wheels on a cobbled pavement between a white van and a straggly tree. For good measure, he put the key fob prominently visible on the passenger seat. Against the dark sky, Wade saw a higgledy-piggledy mix of five- and three-storeys that disrupted the roofline. Wade walked back past the cars crammed on both sides, in a variety of states of repair. Conscious he had already taken twenty minutes, Wade wanted to get back as quickly as possible. He knew he might have to go through this again.

As night settled in, the air had a deep chill, reminding Wade it was winter. Brisk walking kept him warm enough, while his thoughts made him realise he now broke his life into hour-long segments. Even with a hurried pace, he arrived back at the hotel over an hour after he'd left. Wade circumnavigated the reception area and seating. He couldn't find Cassandra and Anya.

Worry gnawed at his insides when the receptionist spotted him. "Mr Cohen!"

It took Wade a few seconds to remember that was his name, for the next few days at least. He looked over at the slim man with slicked-back black hair behind the white, glowing desk.

"Yes?"

The receptionist passed him a white envelope. "Your sister left this for you."

Wade took the envelope and wandered towards the floor to ceiling windows.

"Paladin is coming. Can you bring chloroform ingredients, ten metres of rope, a skateboard, and a bundle of towels? We'll also need a taxi. Wait by the back gate. We're in room two three-three."

Wade looked out over the railway, the blue-tinted glass reflecting his image. He saw a black-suited man standing behind him. He turned and looked at Adrian.

"Lovely to see you, Wade." Adrian's insincere smile barely made it to his cheeks.

Wade nodded cordially. "Adrian. What's wrong with your arm?"

Adrian looked down at the sling. "I have a broken wrist."

"Shame."

Adrian's glance over to the door told Wade more Paladin operatives waited. "Tell me where Cassandra is. We can avoid any unpleasantries."

Wade shrugged and slipped the letter into his jacket pocket. He lowered himself onto a bright red sofa. He wondered where he would find a skateboard. "I was expecting to find them here. I think you might have

Yesterday Pill Iain Benson

scared them off."

Adrian took the seat opposite. "No alternative site?"

Wade gave a wry smile. "I was ditching the car. We're sitting in the meetup spot."

"Your move with the car in Italy was a stroke of genius." Adrian gave a depreciating chuckle. "Using the plates from an old tractor. We were looking for a stolen car."

Wade checked his watch. "If you'll excuse me. I need to leave."

"Come back to us, Wade." Adrian made an expansive gesture with his left hand. "We're the good guys."

Wade shook his head. "My child is involved now."

Adrian winced. "Honestly, there is no point running. The System is close to working out your intention. We'll keep finding you, and quicker."

Wade wondered what the 'System' was, but the last person in time and space he would ask was the person sitting opposite. He twiddled his ring, popping out a pill.

"And we'll keep escaping. Thanks for the information."

The hotel lobby flattened out, zipping away to a distant point. Around the inaccessible pinprick of light, Wade's mind struggled to process the absence of anything. There was no darkness and no light. Reality rushed back into the void, filling his field of vision. The tall buildings around him sent a chill through him that made him shudder.

In the previous scurried walk, he'd fixated his gaze on the distant buildings; now, he looked at the shops as he passed.

A muttered repetition of his list kept it fresh in his mind.

At a pharmacy, he had an idea. He had Anya's card, so he entered the shop, the harsh fluorescent light blinding after the dimness outside. After a few moments, he had his purchases.

The woman behind the till looked him up and down and spoke in English. "You know not to mix these?"

"Bleach, alcohol, and acetone? No. That would be dangerous."

Satisfied he wasn't planning on rendering himself unconscious, she let Wade buy the bottles. A few doors down and he found an outdoor supplies shop, where he got rope and a bucket.

As he paid, he asked the young man behind the counter if he could get a skateboard somewhere.

The youth looked at Wade as though he'd asked where he could find a prostitute. "Sorry, no."

Wade wondered where he would get one as he headed out. Stopping to disgorge a passenger, Wade found his taxi. They reminded him of New York classic cabs, but the sign on the top was *taksi*.

Wade leaned down to the window. "Ramada?"

"Hop in, my friend." The driver had a craggy face, with thick grey eyebrows.

The driver pulled into the traffic, getting Wade back to the hotel five minutes sooner than his last trip. He directed the driver around to the side to wait by the black metal gate at the rear entrance.

"Could you wait? I need to get my sisters?"

"Not a problem, my friend. The meter she runs, though."

"You can have a paid coffee break."

Wade took his new purchases into the hotel. Before heading up, he stopped at the front desk. "Any letters for Cohen?"

The slim, dark-haired man paused before nodding. "Oh, yes, sir."

Wade took the envelope and quickly scanned it, ensuring the requirements and room were the same, before heading up to the second floor. A cleaner vacuumed the hard-wearing red carpet as he found the door. He knocked on the half brown, half white door.

"You're here." Anya looked at the bucket. "Where's the skateboard? And the towels?"

"I would probably have to go back to the nineties to find a skateboard." Wade held up the bucket. "I have everything else, though."

Anya gave him a grin. "I was sort of joking about the skateboard, but we will need towels."

Wade waited until the cleaner went into a room, dragging the vacuum behind her, before swiping the towels off her trolley. "Check."

Juggling suitcases, a bucket and towels down the corridor taxed the three of them. Fortunately, the cases had wheels. Wade pushed a stack of two cases with a pile of towels on top.

"I think we have three, maybe four, minutes." Anya impatiently pushed the lift button.

"What are the towels for?" Cassandra asked.

"Draught excluders." Anya made a relieved noise when the lift dinged.

Looking in the three mirrors in the lift cab, Wade realised how exhausted he looked. Anya dragged a suitcase in a charge across the parking garage and down through a service door onto a white-painted breeze-block corridor. The corridor sloped down to a fire door. Two doors led off to the side. As they passed each one, she had Wade block the openings with towels.

"Mix the chloroform." Anya was in full-on boss mode.

Wade waited for Cassandra to leave the corridor and put the bucket down. He watched Anya drag her suitcase out. Satisfied they were in the clear, he poured the acetone, alcohol, and the bleach in the bucket, stepping back as the cloying gas filled the narrow corridor. Wade pulled his two suitcases out towards the fire door. At the far end, he saw the door open. Adrian looked down through the greenish, billowing cloud.

Wade resisted the urge to salute or give some other signal, instead left without a gesture. The yellow cab remained by the gates.

"Where to, my friends?" the taxi driver asked as they climbed in.

"Fenerbahçe." Anya leaned forward to speak to the driver, switching to Turkish. "You know? The stadium?"

That was all Wade could make out, but whatever she said next made the taxi driver laugh.

When she leaned back, Wade leaned across Cassandra and whispered to Anya: "What did you say?"

"I said we were skipping out without paying our bill and looking for a cheap hotel across the Strait."

"Sounds reasonable." Cassandra gave Wade a shove. He realised he was squashing Bump.

"Sorry," he mumbled his apology.

Their driver took a few turns and joined the motorway. At a bridge, Wade saw no sign of Paladin.

"I think we might get across," he said to Anya.

"It's not the main bridge. You'll know when you see that."

Around them, they passed through modern Istanbul, a mix of glass and concrete, offices, and tenements. As they dropped towards the Bosporus, the hillside had some expensive-looking houses set back from the road.

Anya pointed ahead through the windscreen. "There is the Bosporus."

The suspension bridge spread in a magnificent line across the strait. In the dark, the curving support wires were lit, creating blue sweeps in the night sky. Wade was more interested in the Paladin presence on the bridge. All three of them ducked down as they passed the black-suited figures with their tanks and Range Rovers. The taxi passed unnoticed. Wade allowed a small smile as they crossed from one continent to the other.

The taxi driver looked over his shoulder. "I don't think they deploy the military for not paying hotel bills, my friends."

"You can never be too careful." Although Anya spoke in rapid Turkish, Wade could pick out enough to make sense of what she said.

"Your Turkish. It is perfect," the taxi driver told her.

"I am from Adana."

"But your brother, he is Australian, and your sister is English. You have a strange family, my friend."

Wade sat back. He'd thought he was English.

Cassandra leaned into him. "What is it?"

"I was eavesdropping on the conversation. I'm positive the cabbie said I am Australian." Wade kept his voice low, whispering into her ear.

Yesterday Pill   Iain Benson

"How would he know?"

Wade shrugged. "Accent?"

"Ask Anya when we get out."

Directions from Anya kept the taxi driver moving as they passed the football stadium. On a wide, tree-lined street, they stopped at a three-storey hotel in the middle of a row of similar terraced houses. The cabbie received a generous tip.

"Good luck, my friends!" the driver said. "I have not seen you at all!"

Neon signs flashing *vacancies* in the windows. The night had become too dark to read the sign above the door.

"What did you tell him?" Wade asked.

"We're on the run from the British."

Wade failed to follow the logic of that. "And he's fine with that?"

"A lot of Turks quite dislike the British," Anya explained. "Look around at all the signs in English. Turks feel the British took a bit of their identity."

The reasoning remained beyond Wade. "I heard him say something about me being Australian?"

Anya laughed. "You have no accent when you speak English, but when you speak in Arabic, you speak it like an Australian."

"That's just weird. Am I?"

"Yes. You were born in Alice Springs. You moved to the UK with your family when you were thirteen. At fifteen, you all moved to Germany. You had a knack for languages and ended up working in Tel Aviv, where I met you."

Wade felt the heat drop from his body, exposing him to the chilly night air. Questions swirled around his head. Anya had casually dropped his entire life history onto him in the middle of a dark street in Istanbul. One question protruded into his thoughts more than any other. "My parents?"

Anya gave him a critical look. "That's for another time. Let's get inside before you go into hypothermia."

"I agree. You look pale," Cassandra said.

They pushed through into a cramped hallway.

Anya rang a small bell on an occasional table pressed into a corner by dark wooden stairs. What Wade had thought was a wooden panel opened to reveal an older woman in a blue pinafore dress, her hair tied up with a cloth.

"Anya?" The woman sounded surprised.

"Babaanne!"

Wade's rudimentary Turkish seemed sufficient to translate. "She's your grandmother?"

"Wade, Cassandra, this is my grandmother, Miray." She turned to face the older woman. "Babaanne, we need a safe place to stay tonight."

"Of course. Of course." Miray began fussing. "Oh, your face, my child. What has happened?"

"Partly why we need to hide, Babaanne."

Miray showed them to simple rooms, with beds covered in white sheets, pine bed stands and net curtains looking out onto a dark street. A small shower room gave Cassandra and Wade a chance to get clean. Wade felt grateful for the crisp cotton sheets for the night. He slept well with Cassandra snuggled next to him, awaking to the smell of breakfast.

8

In the dining room, Wade discovered Miray had two other guests. They occupied the table by the back window, whilst Anya had a larger table by a fireplace that contained decorative flowers instead of burning logs.

Anya waved at the two other chairs at her table. "Sit down. Babaanne does the best breakfast in Turkey."

Miray came out of a swing door with a tray. Wade looked on as she placed sesame bread, honeyed bread rolls, sausage, cheeses, and a platter of sliced meats on the table.

Miray smiled at them. "You look better for a night's rest."

"I feel it, thank you," Wade said, in stilted Turkish. That made the woman laugh uproariously. Wade wondered what he'd said instead of what he thought he had said.

Anya grabbed bread rolls and sliced meat. "Don't panic. You got it right. It just sounds funny in your accent."

Wade felt better in fresh clothing. He had had a shower both before and after bed. Cassandra, too, had washed her hair.

Wade let the comment about his accent slide. "What's the plan?"

"We get a train to a small seaport called Mersin and catch a ferry to Cyprus and then to Tel Aviv."

Wade considered this for a moment. "Hopefully, it'll catch Paladin out. Until now, we've been driving."

Miray had overhead. "You should speak to your brother."

Anya shook her head. "I will not involve him."

Cassandra returned upstairs to get ready to leave. Wade pinned Anya in her seat with a look.

"What?" she asked.

Wade stuck to the facts as he knew them. "I saw Adrian in my first attempt at meeting you at the hotel."

"And?"

"He said 'The System' was close to working out our intention."

"That makes sense." Anya looked thoughtful. "We will have to be alert."

"What is 'The System'?"

Instead of answering, Anya asked: "Why was he mentioning it?"

"He was trying to entice me back."

Anya gave a thoughtful nod. "Divide and conquer. We could use that in the future."

"Okay." Wade steered Anya back to his question. "The System?"

She gave an apologetic smile. "The System is why Paladin is the number one security agency for just about every nation on Earth."

"What does it do?"

"It's an AI that reads all the news and extrapolates."

"Clever." Wade had a moment of clarity.

"It is a shame that they charge so highly. Paladin could save more lives but won't intervene unless paid."

The idea of putting a price on people's lives made Wade angry.

"I take it Cassandra was one of those news stories?"

"We never got the full story. When we left, it was still in fragmented pieces," Anya said. "The closer you get to the story's origin, the more accurate it is. All we knew was that it would be the end of Paladin. Craig always said it seemed to be some weird event. He called it the drop-off, beyond which the System provides no more information."

"This may be why they're getting more accurate with us," Wade said, theorising, his mind freewheeling. "We're getting close to whatever causes the end of Paladin."

Anya conceded this point with a tilt of her head and a wrinkle of her lips. The look made Wade smile. Although he had no memory of their time together, he could see that they would have been good together.

She broke the spell, getting to her feet. "We'd best get going. We have a train to catch."

Wade collected his scattered belongings. Cassandra hugged him,

Yesterday Pill   Iain Benson

planting a kiss on his lips. He felt guilty for wondering about his time with Anya. He returned the kiss gently and hoped his errant thoughts went unnoticed.

When Cassandra and Wade got to the dining room, Anya and Miray spoke rapidly in Turkish, far too rapidly for Wade to follow. Both women were laughing.

"Wade, Cassandra," Anya said, waving them over. "Babaanne has got us a taxi to the train station. I've booked our seats to Mersin."

"Stay safe, my little Anya," Miray said, hugging her granddaughter.

"I'll come back, Babaanne," Anya promised.

"When you are at Mersin, see your parents. Your mama misses you."

"We'll see." Anya hugged her grandmother again.

"Thank you." Wade stumbled slightly over the Turkish words.

Istanbul train station reminded Wade of nearly all train stations he'd used before. Even though the exterior here was a vast gothic façade, the interior looked uniform in its layout. A large concourse surrounded by shops with a central area for buying tickets, the floor polished into a mirrored surface.

Anya looked at ease and at home with her bag slung over one shoulder, pulling a suitcase behind her. Wade had a suitcase in each hand, trundling them across the slick flooring, allowing Cassandra to be free to carry herself and Bump. They grabbed pre-packaged sandwiches and coffee from a concourse vendor and headed for the platforms. An extended glass partition with sliding doors prevented their access to the train. Anya showed her phone to the guard on the door. Wade wondered if platform uniforms were the same the world over. He could almost imagine he was at Euston.

The high-speed train was a long silver streak of potential energy desperate to leave the station, the blue stripe only adding to the image. They hauled the suitcases and Cassandra's bump onto the train. Anya checked the reservation tickets as they struggled between the two rows of seats marching down the train.

"We're here." She put her shoulder bag on the table, grunting as she lifted the suitcase onto the plane-style luggage rack.

Wade swung one suitcase up and put the other in the luggage rack by the toilet cubicle.

"Do you want the aisle or window seat?" Wade asked Cassandra.

"I'd best take the aisle seat. I'll probably have to go to the loo."

Wade squeezed between the table and the chair, dropping onto the light blue fabric, glad he was facing in the direction the train would travel. Anya sat opposite, watching the carriage. He took Cassandra's hand but disconcertingly looked at Anya, inducing a disconnect. Wade shook it off and gazed at the scenery instead. The platform gave a good view over offices and businesses, but he mainly saw the other passengers embarking. As the train filled up, the noise level increased. They'd beaten the rush, either by intention or accident. The overhead racks filled rapidly, and the lids slammed down. Latecomers had no space, forced into keeping their bags on their knees. He half-expected somebody to take the seat next to Anya. Despite people taking most other chairs, that one remained empty as the train smoothly started moving.

After an hour, Wade checked his watch. It felt like they were still travelling through Istanbul, though it seemed unlikely. The suburbs of each city down the coast merged into one. The screens periodically punctuating the ceiling told Wade that they were travelling at a hundred and eighty kilometres an hour. When his view became a close-fitting stone wall, Wade looked over Cassandra and the aisle to the window on the other side. He was a little surprised to see sunlight sparkling off the small, cresting waves in a large body of water. Wade played a mental game of people watching. He constructed stories about his fellow passengers. At Izmit, he got a dozen fresh faces but lost twice that. The seat next to Anya remained empty. A curly-haired man in a camouflage jacket checked the reservation ticket but moved on down the carriage.

"Did you book four seats?" Wade asked.

Yesterday Pill   Iain Benson

"Of course." Anya looked up from her phone and gave a smile. "It saves having somebody we don't know sitting there."

Wade gave a sideways, envious glance at Cassandra's book. "You didn't bring a book for me, did you?"

Anya laughed and shook her head. "You weren't reading one."

Wade thought back. "I was, but it wasn't in the bedroom."

"What were you reading?"

"The same he always reads." Cassandra gave him a quick, amused glance, interrupting him. "History books."

Wade shrugged, feeling a little on the defensive. "They fill the gaps in my knowledge. Remember, my memory started five years ago. I need to relearn what I might have known."

Anya shrugged. "That sounds more sensible than the horror books you used to read."

Ankara saw more passengers with a fresh batch for him to create their histories. Beyond Ankara, Wade found the landscape much more boring than around Istanbul, with scrubby desert to the horizon. When the hills grew into mountains, the scenery became momentarily more interesting until the train flashed into a tunnel.

Wade sighed and pulled out the sandwiches.

Cassandra put down her book. "A little early, isn't it?"

"I am bored. I can only watch the arrow on the screen move imperceptibly for so long."

Wade wondered how long he could make two triangles of a sandwich last. He stared at it, trying to read the writing on the side.

Anya gave him a pitying look. "When we get off in Adana, we'll find you a book."

"Meanwhile, I'll try to work out what *marul* means."

"Lettuce." Anya gave him a sunny smile.

"Makes sense. It has lettuce in it."

Light flooded the carriage as they shot from the tunnel. Wade blinked, looking out over a reddish landscape of deeply crevassed hills.

Iain Benson   **Yesterday Pill**

There was no more arguing with his stomach. Wade ripped open the sandwich.

Halfway through the second triangle, noise, heat, and air enveloped and engulfed them. He watched Anya mouth an 'O'. The seat he was in compressed forward, sending Wade crashing into the table. He doubled up, pain ripping through his chest as ribs cracked. Beside him, Cassandra, hit by flying shrapnel, fountained blood from a shoulder wound. Debris and a seething cloud of flame flew above his head. His hearing had gone. Tears blurred his vision, creating swirling patterns in the yellow, orange, and red crashing about him. He could feel his skin burning, the world turning as the carriage left the tracks. Wade fought against the scream as he moved his shoulder to pull his ring from his pocket.

Agony coursed down his arm, almost causing him to black out.

He could see a metal seat strut emerging from his shoulder, pinning him to the seat.

Each breath came with ragged, burning pain, blood bubbling on his lips.

He could not concede to the pain. That would be the end.

Anya lay, burned inches from him, Cassandra's arm dripped blood onto his leg.

Against the mind-numbing torture, Wade depressed and twisted his ring. Almost the last of his strength used to push and get what he hoped was a single dose. Consciousness almost faded, he pressed it to his lips.

The roiling flames froze, eddying patterns of fire churned within the static image. Alongside the frozen view, the pain ceased. It vanished to a point deep within him, returning as hunger and boredom. Harsh light from the fluorescent tubing fought against the tunnel's darkness outside the window. Neither woman seemed to notice his jerky arrival.

Puzzled, Wade looked at his watch. He had come back fifty minutes, not an hour.

"Do you have to be somewhere?" Cassandra asked.

"Sorry?" Wade didn't understand and wondered if he'd jumped

Yesterday Pill   Iain Benson

back into the middle of a conversation.

"You've checked your watch twice in a minute."

Wade understood. "Bored. I'm thinking of eating my sandwich."

Anya looked up from her phone. "You should eat it."

"I might go for a walk instead."

"You are going to want me to get up, aren't you?" Cassandra over-dramatically placed her book down. With a theatrical sigh, she slid out. Wade followed suit without the theatrics.

"Where are you going?" Anya asked.

"I thought I'd go looking for another sandwich."

Anya pointed to the sandwich. "What's wrong with that one?"

Wade had a moment of inspiration. "The ingredients on that are in Turkish, and said it contained," he switched to stilted Turkish, "we were an explosion."

Anya nodded. "That's radish and lettuce."

Wade gestured over his shoulder at where the explosion had been. "Does anybody want a fresh coffee?"

Anya handed him the payment card. "Turkish, black, please."

Cassandra nodded with a smile.

Wade headed down the narrow aisle, rocking slightly in time with the train. He had no way of knowing if a missile had hit them or if there was a bomb on board. As much as it depressed him, Wade would have to watch to find out. He went through the sliding door into the next carriage down. Wade had reached the first carriage. Through a small porthole, he saw a plain blue metal wall. Wade decided that was the engine. From the scorching memory, the explosion had come from behind him, not in front. He turned around and came back.

"It's the other way," Cassandra said, watching him approach.

Wade gave her a sarcastic smile. As he headed down the carriage, he tried to examine the bags he could see on desks and in any open luggage racks, searching for anything bomb-like. They all looked suspicious. Wade moved through the carriages until he found the buffet car. He bought three coffees and returned. According to his watch, he had about five minutes before the explosion.

"I forgot my sandwich after all that." Wade put the paper cups on the table between them. "I'll be right back."

With his body between Anya and Cassandra, he held up five fingers to Anya. She gave an imperceptible nod as light burst into the train.

The time approached rapidly. Wade looked for a helicopter gunship or tank in the countryside, seeing nothing. At the door, he passed through to the next carriage down and put on his ring. Wade took out a pill, feeling like a traitor to Anya and Cassandra. Instead of rescuing them, he watched. Wade knew he had to wait until the actual explosion to jump back. His timing had to be perfect.

The explosion held its own beauty, billowing out from the top left. A deadly flower blossoming from the enclosed luggage racks. The carriage metalwork peeled away, lethal debris erupting in rays. Wade twisted to the side as the devastating heat and pressure wave reached the door. Glass in both doors creaked and cracked, shattering, and exploding outwards in a fountain of diamond shards. The whole train shifted sideways, bending unnaturally. Wade had seen enough, taking the pill, hoping it was long enough.

The noise and debris froze, vanishing and replaced with the tunnel through the window.

He looked at his watch. Definitely fifty minutes. "Weird."

"What is it?" Anya asked, obviously clocking his return.

"The jump back was fifty minutes, well, fifty-one."

She agreed. "Weird. I take it you'll be going around this one again."

"Even if I get it this time, I will."

Cassandra looked at them both oddly. "What are you talking about?"

"There's a bomb on board." Wade gave her a level look. "There's no time to go into the details of how I know. I need you to get up. I've got to find it."

Yesterday Pill   Iain Benson

Bemused, Cassandra slid off the chair, allowing Wade to get up. He went to where the explosion had been. It had to be a bomb. Hitting the correct carriage on a train travelling at two hundred and fifty kilometres an hour would tax even Paladin. Wade rationalised it would be far easier to put a bomb on board, triggering it when it was away from houses. Paladin even had the good grace to wait until they were away from the tunnel to minimise infrastructure damage. He shook his head at their casual disregard for the lives on board.

He opened the cover to the overhead rack, attracting stares from the nearby passengers. A dozen bags jammed into the small space offered a lot of choice.

"Hey!" a passenger, a man in his early twenties, tried standing and twisting as Wade pulled bags off the rack. He pulled the first two out roughly before remembering he was looking for a bomb.

Wade held up a green canvas bag and asked in Turkish: "Yours?"

The young man nodded and snatched the bag. Wade decided no bomber would treat a bomb that way, so he returned to removing the remaining bags, placing each one on the floor.

Wade looked up at an imposing figure in a pale brown suit hovering over him. "What are you doing?"

Wade looked up at the white-bearded face. He saw no point in lying; they would have no memory of this. "There is a bomb."

Gasps echoed around the carriage from those that had heard. The young man pushed his own bag away from himself.

Wade pulled open a zip.

Anya came over. "How long have we got?"

Wade checked his watch. "Forty minutes."

Anya shrugged. "Ages."

The current bag was a black leather holdall. Wade unzipped it, the onlookers watching with horror and intrigue. A collective sigh went around them as Wade found clothes. Four other bags came down, all innocuous. He took the fifth bag down, a camouflage duffle bag.

Wade looked at the stitching, fastening it shut. "I think this is it. Anya, pass me a knife."

"Here." Anya passed down a sharp-bladed knife.

Wade put the blade against the fabric. "Does anybody want to claim this bag before I cut it open?"

Anya translated, but the passengers were quiet.

Wade carefully ran the blade around the bag, slicing through the fabric. Inside, he found plastic wrapping. Somebody in the crowd swore as Wade pulled back the camouflage cover.

Wade did not remember if he was an expert in bomb disposal, but he knew he was looking at a bomb. White plasticine inside a plastic tub, with wires and a black plastic and metal box. Wade was about to use the knife to open the black plastic box from where the strands emerged, but the crowd's sudden gasp halted his hand.

"Everybody, please leave the carriage." He lifted it carefully, although there should be no way it was movement detonated, with the train rocking regularly.

"Be careful." Cassandra had worried furrows at the top of her nose.

Wade gave a reassuring smile. He looked over at Anya. "If there's an explosion, point out the right bag to me, and I'll go again."

"Better idea." Anya took the bomb off him. "I'll defuse it."

Wade shrugged. "As long as one of us remembers."

"Neither of you are making any sense." Cassandra narrowed her eyes at them. "When this is over, you are going to explain what's going on."

Wade gave her a dubious look. "It's unlikely I will get a chance."

She gave him a stern look. The passengers shuffled from the carriage, and she joined them. Anya placed the bomb on the table. She took her screwdriver from her bag and removed the plastic cover on the box with wires. Inside, Wade expected to see a clock, but found a small chip connected to dozens of thin strands of black wire.

"I don't think we can cut the red wire." Wade tried to make a joke, but Anya was not in the mood.

Yesterday Pill — Iain Benson

She turned to look at him. "Which shall I do? Pull the wires, pull the detonators from the plastique, or smash the controller chip."

Wade shook his head. "I don't know. It is my first time seeing the bomb before it explodes. They all sound both sensible and dangerous at the same time."

"In that case, stand by the door. I'm going to smash the control box. How long before you can jump back?"

Wade checked his watch. "Ten minutes in five, four, three, two, now."

Anya checked her watch. "I'll do it in nine minutes from now. Go into the other carriage. If there's no explosion in the next ten minutes, you'll still have to go back, as Cassandra now suspects something."

Wade set his alarm on his watch and retreated to be with Cassandra.

Cassandra watched Wade approach with worry etched on her face. She peered through the glass at the hunched form of Anya. "Does she know what she's doing?"

The other passengers appeared quite keen to know the answer. Wade looked around them. "She's fairly confident."

"Fairly?" a passenger asked, their voice highly pitched.

Wade pulled Cassandra to one side and showed her his ring. "This produces a quantum connection that allows me to travel back an hour."

"No. It doesn't." Cassandra seemed quite confident.

Wade twisted the signet ring, popping out the pill. "It does."

"How does it work?" Cassandra asked. "Why have you never told me about this before?"

"I don't know." Wade looked her in the eyes. "I have told you before. But you didn't remember because I had to jump back."

"How long have you known?"

"I found out in Le Mans."

Cassandra looked puzzled. "That hallucination with being beaten up?"

Iain Benson   Yesterday Pill

Wade nodded. "It wasn't a hallucination."

The glass buckled towards them. A precursor to the sound following as the explosion mushroomed through the carriage. Wade's fist closed around the small pill, protecting it. Around Wade, the passengers yelled and screamed as the train rocked on the tracks. There was a calmness around Wade.

Cassandra's analytical mind momentarily crumbled: "Anya!"

Wade's watch beeped. Calmly, he took the pill and started again.

He set his watch and twisted the triangular box with his sandwich inside.

Cassandra put down her book. "A little early, isn't it?"

"Passing time." Wade fiddled with the opening.

"You might as well eat it," Anya said.

Wade followed her advice and ate the sandwich. It reminded him of service station sandwiches. After forty-five minutes, his watch beeped.

"What's that for?" Cassandra asked.

Wade turned it off. "It means it's time to defuse a bomb."

Cassandra laughed. "No, really. What does it mean?"

"Can I get up?"

Cassandra shook her head, inserted her bookmark, and placed the book on the table. With a theatrical sigh, she stood.

"Where are you going?" Anya asked.

"To get the bomb."

Wade walked back down the train to where the young man who'd owned the canvas bag was sitting. Wade opened the rack and moved his bag to pull clear the camouflage duffle.

"Hey!" the young man said.

Although he felt no sorrow, Wade apologised.

He put the bag on the table between Anya and Cassandra. "May I use your knife?"

Anya quickly understood, passing Wade a blade. He used it to slice around the bag, revealing the bomb.

Yesterday Pill   Iain Benson

Wade pulled them out and knocked the bag to the side, clearing the table.

"We'll need to clear the carriage." Anya looked at the bomb. "What did I do last time?"

Wade avoided Cassandra's confused mutterings and expression. "You smashed the control box."

Using her screwdriver, she lifted the lid on the control box and looked inside. "That seems like the first thing I would try."

"Wade?" Cassandra asked. "How did you know about the bomb?"

"I'll explain in a minute." He knew it was a false promise.

Anya got to her feet and raised her voice. In Turkish, she passed on the message to the other passengers. "Passengers, could you please move down a carriage? We have found a bomb. I will need to disarm it."

Mutterings and shuffling bodies in seats susurrated around the carriage as people turned to look. Anya obliged by holding up the bomb. It sped up the evacuation. Wade helped Cassandra out of her chair and led them down the aisle.

Wade checked his watch. "We have two minutes, folks."

People scrambled from the carriage, although Wade knew they were no safer than one carriage down.

Before joining the other passengers, Wade leaned over Anya.

"Pull the wires."

She gave him a thumbs up.

"Does she know what she's doing?" asked a voice. Wade identified the owner this time as the bearded man in the pale brown suit.

Wade gave his most reassuring smile. "She does."

Cassandra tugged his sleeve. "Wade, how did you know?"

The explosion again rocked the train. Wade sighed as around him, the people screamed, clutching each other.

Cassandra moved towards the shattered, twisted doorway. "Anya!"

Wade's watch beeped. He took the pill.

Wade looked at Anya. "I seriously hope you get it right this time. It is getting repetitive."

"Are you talking in your sleep?" Cassandra asked.

Anya looked up from her phone and arched an eyebrow.

"I'll explain in a bit," he told her.

"What's the matter?" Cassandra put her book down.

"I am going to get coffee."

"You are going to want me to get up, aren't you?" Cassandra sighed, sliding along.

Wade squeezed her shoulder as Anya passed the contactless card. At the correct locker, he opened it up and pulled the camouflage bag out. A glance back at Anya and Wade could see her watching him.

"Hey!" said the youth.

"Just getting my bag." Wade showed the camouflage duffle.

Wade slung the bag over his shoulder and headed down the train towards the back. Each time the bag banged on a seat back, his breathing stopped, and his heart skipped a beat. He had to remind himself that if anything happened, none of this would ever have happened. Wade retraced his steps back to the buffet car past the sleeping carriage. The man working behind the counter selling coffee, fruit and sandwiches was the only employee Wade knew on the train. He put the bag on the counter.

"Can I help you, sir?" the sales assistant asked.

Wade put the duffle bag on the counter. "Do you have a knife?"

The assistant looked perplexed and placed a plastic knife on the counter. "Is this all right?"

"A proper knife?"

"I have scissors." The assistant put a pair of scissors on the counter. Wade gave a quick smile and sliced open the bag.

"Is that a bomb?" The assistant paled and tried to step back into the drink shelving behind him.

"It is." Wade rested his hand on the window. "I found it in our carriage. We need to get it off the train, as it will explode in about thirty minutes."

Yesterday Pill   Iain Benson

"The doors won't open if we're moving." The assistant could not remove his eyes from the plastique and wires.

Wade kept his calm. "Can you contact somebody who can open a door, or do you know of a way of opening a hatch in the roof or floor?"

The assistant almost imperceptibly shook his head. "They seal the train for the speed."

It sounded like a rote remark to Wade. "Are you able to contact the driver or somebody else in charge to get the train stopped?"

"We cannot stop the train."

Wade sighed and resisted the urge to roll his eyes. "How about contacting the driver?"

"Are you hijacking the train?" The sales assistant sounded petrified.

Wade lost his temper a little. "And do what? Demand you take me to Afghanistan? It's not a plane. It will go down the tracks and stop at the next station. If we get that far before the bomb goes off."

"I cannot talk to the driver."

Wade scooped it off the counter. "I'll just have to defuse it then."

Returning to his carriage left a trail of whispers and passengers craning their necks to look at his retreating form. He placed the bomb on the table.

"Is that a bomb?" Cassandra asked.

Wade nodded. "A big one."

"Was that in the duffle?" Anya asked.

Again, Wade nodded. "So far, you have smashed the control box and pulled the wires out."

"I can see why I left pulling the detonators out until last." Anya twisted the bomb around and looked underneath it.

Cassandra slid out of her seat. Around them, other passengers were looking concerned. "Should you be doing that?"

"Given Wade carried it around, I'm guessing it's safe. Where did you go, by the way?"

Wade succumbed and rolled his eyes. "The only person I've seen on the train who works for the train is in the buffet car, so I went to see him. You'd already blown up four times, and it's depressing watching that."

Cassandra held Wade's arm, pulling at it. "You're not making any sense, Wade."

Wade levered Cassandra's fingers from the material of his jumper. "I will explain soon." He checked his watch. "But we now have ten minutes. We need to work out what to do, so you need to clear the carriage. Could you get everybody into the next carriage, please?"

Cassandra scowled at Wade and stormed down the corridor. "Hi, everybody, could you all move into the next carriage?"

"Is that a bomb?" asked the man in the brown suit.

Wade gave Anya a wry smile. "People are very observant."

"You'll need to go as well." Anya jerked her thumb toward the door.

"Why did you leave the detonators until last?"

Anya pulled one, making Wade wince. "Detonators are miniature bombs. When they explode, they still explode."

The detonator tube felt smooth as Wade ran his finger down it. "Are they safe to remove?"

Anya responded by removing all four tubes. "Perfectly."

Wade put the plastique into a stack and moved it away from the tubes. "Would they damage train tracks?"

"Are you going to flush them?"

"It's a thought."

Anya looked like she was considering it. "Let me try something else first."

Watching her as he backed down the corridor, he saw her use her knife to slice through the rubber caps on the detonators.

His heart raced, expecting the explosion.

She slid wires from tubes with a steady hand, leaving an empty plastic container. Wade checked his watch. She had less than two minutes. Anya placed her knife down and stretched her fingers, wiggling them. It had to be tough; Wade empathised with her tension. Closing her eyes and

Yesterday Pill   Iain Benson

centring her mind for a precious few moments, Anya picked up her knife and worked on the other detonators.

After removing the last one, she stretched, wiggling her shoulders.

Wade's watch beeped. Anya jerked as the electric charge ran through her fingers. Better them than the detonators.

She looked at him. "We're all clear."

Wade came back to the table. "Do I need to run through this one last time?"

"You might." Anya's brow furrowed. "Probably a good idea. Cassandra is quite suspicious, and she appears to have fallen out with you."

"What do you mean?"

"When you told her you got depressed watching me get blown up, she wouldn't have understood. Did you mean that, by the way? Did you find it depressing?"

That question surprised Wade. "Yes, of course I did."

Anya smiled. "And that's why she's cross. I'd not mention this, next time around, if I were you."

Wade twisted and pushed his ring.

He felt much more relaxed as the world snapped back into three dimensions.

He opened his sandwich, setting the alarm on his watch.

"Anybody want a coffee?" he asked.

"I'd love one." Anya fished out her payment card. "Turkish, black."

"I suppose this means you'll want me to stand up?" Cassandra squeezed his arm and leaned towards him. "I'd love one."

She grunted as she slid herself out of her seat. After Wade had spun her around like they were dancing to get past, making her giggle, she sat back down. Wade felt happier now he'd repaired the previous, unremembered, slight.

He headed to the buffet car, stopping by the locker with the duffle bag.

To the young man, he gave a smile. "Excuse me."

"No problem," the man replied with a smile.

Wade pulled the duffle from the rack and headed off down the corridor, thinking of a way of defusing without worrying Cassandra. He wondered about doing it in a lavatory. Anya had all the tools. As the sales assistant behind the counter made him his coffee, he pierced a creamer with scissors. Wade had an idea.

"Excuse me?"

The assistant turned. "Yes?"

"May I have your scissors?"

Looking perplexed, he passed Wade the scissors. Wade placed the bag on the counter and sliced around the top, exposing the plastic-encased bomb.

"Is that a bomb?" the assistant paled and stepped backwards.

"I'm a member of Interpol. We had a report of a bomb on the train. I've found it. Now I need to defuse it. My assistant usually has my tools, but she forgot. It is a little embarrassing, truth be told."

"You know how to defuse it?" He looked slightly more relaxed.

"I should think so." Wade gave him a winning smile. "Would I be able to have a tray? I can't carry both them and the bomb."

"I cannot let customers have a tray."

"You wouldn't want me to drop the bomb, would you?"

The sales assistant placed the cups on a black plastic tray. Wade added the bomb. "Dispose of that bag for me, thanks."

Between the sleeping cars and the carriages, Wade went into the toilet cubicle. Even balancing the tray on his knee with the cups on the floor left him with insufficient room to operate. He needed the space of a table.

Wade returned to his seat. Again, the ripples of whispered comments followed him back. Cassandra squeezed back into the aisle as Wade placed the tray on the table.

"Is that a bomb?" Cassandra sounded freaked out.

"I found it in the toilet."

"And you brought it here?" Her intonation rose.

Yesterday Pill   Iain Benson

"I have a feeling I can disarm it." He slid a detonator from the plastique, making her and several other passengers exclaim. "I'm certain I can."

"How do you know this?" Cassandra asked.

"Yes, how do you know this, Wade?" Anya sounded vaguely amused.

Wade knew Anya knew this wasn't his first time. "I don't know. It's like driving a car, I guess. I want to be on the safe side, so can you get everybody into the next carriage?"

Anya nodded. She passed Wade her knife. "I think you might need this. I'll watch from the door. If you don't mind?"

Wade smiled. "It's always good to have a backup."

"Can't you leave it?" Cassandra asked.

Wade levered off the lid from the control box. "There's no obvious timer. It might be a remote detonator or on a hidden timer. We don't know when it will explode. I know it's here for you, though, so please go in the next carriage."

"Be careful." Cassandra looked worried.

Wade patted Bump. "I will."

Anya cleared the carriage.

"Is that a bomb?" asked the brown-suited man.

Wade nodded. "Don't worry. I'm an expert."

Following Anya's actions, he slid the detonators from the plastique and placed that to one side. With the knife, he sliced through the rubber top and pulled the wires out.

He held up a thumb as the train burst from the tunnel into the light. He finally cut the wire to the battery, making all four wires spark with an audible crack. Wade's alarm on his watch beeped. He stopped it.

Anya let the passengers back into the carriage on seeing Wade's thumb. As they returned to their seats, the man in the brown suit started clapping. Wade felt slightly embarrassed as the applause rippled around the carriage.

Anya slid back into her seat and made the knife vanish into the folds of her shoulder bag. "You made that look easy. Almost like you've done it before."

Wade shook his head. "I had a wonderful teacher."

Anya laughed as Cassandra returned. "What's funny?"

Anya looked up. "Just laughing with relief."

Cassandra squeezed back into the seat. "I know what you mean."

A woman in her early thirties paused by their table and looked at the pile of explosives. "Thank you."

Wade shrugged. "It saved me as well."

Cassandra pointed at the plastique. "Is that safe?"

"Perfectly," Wade said. "I wouldn't advise allowing a small child to make models from it, but it won't explode."

Anya raised her paper cup, smiling. "That's a job well done."

Wade sipped his slightly cold coffee and returned to watching the scenery blur past.

Yesterday Pill   **Iain Benson**

9

Another hour passed. Anya suddenly put her phone away. "Time to move."

"Shouldn't we wait until we're in the station?" Wade asked.

Anya shook her head. "Thanks to mobile phones, people know about the bomb."

"Ah." Wade would have to go back a day. Over an hour had passed since defusing the bomb. Having another breakfast at Anya's grandmother's hotel sounded appealing. He had time to wait and see how Anya's escape panned out.

"Reporters and a TV crew are waiting at the station." Anya packed her bag. "As they put a bomb on the train, Paladin will also wait. They know the bomb did not work."

Wade retrieved their suitcases. A few passengers gave Wade a grateful smile as they travelled down the train. He didn't feel he'd earned it; Anya had made the dangerous attempts. They stopped at the last seating carriage, with the sleeping cars and buffet car the only ones farther back.

Konya station appeared abruptly in the windows, white pillars flashing past, slowing as the train came to a stop. For Wade, it was a heart-stopping pause before the doors hissed open. Anya took the steps down onto the platform first, checking down the platform towards the exit. A slight motion of her hand for Cassandra and Wade followed both women.

Most passengers headed for the station escalators. Instead, Anya led them towards the opposite end. Paladin would be around, Wade knew. He looked for them, but they had to have taken excellent hiding places. He could see a camera crew filming the train for the local news. Assuming they were local news and not Paladin. Wade felt paranoid, but knowing that people *were* out to get him.

The platform sloped down to a siding, relieving Wade, who'd feared they would have to climb down. It was tempting to abandon the suitcases as Wade struggled across the cinders and gravel towards a train turntable and train sheds.

Concrete made the going easier after they reached the shadows and perceived safety of older train carriages. They crowded around, looking like sleeping behemoths in the overhead sun. Anya led them to a locked metal gate on rollers. She pressed a button on a plinth, sending the gate trundling open with a grating squeak. Even though it was winter, the air felt warm in the sun, away from the wind.

Wade saw a diner with seats outside. "There, that looks promising." They crossed the quiet road to the small café.

"You two wait here," Anya said. "I'll be back with some transport."

A coffee and ciabatta later, Anya returned in a dark blue Transit.

"A van?" Cassandra's eyebrow arched.

"To get across Turkey, it's perfect." Cassandra leaned over and opened the door. "It has a full tank of diesel, and the owner has gone home for the day. By the time he misses it, we'll be in Tel Aviv."

After the previous cars, the van felt like a tank as Anya navigated her way out of Konya. "I came here on a school trip as a kid."

She drove them from the city via a road broader than most motorways in the UK. Trams trundled in both directions down the central reservation.

She pointed at an angular white building set back from the road and partially hidden by conical trees. "Have you heard of Whirling Dervish? That's where they whir. There's a big amphitheatre inside."

"And that?" Cassandra asked as they passed a group of stadia.

"No idea. Those buildings look new."

As they left the town's outskirts, the landscape flattened out, desolate. The sky filled with heavy clouds as the Transit headed down an almost deserted road. In the distance, Wade felt he could see mountains. As the miles rolled under the wheels, they never seemed to get any closer until they suddenly surrounded the vehicle. A brief pause at a service station and back on the move again. Wade missed the leisurely recharging stops. The mountains provided more varied scenery, though it occasionally vanished as

Yesterday Pill   Iain Benson

they drove into tunnels. Something about the vista allowed Wade to relax momentarily.

Even though darkness crept into the sky, Wade liked it. "It's beautiful here."

"It's all right up here," Anya said, speaking across Cassandra. "When you get down to Adana, it gets boring."

"What's wrong with it?" Cassandra asked.

Anya tutted, as though cross with mentioning it. "It's where my parents moved to, leaving Istanbul behind just before I was born. I prefer Istanbul, as Adana is like how Turkey used to be."

"What do your parents do?" Wade recognised Cassandra's inquisitive tone. He'd thought she could be an interrogator.

"They run a guest house on the lake in Adana." Anya included all the pent-up venom she'd accrued during her childhood in that brief description.

The tone would not deter Cassandra. "It sounds idyllic."

Anya twisted in her seat to look at Cassandra. "There was nothing to do. I moved back to Istanbul to live with Babaanne, but had to come back to help when I was sixteen."

Cassandra squeezed Anya's arm. "I think all kids feel that way about where they grow up."

"I could see all this stuff happening around the world on the TV, and Adana felt like a backwater, missing out on it all."

Wade was thinking about his parents and who they were. "When did you last see your parents?"

Anya went quiet for a moment. "I had a big argument with my mama when I was in my early twenties. I think that was it."

"What about mine?"

Anya sighed. Her tone filled with sadness. "There is no easy way to tell you."

"How did they die?" Wade knew what Anya's tone meant. He tried to keep his tone light, but the feeling of darkness swelling inside him made him spit the words out.

He felt Cassandra's hand squirm into his.

Anya was silent, allowing the gloom gathering outside to provide a metaphor for his feelings. He found the silence worse than knowing. It gave space for horrors to take the place of rational thought.

Blowing a long stream of air out through pursed lips, Anya eventually spoke. "They died in a plane crash."

Wade was a little confused. In the silence, his mind had conjured the idea he had killed them. "From your reaction, I thought you were going to accuse me of murdering them."

"There was nothing you could do." Anya had a firmness in her voice.

Wade wondered if he'd always believed he could have saved them. Perhaps he could have done but chose not to do so. "When was this?"

"Eight years ago."

Wade desperately wanted to know why he hadn't used a pill, even though it was in the right time frame. He squeezed Cassandra's hand, knowing he could not ask Anya that until they were alone. Not knowing gnawed away inside him. He'd spent years unable to dwell on his past. Now he longed for that time again.

They stopped at a service station so Cassandra could go to the toilet after Bump played football with her bladder. Wade suspected she was trying to be light-hearted in the face of his grim ideation.

Wade caught Anya's arm as she was heading to follow Cassandra. "Why didn't I use a pill?"

"You tried, once," Anya said, coming to stand in front of him, her features in shadow, the light from the fuel station a halo through her dark hair. "You found out after nearly a week, jumped back and begged them not to get on that flight."

"I don't understand why they would."

Anya looked at the shop where the toilets were. She bit her lip. "Your parents thought you were having delusions. They thought it before you rang. After you joined Paladin, you and they became estranged."

Yesterday Pill   Iain Benson

Cassandra emerged, pausing briefly to look through the shelving, giving them a few more moments. Anya turned back to Wade with love and hurt in her eyes. "I'm glad you have lost those memories, Wade. They made you sad. As happy as we were together, you are so much happier with Cassandra, without the baggage you had with us."

Wade felt the sadness of which she spoke. "It's like I'm two people."

Anya nodded. "You were my Wade. You're now Cassandra's Wade."

Their conversation curtailed with the return of Cassandra. She kissed Wade. "You'll be okay. It's grief."

Wade nodded. "Yes, I will be. I didn't know this morning. Now, I half wish I didn't know."

"It's important." Cassandra squeezed his hands. "You pretended you were okay after I found you. You pretended not knowing who you were didn't matter. I've always known it did."

"I can't imagine losing my entire past." Anya tilted her head. "It must have been tough for you."

Wade's darkness lifted in the face of so much support. He smiled. "Enough esteem bolstering. We need to get moving."

Anya drove them to the coast, leaving Wade to his thoughts. As they turned onto the promenade road, Wade looked out on the darkened houses and shops on one side, the container storage on the other side. He'd been expecting a seaside town, but it seemed they'd come in the port's industrial side. Up ahead, in the dark, a dome of light betrayed the ferry.

All three of them could see the army and police at the entrance to the port. Anya continued down the road, shrinking back into the seat. Their van merged in with plenty of other business traffic travelling to and from the port warehousing. Across the port, the warehousing became hotels. The lights and garish colours at least felt appropriate for the seaside.

Cassandra said what they were all thinking. "That was a lot of activity."

Anya pulled into a hotel carpark. "Paladin knows we're in Turkey, heading in this general direction."

"How can we get past them?" Wade again considered going back a day, redoing it differently.

Anya seemed to read his mind. "I may have an idea. It's not something I would want to do. I doubt Paladin will have it covered."

Wade wondered where she was going. "What is it?"

"We're going to fly."

Cassandra gasped. "But airports are heavy with CCTV."

Anya nodded. "We'll deal with that if we need to."

Wade had a feeling that they would have to deal with it, possibly several times. He trusted Anya. That thought made him chuckle. A few nights ago, she'd walked into a restaurant with a shotgun, saving their lives at gunpoint.

"What's funny?" Cassandra asked.

"Doesn't matter," Wade replied.

Anya slid out. "I need to make a phone call."

Wade could only catch snippets through the closed door, understanding less with his imperfect Turkish.

Cassandra added to the complication of listening. "What's she saying?"

"I don't know enough Turkish, and she's talking very fast," Wade told her. "I've got that she's talking to somebody called Ozzy."

Anya's mood when she got back into the van was thunderous. "I asked nicely. Now we ask more personally. Let's see him say no to my face."

She grated the Transit's gears to put it in reverse and headed back towards the port. They drove straight past, not even glancing at the dark blue suited police or pale green soldiers. Several black-clad Paladin operatives dotted among them. He silently wondered if the System now knew their plan and their itinerary. The other option had this kind of presence at every port. It struck Wade that they would also patrol the borders. Turkey might be a big enough country for them to get lost in it. Eventually, the locals would tire of looking for them. Paladin could probably keep it up, kettling them, but Wade felt they would slip through whatever

Yesterday Pill   Iain Benson

dragnet Paladin could construct.

Being besieged in Turkey was possible, but not ideal. The longer it took for the truth to come out, the more chances they had to slip and for Paladin to find them. Though the public would forget about the restaurant explosion, Paladin would never stop looking.

Anya's mood translated into aggressive driving. Rocketing through the darkness, temporary pools of civilization flashed past the windows. Wade noticed there was no satnav. She knew where she was going. Anya turned off the major road onto a strip of single carriageway tarmac, barely slowing. She overtook a large truck, the horn from the vehicle fading rapidly with distance. The road was relatively straight and virtually empty. Up ahead, in the pre-dawn deep indigo sky, Wade saw a dome of light, which resolved at speed to a provincial airport.

Anya finally slowed and came to a stop just outside the fence. She slipped her baseball cap on her head. "You're going to have to get in the back."

Wade didn't argue. He helped Cassandra down and used the side slide door to climb into the back, getting a momentary flashback of Le Mans. The van's back smelled of scorched metal. A stack of wood occupied bolted shelving on the far side. Though he feared they would get tossed around as Anya attempted the speed record for a van, she drove sensibly. Wade pressed into the corner by the back doors, his legs making a vee-shape for Cassandra to sit in, using him as a cushion. He could feel a protrusion that would leave a bruise on his lower back. Through it, he felt every bump.

He could barely see through the front windscreen; the bright lights of a security gate reflecting off them. Anya wound down the window.

"Oil for Dogan," she said through the window.

Security was light, with Anya allowed to continue with no checks or paperwork. When Anya stopped, Wade and Cassandra opened the door and stepped out. The air held a chill after the van's warmth, the scents of kerosene hanging in the still air. Wade found the vast expanse of concrete and tarmac to be overly bright. The waves in the main terminal building's roofline reminded Wade of waves, not the sky. It was too reflective, making it hard to look at in the harsh lighting.

Anya parked next to blocky hangers, gaping entrances to private planes arrayed like a carpark. She headed towards a two-storey concrete block of a building with small windows on the top floor. A few were dark, but most already had lights shining from them. Wade could see the silhouettes of early risers starting their work for the day.

They followed Anya through a pair of double glass doors onto a long corridor with a staircase at the end. Wade looked down at workshops before scurrying to catch up to Cassandra and Anya as they took the switchback onto the top floor. Wade caught them up, discovering dozens of offices along the top floor, each with a small sign beside the door. A small picture of a hawk etched into the brass plaque announced Dogan-Air.

Anya pushed the door open with rather more force than necessary.

"Annie," a man's voice came from inside. His follow up Turkish was too rapid for Wade to follow, but it sounded irritated.

Wade followed her inside and found himself in a small square office with a narrow desk and laptop against one wall, under a large map showing the Mersin coast. A window looked out onto the carpark and terminal building beyond. The occupant, who Wade assumed was Ozzy, wore a pale grey tee-shirt and jeans. Wade guessed he was about their age, with a fuzzy beard and dark, close-cropped curls. He rattled off rapid Turkish.

"Ozzy, stop." Anya held up her hand and pointed to Wade and Cassandra standing by the door. "This is Wade and Cassandra."

Wade stepped into the room a little more.

"You are pregnant?" Ozzy stared at Cassandra's bump.

Cassandra supported her bump with both hands. "Yes."

Ozzy gave Anya a stern glare. "Annie, you cannot do this to me. I could lose my plane, my licence, my business."

Anya prodded him in the shoulder with a stiff finger. "You wouldn't have any of this if it wasn't for me."

Yesterday Pill   Iain Benson

"Gah!" Ozzy slapped the palm of his hand against the wall.

The Turkish flowed between the two of them with quite a lot of gesticulating.

Cassandra leaned into Wade and lowered her voice. "Can you understand any of this?"

Wade slipped his arm around her shoulder. "Very little."

"Anything?"

"Something about a debt and time to repay."

Wade tried to follow the argument. The two seemed to have a long history, and they were trawling it all up. They spoke in incomplete sentences, with a slang smattered through the tirade.

Wade stepped forward and coughed. "Look, I get it. You can't take us. We'll find a different way. I don't know what, if anything, you owe Anya, but I can't have somebody else risk anything for Cassandra and me."

Anya's mouth slightly opened as she gaped at him. "Wade?"

"I'm sorry, Anya, but this is Ozzy's life."

Anya's anger dissipated. "In this, Wade, you don't know the complete story."

Wade acknowledged that. "You're right. I don't. But we have got this far. We can get past Paladin."

Anya took a deep breath and returned her gaze to Ozzy. "Wade's right. We can't ask you to do this."

"Paladin?" Ozzy looked puzzled.

Anya's brow furrowed, exactly like Ozzy's. "Have you heard of them?"

Wade realised how much alike the two looked. It was hard to see Ozzy's face shape, but around the eyes and the nose, Wade decided they were siblings.

He ignored his sister's question. "What did they do? Did they put those bruises on your face?"

Wade took over. "They're trying to kill Cassandra. They blew up a restaurant. And, yes, they put the bruises on her face."

"The one in the UK?"

Wade nodded. "We hope we can find why they want Cassandra dead and find proof of being behind the attack."

Ozzy rubbed his beard. "That's why you want to go to Tel Aviv."

"Paladin is dangerous." Anya perched on the narrow table. "I was desperate. But I shouldn't have rung."

"Okay, I will help." Ozzy sounded as positive about helping as he had been about not.

"What?" Anya shook her head. She'd gone the other way and had decided not to involve her brother.

"Do you think I don't know what happened to you?" It was Ozzy's turn to prod Anya's shoulder. "Or what you had to do to get the cartel off my back? I'm not stupid, Annie."

Wade wondered at Anya's history. It made him wonder about his own, too. He shook his head, bringing his focus back to the present. "Cartel?"

Anya glanced towards Wade. "It's a story from a long time ago. I have neither the time nor the inclination to go through it now."

Her tone led Wade to believe her. He gestured with his palms out to show supplication. "Noted."

"I've lost track." Cassandra's gaze swept over them. "Is Ozzy taking us or not?"

Ozzy and Anya spoke together, but disagreed.

Ozzy grinned. "It's not up to you, Annie."

"Are you going to drug me and drag me on?"

"If I have to!"

Anya pushed off the desk. "Then yes, Ozzy is taking us."

Ozzy pulled the laptop towards him and tapped a few keys. "I'll make a flight plan for Cyprus. I'm going to miss it. It's about five-fifty klicks to Tel Aviv. That's a tank there and back. I'll put in half a tank."

"Why?" Cassandra watched Ozzy's process closely.

"I'll have to land to refuel. Having a full tank would look suspicious."

Wade detected how Ozzy pronounced every syllable. Something more noticeable on 'suspicious'.

Anya looked grim. "We'll have to jump out and run for it."

"It's going to have to be that way. Israel air traffic cannot know I've brought passengers, or that's me done."

Cassandra seemed keen to understand. "Where are you heading for?"

"I can't go to the main city airport." Ozzy sounded like he was thinking aloud. "I am going to aim for Herzliya. It's a provincial airport mainly used for pleasure flights and pilot training. After that, you're on your own."

Wade thought about what came next. "How far is the city?"

Ozzy turned back to the computer and touched the screen a few times. "About twelve klicks."

Anya nodded. "That's doable. We'll have to move quickly."

Cassandra laughed. "Don't we always?"

Wade brought up the rear as Ozzy led the way back down the stairs and across to the hangers. While Ozzy filled the fuel tank, Anya removed the plates from the van.

"Wade," she called. "Grab the bags."

Wade felt resigned to his pack mule role, carrying the bags into the aircraft. Up close, the craft's size surprised Wade. He leaned on the strut, connecting the wing above his head to the plane's body. The hawk motif on the side, wings spread as though landing on the wheel struts. Wade split the Dogan-Air red lettering as he opened the door. He put the cases behind the rear pair of seats. Ozzy took a great deal of pride in his plane; it smelled of lemons without a single speck of dirt inside.

Anya spoiled the aesthetics by tossing the dirty van licence plates onto the carpet. Wade caught sight of her face. She knew how much Ozzy liked a clean plane, and she dirtied it on purpose.

Ozzy noticed the plates on the floor and gave his sister a hard stare as he stooped into the cabin. "All aboard."

Anya slipped in to take the seat beside her brother, with Cassandra and Wade taking the two cramped back seats.

Ozzy put on a clipped English accent. "Ladies and gentlemen, welcome to Dogan-Air. I am Ozan Dogan, your pilot for this short flight. It's currently mild, with some clouds in Tel Aviv. We should arrive in Israel at noon."

The engine throb thudded into the cabin as Ozzy flicked switches. The pitch increased as the plane taxied from the hangar.

Ozzy slipped on a headset and pressed the earpiece. "Çukurova tower, this is dog-oh-oh-one, ready for take-off."

With a roar, the propeller blurred, pulling the small plane along the runway, bright white lights lining the path it took. Within moments, Wade could no longer feel the ground bouncing under the wheels.

Ozzy raised his voice over the engine noise. "I saw on the news that you defused a bomb on the YHT. You saved many people."

Wade felt a little duplicitous taking credit, but knew Cassandra had to be kept in the dark. "It would have been a horror show had I not."

Ozzy's following words surprised Wade. "They are trying to claim you planted the bomb and had to defuse it because it was about to go off while you were still on the train."

Wade sighed. People would believe that if the papers said it. He wriggled and pulled his signet ring from his pocket. Keeping it out of Cassandra's eye line, he slipped it onto the ring finger on his left hand. There was no immediate danger he could see, but Wade felt constrained by the plane. He lacked room to manoeuvre while they were in the air. Judging by the way Anya stroked her necklace, she felt the same way.

Darkness completely enveloped the plane. Looking through the window, Wade sensed no movement. The light on the wingtip flashed on and off, momentarily illuminating the wing's underside. Beyond, Wade watched the sunrise, red light tinging long thin clouds on the horizon. Wade stared at it, entranced.

Ozzy looked at his sister. Though he spoke Turkish, it was slow

Yesterday Pill   Iain Benson

enough and simple enough for Wade to follow. "Annie, what have you been up to for the past eighteen years?"

"Saving the world."

"I never had time to thank you." The flashing light on the wing momentarily illuminated Ozzy's smile. "Thank you. I don't know how you did what you did, but it meant I got my life back."

Wade's curiosity got the better of him. He leaned forward. "What happened?"

"An Armenian drug cartel got their claws into me." Ozzy sounded deeply regretful. "It was only a matter of time before I wound up dead."

"Paladin had wanted me to join for a while." Anya, too, had a tone of reminiscing. Wade hoped to elicit more information about his past. "They agreed to remove the cartel if I joined."

"How did they do that?"

Anya scowled. "They funded a rival cartel."

Wade recalled Adrian telling him they were the good guys. It certainly sounded like he was lying. The cab lapsed into silence.

10

"Is that Cyprus?" Cassandra peered down at the sliver of land that vanished off into the early morning murk.

Ozzy didn't need to look. "It is."

Wade felt he'd dozed off as he came awake as Ozzy banked the plane, heading to the thicker land on their left. The sun appeared much higher, blinding them as it bounced off the buildings, making up Tel Aviv.

Ozzy was talking into the headset. "Tel Aviv, I repeat, it is an emergency landing required. I'm on fumes here." There was a pause while he listened to the tower in Israel. "GPS failure. I aimed for Cyprus and missed. I can see Herzliya."

Wade saw they now were over land.

Ozzy was still talking. "I am going to be there in under a minute. I either come down and buy some fuel, or you scrape me off the runway. That's unnecessary!"

As he wondered why Ozzy's last two words were more panicked, Wade could hear another noise above the propeller. He twisted in his seat, looking everywhere, trying to pinpoint the whomp noise.

He attracted Ozzy's attention. "There's a pair of helicopter gunships behind us."

Wade learned a new profanity as Ozzy muttered *bok*.

Below them, the runway approached at speed. Wade decided to pre-empt the expected missiles and took a dose.

As the world snapped back into three dimensions, Wade wondered what exactly he could do differently this time.

"Could you fly lower, come in under the radar?"

Ozzy's eyebrows knitted together in the same way as Anya's when something puzzled her. "That would be suspicious and pointless."

"Pointless how?"

Ozzy used his hands, waving them over the instrument panel.

Yesterday Pill   Iain Benson

"Technically, there is no under the radar at an airport. It forms a dome. You can avoid it using valleys and buildings, but the airport is in a flat area on purpose."

Cassandra took his hand. "What's bothering you, Wade?"

"Paladin knows we're coming. They have helicopter gunships."

"That's specific," Ozzy said.

"They can't know." Cassandra sounded sure of that, but Wade knew differently. He knew Paladin knew. Or would know, soon.

Wade felt trapped as the plane banked.

Anya took matters into her own hands. She unclipped her belt and slipped under the instrument panel with a screwdriver. After a few profanities in several languages and deep throated grunting, she pulled out a slim aluminium box that she slapped onto the seat.

Ozzy sounded a little panicked. "Annie, that's the transponder!"

Muffled from having her head in the instrumentation, she explained. "I know. You're about to lose GPS."

Ozzy batted at his sister's side, trying to pull her out. "Bok. I'm flying blind now."

Anya contorted herself back out from the tight space. "Aim for the land. It's over there."

"You know it's illegal to fly without that. Other planes can't see me. Air traffic will think I'm hostile. Did you want helicopter gunships? We are now more likely to get them."

Wade hoped Anya knew what she was doing. She'd seemed confident of what to remove. She could have sent them crashing into the sea. He probably would have done. He wondered if she knew planes or discovered what she could remove by jumping back each time she failed.

"A little dramatic." Anya opened the aluminium transponder component. "They're more likely to have the police meet you."

Wade leaned forward to watch as Anya placed the flat screwdriver blade next to the most prominent black chip. She tapped it.

"Great," Ozzy muttered. "That's completely fucked."

Anya reached into her bag and pulled out a wad of euros. She dropped them on his lap. "Buy yourself a new one."

Wade looked all around, pressing his cheek against the cold glass, trying to spot the helicopters as they came in on final approach. Through the front window, he could see the line of land expanding. A strip of yellow and grey had to be the airport.

Ozzy pointed at his headset. "Tel Aviv Tower wants to know who we are."

Anya took the headset from him and slipped it on her head.

"Tel Aviv Tower. I've had a massive electric malfunction. There are sparks everywhere. I've seen an airstrip, and I'm aiming for it. Navigation is toast. My fuel is low, and."

She switched off the headset.

"Jesus, Annie!" Ozzy snatched back the headset. "You're going to get us killed."

Anya shrugged. "Would you like me to break your headset as well? For authenticity?"

Ozzy shook his head. "Whatever you're doing had better be worth this."

"It is," Anya told him. "When we land, head down the runway, at the far end, turn around and taxi back to the buildings."

Wade got the feeling that Anya now knew more than she was saying. That meant she'd been the one to jump back this time. He could spot the signs. She got more confident in her actions. He wondered if he was that obvious.

Ozzy missed the change of demeanour. "I take it I pause long enough for you to get out and behind the baffles before I've finished turning?"

"Perfect." Anya patted his arm.

"This is the kind of shit the cartel used to have me pull."

"Unlike the cartel, you'll only ever do this once for us."

Ozzy kept his bitterness even after all the time that had passed.

Yesterday Pill   Iain Benson

"That's what they said."

Beneath their wings, the sea became land like Ozzy had thrown a switch. The blue became green. Ozzy approached low and fast.

"The only time." Anya reached over and hugged him. "Also, unlike the cartels. Thanks, little brother."

Ozzy gave his sister a lopsided smile. "Next time you ring me in the middle of the night, I hope it's because you're coming to dinner. Jaz and Marie have never actually met you."

His problems had occupied his mind so much Wade realised he'd never stopped to consider that Ozzy had a family. "You have a family? Are Jaz and Marie your children?"

Ozzy gave a small laugh. "Jasmine is my daughter. She's six. Marie is my wife."

Wade felt awful. "I can only apologise for putting you at risk."

"Don't mention it."

Their landing dragged Ozzy's attention back to flying. The wheels hit the hard concrete runway with a lurch so hard that the plane bounced.

Anya gripped her belt as they slewed down the runway. "You normally do better landings than that."

"It's for the cameras." Ozzy grinned. "I've got no instruments, remember?"

Anya unclipped her belt and grabbed her bag. "We're going to have to be quick."

Cassandra and Wade unclipped their belts and extracted their cases. Wade wondered about the suitcases. They had clothes and toiletries in them, but this wasn't a holiday. "Shall we leave the bags?"

As the plane slowed, Anya paused, thinking, making Wade reassess his thought that she'd jumped back. This could all be improvisation unless this was one of those minute changes she had mentioned.

"Yes."

"I'm going to miss clean underwear," Cassandra said.

Anya opened the door in preparation. "Ozzy, we'll come back and get our cases and have dinner once we destroy Paladin. Soon!"

The three clambered from the plane through the small door as it turned slowly.

Ozzy reached over and pulled the door closed. "Good luck, sis."

Wade helped Cassandra over a wooden baffle. Long wooden support struts dug into the soil, propping up the orange and white painted plyboard. It looked unlikely to protect any aircraft unable to stop, but probably cheap to replace if something crashed into them. With Ozzy's plane between them and the low buildings at the airfield's far end, they scooted behind them and lay down. Wade watched. He put his head low, looking around the baffle. Ozzy's plane trundled down to the buildings. Half a dozen police vehicles, lights flashing, swung in through the gate, kicking up gravel as they surrounded Ozzy's plane.

Cassandra was peeking out as well. "I hope he'll be okay."

Anya looked a little dubious. "He can talk his way out of anything. He'll be fine."

The propeller on Ozzy's plane was still spinning as two black helicopter gunships appeared.

Anya breathed out a single word: "No."

Air to surface missiles erupted from the lead gunship. Plumes of smoke behind each of them. Pure white that belied the devastation they caused as they connected with Ozzy's plane. Orange blossomed up from a newly created crater on the runway. Police, mechanics, and pilots blown backwards as debris from the light aircraft rained down. The explosion's boom arrived after a moment; a single dull crump followed by a wash of heat.

"Ozzy!" Anya's voice cracked up, tears causing her eyes to glisten.

Wade knew there was nothing he could do within an hour.

He dialled through to a day on his ring. Ozzy's life was worth the headache.

The expanding mushroom froze into a planar representation of itself.

Yesterday Pill   Iain Benson

Wade was expecting to be back on the train and having to defuse the bomb again. Instead, the scene resolved into a roadside café; he still had the taste of coffee and ciabatta on his lips. Anya pulled up in the blue Transit.

"A van?" Cassandra asked, as Wade's mind was racing.

Anya opened the passenger door, allowing Cassandra to climb in. "To get across Turkey, it's perfect. It has a full tank of diesel. The owner has gone home for the day. By the time he misses it, we'll be in Tel Aviv."

Wade took the third seat next to the window. By his calculations, instead of twenty-four hours, he'd come back twenty. Wade had insufficient knowledge about the pills to know whether they always jumped the same amount. Nor could Wade be sure when Anya described it as 'a day' if it was a whole day. It was undoubtedly yesterday.

"I came here on a school trip as a kid." Anya's words echoed with déjà vu for Wade as they left the city. "Have you heard of Whirling Dervish? That's where they whir. There's a big amphitheatre inside."

Cassandra pointed at architectural-looking buildings opposite. "And that?"

"No idea. Those buildings look new."

Wade was wondering how he should play out the coming day. He knew how it went previously. As far as he could work out, he could either tell Anya to drive to Tel Aviv or come up with some way of having Ozzy survive the trip. For the time being, he'd keep things the same. Anya had reconnected with her family, and he felt that was important. However, Wade decided not to reopen the wound of asking about his parents. He knew now how they had died. He didn't need Cassandra knowing as well.

As they climbed through the mountains, he repeated himself. "It's beautiful here."

It was still beautiful; the mountains' jaggedness broken only by the softness of trees. The road held little traffic as the light left the sky, long shadows trailing across treetops.

Anya replied, her tone light enough, but he could detect the undercurrent of resentment he knew boiled there. "It's all right up here. It is seriously dull when you get down to Adana."

"What's wrong with it?" Cassandra asked.

Anya clicked her tongue. "It's where my parents moved to, leaving Istanbul behind before I was born. I prefer Istanbul, as Adana is like how Turkey used to be."

Cassandra continued to press, although Wade now knew memories of childhood were unwillingly coming back to Anya. "What do your parents do?"

"They run a guest house on the lake in Adana."

Despite Anya spitting the word 'Adana', Cassandra ploughed on as Wade knew she would. "It sounds idyllic."

Anya twisted in her seat to look at Cassandra. "There was nothing to do. I moved back to Istanbul to live with Babaanne, but had to come back to help when I was sixteen."

Cassandra squeezed Anya's arm. "I think all kids feel that way about where they grow up."

"I could see all this stuff happening around the world on the TV, and Adana felt like a backwater, missing out on it all."

Wade knew his line came next. "When did you last see them? Your parents, I mean."

Anya glanced over Cassandra at him. Had there been something in his tone? He'd hoped to keep his spontaneity, but perhaps she'd been through this enough to know he'd jumped back.

"I had a big argument with my mama when I was in my early twenties. I think that was it."

Wade nodded and chose deviation over returning to the still smouldering ruin that was the renewed loss of his parents. "You should see them. While you can."

"Yours." Anya took a deep breath, realising where the conversation would go.

Wade's heart caught in his chest as Cassandra ensured the timeline remained on track. "Do you know what happened to Wade's parents?"

Anya looked at Wade. Wade struggled to keep the emotion off his face. He knew Anya could read it, anyway. She looked like she was waiting for his permission to continue. He gave a slight nod.

"They died in a plane crash about eight years ago."

The sadness again caught the back of Wade's throat. Even though he knew, it was like hearing it for the first time. He expected it would be like that for some time to come. His breathing turned shallow as he fought back the tears.

Cassandra's hand squirmed into his. He squeezed it. Wade lapsed into silence. He still needed a way to Tel Aviv, but now the thoughts of his parents crowded in, complicating his planning.

As Cassandra vanished into the stone block housing the toilets at the service station, Anya stood facing Wade, a hand on her hip, her head cocked.

"How far back did you come?"

As though the pressure from Anya was the trigger he needed, Wade knew what to do. What he wasn't going to do was tell her that Paladin had killed her brother.

"I came back a day." Wade hoped she didn't ask him about what came next.

"You already asked about your parents, didn't you?" She placed a gentle hand on his forearm.

"I did. It was no easier hearing it twice."

"I'm glad you have lost those memories, Wade. They made you sad. As happy as we were together, you are so much happier with Cassandra, without the baggage you had with us."

"Thank you."

"Now, what do I need to know about what's coming up?"

Wade knew that what he said next would affect how the rest of what he knew about would work out. "You don't need to change anything."

Anya gave him a long look, but Cassandra returned before she could interrogate him further.

Cassandra kissed Wade. "You'll be okay. It's grief."

Wade nodded. "It was a long time ago. I don't remember."

Cassandra squeezed his hands. "You pretended you were okay with not knowing who you were after I found you. You pretended it didn't matter. I've always known it did."

"I can't imagine losing my entire past." Anya tilted her head. "It must have been tough for you."

"It has been. Denial is a wonderful thing."

They drove into Mersin. Past the container port and the ferry terminal, where the army, police, and Paladin operatives congregated around the entrance. Anya shot Wade a glare and drove past.

"That was a lot of activity," Cassandra said.

After pulling into the same hotel car park as before, Anya turned off the van's engine. "Paladin knows we're in Turkey, heading in this general direction. We probably could have guessed they'd be here."

A steady look at Wade accompanied the last sentence.

Wade shrugged. "I think the border into Syria is going to be equally difficult to get across."

Anya nodded, as though accepting this as a route they may have taken that would require a jump back. She held up a finger. "I may have an idea. It's not something I would want to do. I doubt Paladin will have it covered."

Wade adopted a curious look that he hoped he looked convincing. "What?"

Anya triumphantly announced: "We're going to fly."

Cassandra gasped. "But airports are heavy with CCTV."

Anya checked with Wade. "We'll deal with that. If we need to."

Wade nodded. "Sounds like a plan."

"I need to make a call." Anya picked up her phone and stood beside the van.

After a few moments of frantic conversation, Cassandra leaned onto Wade's shoulder. "What's she saying?"

Wade shrugged a little, constrained by Cassandra's shoulder. "She's talking too fast. I don't know enough Turkish. She's talking to Ozzy."

"An Australian?"

Wade laughed. "No. It is their name."

Anya slammed the door as she climbed back into the van. "I asked nicely. Now we ask more personally. Let's see him say no to my face."

Anya's driving was just as aggressive and rapid as Wade remembered. Once again, after turning onto a provincial road, she pulled over to the side. Dawn tinged the horizon.

Anya pulled her baseball cap down on her head. "You'll have to get in the back."

Wade acquiesced, sitting against the bolted shelving, putting his legs into a V and welcoming Cassandra into them. She tilted her head back onto his shoulder. This corner smelled of sawn wood and preservatives.

"That looks uncomfortable." Cassandra pointed at the other corner. "What's wrong with that one?"

Wade could see the protuberance that had left a bruise. "That metal bolt would dig in my back."

She snuggled in close. "I suppose it's not for long."

"Oil for Dogan," Anya said as they reached the airport.

Once again, the guard waved her through the gates. She drove to the blocky hangers. Cassandra extricated herself. Wade followed, locating Ozzy's plane amid the other private planes parked in the hangar.

Anya's angry walk to the offices once again surprised Wade. He hurried with Cassandra to catch up at the double glass doors. They climbed to the next floor, walking along the hard-wearing carpet to Ozzy's office. Anya slammed the door to Dogan-Air open.

"Annie!" Ozzy said before launching into possibly the same Turkish as previously. Wade followed Anya into the cramped room with Cassandra.

Wade tried to pick out words doing slightly better than previously.

Anya held up her hand. "Ozzy, stop." She pointed at Cassandra and

Wade. "This is Wade and Cassandra."

Ozzy looked around Wade at Cassandra's bump. "You are pregnant?"

Cassandra cupped Bump. "Yes."

"Annie, you cannot do this to me. I could lose my plane, my licence, my business."

Wade almost winced ahead of time as Anya's stiffened finger prodded her brother in the shoulder. "You wouldn't have any of this if it wasn't for me."

"Gah!" The slap of Ozzy's palm on the wall was loud as they both launched back into Turkish.

Cassandra whispered to him. "Can you understand any of this?"

Wade slipped his arm around her shoulder. "Very little."

"Anything?"

Wade knew what the conversation was about, helping him pick out other words, such as 'Albanian Cartel'. "Ozzy owes Anya for saving his business."

Wade watched the sibling back and forth. Knowing how he had changed Ozzy's mind before, he coughed and stepped forward. "Look, I get it. Taking us is dangerous. We will find a way without you. I don't know what the debt is that Anya speaks of, but I can't have somebody else risk anything for Cassandra and me."

Anya's mouth slightly opened as she gaped at him. "Wade?"

"Anya, this is Ozzy's life."

Anya's anger dissipated. "In this, Wade, you don't know the entire story."

Wade acknowledged that. "Correct. But we can get past Paladin some other way."

Anya took a deep breath and returned her gaze to Ozzy. "Wade's right. We can't ask you to do this."

"Paladin?" Ozzy's puzzled tone was no surprise.

Anya looked puzzled in return. "Have you heard of them?"

Yesterday Pill　　　　　　　　　　　　　　Iain Benson

"What did they do?" Ozzy scrutinised the swelling and bruising on Anya's face. "Did they put those bruises on your face?"

Wade stepped in, halting Anya. "They're trying to murder Cass. They blew up a restaurant. And yes. They beat Anya."

"The restaurant in the UK?"

Wade nodded. "We hope we can find why they want Cassandra dead and find proof of being behind the attack."

Ozzy rubbed his beard. "That's why you want to go to Tel Aviv."

Anya leant against the table. "Paladin is dangerous. Sorry, I shouldn't have rung. Desperation will do that."

"I will help."

"What?" Anya made vague gestures with her hands.

Ozzy prodded Anya's shoulder. "Do you think I don't know what happened to you? Or what you had to do to get the cartel off my back? I'm not stupid, Annie."

Cassandra's gaze had been tracking the to-and-fro. "I've lost track. Is Ozzy taking us or not?"

"No!" Anya said.

"I will," Ozzy said at the same time. "It's not up to you, Annie."

"Are you going to drug me and drag me on?"

"If I have to!"

"Then yes, Ozzy is taking us." Anya stood away from the desk.

"I'll make a flight plan to Cyprus." Ozzy opened his laptop. "I'm going to miss that. It's about five-fifty klicks to Tel Aviv. That's a tank there and back. I'll put in half a tank."

"Why?" Cassandra asked.

"I'll have to land to refuel. Having a full tank would look suspicious."

Anya sighed. "We'll have to jump out and run for it."

"It's going to have to be that way. Israel air traffic cannot know I've brought passengers, or that's me done."

"Where are you heading for?" Cassandra asked.

"I can't go to the main city airport." Ozzy sounded like he was thinking aloud. "I am going to aim for Herzliya. It's a provincial airport mainly used for pleasure flights and pilot training. After that, you're on your own."

Wade felt now was the time to pitch his plan. "I have a better idea."

All three looked at him. Anya spoke up. "Go on."

"Book your flight plan to Herzliya."

Ozzy interrupted. "I'll have to put your names in."

Wade's smile broadened. "You're not taking us. You're taking our bags. Bags required by people already in Tel Aviv."

Anya clapped. "Genius."

Ozzy redid his flight plan as a baggage trip and led them to his plane. While he filled it and readied it, Anya removed the van's plates. "Wade. Grab the bags."

Wade removed the bags. Had Paladin found the van here, using it to work out their destination? "It might be a good idea to stash the van as well."

Anya nodded, driving the van away while Wade packed the bags behind the seats. Cassandra climbed in first, followed by Wade, squeezing into the two rear seats. Ozzy climbed in, going through his pre-flight check. Anya arrived, slightly out of breath. She tossed the plates on the carpet.

"Annie! I've only just steam cleaned that carpet."

Anya climbed into the seat beside her brother. "Just get us out of here."

Ozzy flashed her a grin. "Ladies and gentlemen, welcome to Dogan-Air. I am Ozan Dogan, your pilot for this short flight. It's currently mild, with some clouds in Tel Aviv. We should arrive in Israel at noon."

Ozzy gunned the engine, taxiing to the runway.

"Çukurova tower, this is dog-oh-oh-one, ready for take-off." After getting the plane into the air, Ozzy tapped the earpiece and glanced over his shoulder. "I saw on the news that you defused a bomb on the YHT. You saved many people."

"It was fairly easy," Wade said. Cassandra gripped his fingers.

Yesterday Pill   Iain Benson

"They are trying to claim you planted the bomb and had to defuse it because it was about to go off while you were still on the train."

"Hopefully, we can correct that misbelief," Wade replied.

As Anya and Ozzy talked, Wade decided to get some sleep. Engine noises and the slight rocking soon lulled him.

11

Wade brought himself around with a swig of water, watching as the sea became land and the runway appeared.

"Israel tower," Ozzy said into his headset. "This is Dog-oh-oh-one bringing some lost luggage home."

Wade leaned forward. "When you get down, head to the end and turn slowly."

"We'll jump out, hidden by the plane." Anya gave a knowledgeable nod. "We can hide behind the baffles."

The landing by Ozzy felt almost serene. He glided in and trundled along the runway.

"Everybody out!" Anya led by example as the plane turned.

Wade helped Cassandra down, closing the door. "See you in a minute."

Ozzy flipped a salute. "At the other end."

The three of them scrambled over the baffles, hiding as the plane moved slowly down the runaway.

Anya adjusted the strap on her bag. "Time to move."

He helped Cassandra to her feet. The three of them scrambled off the concrete and across scrubby, dried-up grass to a simple fence topped with razor wire. After a bit of searching, they found a broken fence panel. He pulled it back, the mesh link fence unattached from the supporting metal strut.

"Handy." Anya gave a little chortle as they passed through.

The three headed down the sandy dirt track that paralleled the fence. The air carried the scent of dried dust and menthol wafting from the scrubby bushes beside the path. A white-shirted security guard stopped them at the airport's main entrance.

Wade passed over his Cohen passport. He slipped unconsciously into Hebrew. "We're here to pick up our bags."

Yesterday Pill   Iain Benson

The security guard looked in his early twenties, with a half-grown beard and dark glasses. He barely glanced at the passport and his computer screen. "Go on through."

Ozzy was pulling the cases off the plane while the ground crew refilled his aircraft.

"Thank you." Anya smiled at her brother.

"Not a problem." Ozzy returned the smile. "If you need Dogan-Air again, you have our number. Good luck!"

Wade shook his hand and took the cases. They watched as Ozzy boarded his plane and headed off back down the runway.

Wade smiled at Anya. "I like your brother."

"I always thought you might. If you two met."

Wade's eyebrows went up a little. "When this is all over, you need to get back to your family."

She gave a sad little smile.

"Do you think they can get us a taxi?" Cassandra asked. "One with air conditioning?"

Wade had to admit the weather felt unseasonably warm. He shared the water bottle around, draining the last few mouthfuls himself.

He trundled two cases behind him over to the security desk.

The security guard that had let them in looked up from his graphic novel. "You don't need me to let you out. Push the button that says 'exit'."

Wade gave an acknowledgement smile. "Thanks. I was wondering if somebody could call us a taxi. Ours wouldn't wait."

The guard seemed surly beyond his years and simply shook his head. "We're not a public service. Download *Ryder* or something."

The guard returned to his comic. Wade shook his head and scowled as Cassandra and Anya joined him.

He jerked his thumb toward the security guard. "He said to download *Ryder* if we want a taxi."

Anya sat on her case and pulled out her phone. "It's not a bad idea."

Wade put the water bottle up to his lips, only to discover it remained empty. The air temperature caressed Wade's skin. Although only in the high teens, it held a residual heat that had him removing his jacket and wishing the water bottle still contained water.

"Two minutes." Anya put her phone away.

She took a full water bottle from her shoulder bag. Wade looked at it. She could see him watching, making a dramatic show of sipping from it, and relishing each drop. She laughed and tossed it to him. He took a slug and passed it back.

"Thanks."

"Don't mention it."

The two minutes waiting for the taxi dragged, Wade wished he could twist the dial of his ring in the opposite direction and go forward. Thinking about what that meant in terms of free will made his head hurt. Instead, he hugged Cassandra, only for her to push him away, irritated by the heat.

"It's too hot for cuddles."

Alongside the airstrip, an information board gave humidity, wind, and temperature. "It's eighteen point four degrees."

"Too warm."

The sound of tyres kicking up gravel announced a white saloon taxi.

"Three? Is it?" The driver was in his early thirties, grey streaking through his black hair.

Anya nodded. "We have luggage."

The driver popped up the boot for Wade to stow the bags. With a playful smile, Anya passed him her suitcase. She seemed much more relaxed than the week previously. Wade rolled his eyes and tutted theatrically, adding her bag to the group already in the boot.

As Wade closed the rear door, the driver was looking at his large screen map. "You're off to Paladin Tower?"

"We are." Anya sounded cheerful.

The cab driver's eyes narrowed. "Do you work for them?"

Anya laughed. "Oh! No! We're staying nearby. I couldn't find the

Yesterday Pill   Iain Benson

hotel on your app, so I put that because it's close."

The driver relaxed and drove them down the main road into an area of high-rises, white plaster, glass, and steel, creating striped shadows on the road. The driver took a side street and drove them along the seafront. Up ahead, skyscrapers rose above other, lower, multistorey buildings. Mere foothills to the monolithic mountains of metal and mirrored glass. Wade looked for anything familiar, asking himself if he recognised the gardens with a central fountain or the harbour with its dinghies.

"I don't recognise anything."

Cassandra squeezed his hand. "Neither do I!"

"You haven't been here before." Wade found it challenging to keep the bitterness out of his tone.

Anya flicked through her phone. "We can revisit familiar places, see if your memory returns."

That idea gave Wade hope, but they had more pressing needs. "We'll add it to the list of things to do when this is over."

Anya turned to the driver. "Our hotel is being cleaned until four. Do you know anywhere we could get something to eat and drink near there?"

The taxi driver looked pleased to be asked. "There is a lovely brasserie on the corner."

"Sounds perfect." Anya flashed her full, bright white smile.

"Because you booked through the app, I'll still have to drop you off at Paladin Tower." The driver pointed diagonally up to the left. Wade looked in that direction, where he saw a building with blue glass curving off around and into a more ordinary-looking white block of a building.

"Not a problem." Anya put her phone away as they swept around a grassy central reservation filled with papery-looking palm trees.

Wade extricated the cases while the two women climbed out. About halfway down the road, they passed a darkened Chinese restaurant. A convoy of three blacked-out Range Rovers came up, partially hidden by the central reservation. The darkened restaurant window became a mirror as they passed, allowing Wade to see Adrian in the back with the window down.

Wade attracted Anya's attention. "Adrian's here."

She touched her bruised and swollen eye socket. There was a personal element in this for her. "Good to know."

At the corner, they found the promised brasserie. Anya slumped into a metal and wickerwork chair and waved her hand at the waitress. Wade held a chair for Cassandra.

A waitress in a white vest top and black pleated skirt approached. She used English. "What can I get you?"

"Black coffee please," Wade replied in Hebrew, sitting.

Cassandra put her hand up a little. "Decaf cappuccino."

Anya looked up. "Can you do Turkish?"

"We can."

Anya smiled. "I'll have that. Could we get the food menu?"

The waitress nodded, returning after a few moments with three small paper menus.

"Was this place here when we were?" Wade looked about, still trying to find something even vaguely recognisable.

Anya shook her head. "It was like a fifties bar, full of kids on mopeds who thought they knew what the fifties was like."

They went silent as their server gave them coffees. "I hadn't realised Paladin's headquarters would be so big. Do you know where we're going?"

Anya sipped at the treacly black coffee. She looked pensive. "I have a vague idea. We're going to have to split into two teams if you still want to find out why they're trying to find out why Cassandra's so important to them."

"I am." Wade was certain. Anya's approach made sense for the short term, but long term. Only having Paladin want to abandon their search for Cassandra would keep them safe.

"I think the details on who ordered the hits on the restaurant and train will be on their main server. Probably only accessible from a few

Yesterday Pill   Iain Benson

terminals. I'm thinking of heading to the server room."

Cassandra stopped Wade asking where he would go by asking: "And us?"

Anya sighed. "You'll have to stay in the room."

"This is my life, Anya." Cassandra's tone was one Wade knew very well. "I am going."

Wade took Cassandra's hand. "Cass, we've come so far. We can't take you into the lion's den. All it takes is for one slip, and it'll all have been for nothing."

Cassandra's opinion remained solid. "Then keep me safe."

Anya leapt on that remark. "That is what we are trying to do."

"I am not staying behind."

It was Wade's turn to sigh. This was an argument for closer to the time. He changed the conversation's direction. "Once we're inside, where do I need to go? Pretend I don't remember anything."

Anya paused, reviewing her memories. "We first found out about Cassandra when Craig translated the System's output. I guess his lab is on the sixteenth floor."

Cassandra looked puzzled. "The System?"

Wade realised she didn't know. He echoed her words. "What's the System?"

Anya momentarily gave him a confused look, and then comprehension cleared her features. "It's the AI that works out how the future will pan out. The further into the future an event is, the less accurate the prediction is."

Cassandra nodded, quickly picking it up. "Like the weather?"

Anya agreed. "Exactly. On a social scale. Craig never really explained how it all worked. It is stunningly accurate, and it's how Paladin became so big."

"If it's accurate, I can understand that." Cassandra looked thoughtful. "I've read papers on social extrapolation. I'd no idea it was already in use and working so well."

Anya shrugged. "It's a big secret. Paladin never reveals how it works, even to their staff."

Wade thought of a question. "But Craig knew?"

Anya nodded. "Paladin was never really Craig's idea, but he'd been there at the beginning."

Wade made a check. "Sixteenth floor?"

"When we left, yes. But that was years ago. I don't know if it will still be the research labs."

Wade had been hoping for certainty. "It's a starting place."

They ordered food and ate. While the three were in the restaurant, Wade had a view covering the front door, and Anya watched the rear entrance. Their corner table allowed the two of them to stay vigilant without being overt about it.

As the waitress left, having deposited additional coffee, Anya received a message.

She glanced at it. "We should head to the accommodation now."

Wade's eyebrows involuntarily raised. "I thought the hotel was a ruse?"

Anya shook her head. "I think we'll be going in very late. There will be too many people there during the day. Some people work at night, but fewer. Also, they might not be monitoring the video feeds as closely during the night shift. I suggest grabbing a nap before we go in."

Wade could see her wisdom. They were so close. A small part of him wanted to rush in immediately. Answers lived down the block from them. His time of innocence had ended when Anya had rescued them from the restaurant. They had come thousands of kilometres and were now metres from the end. Wade reached over and squeezed Cassandra's hand.

"We're almost there."

She smiled back. "One more night, and we can go back home and normality."

Wade knew a return to normality was impossible. He had seen and learned too much. Wade consoled himself that they would find their

Yesterday Pill   Iain Benson

answers that night.

As they crossed the road outside the restaurant, Wade swept his gaze around, looking for anybody who might be a Paladin agent. Their adversary's home base dominated the skyline, casting a long shadow down the street, both figuratively and literally. Anya led them to their base of operations for the night.

"I was expecting a hotel." Wade looked up at the three-storey narrow building with a balcony on the top floor.

"The hotels are all some distance from here." Anya went to the key safe beside the door and entered the combination on her first attempt. Much less stressful than their previous encounter with a key safe in the Italian Alps.

Suitcases deposited in the minimalist lounge Wade felt the tension drain away. A pale wooden staircase led up, hopefully to a shower and a bed. The surfaces glistened as though recently cleaned, but the air held a slight mustiness that suggested they were the first to stay there for some time.

12

Anya awoke Wade. He came awake immediately and glanced at his watch. Beside him, Cassandra slept soundly, breathing deeply, lying on her side. Anya placed a finger on Wade's lips. He nodded to show he understood and slipped from the double bed. It had been extremely comfortable, exactly the right firmness. Anya headed out. Between two tall wardrobes, the dressing table held a mirror and his clothes. He slid them off quietly, following Anya downstairs. The light from the kitchen illuminated the wooden staircase enough for him to leave Cassandra sleeping. He slipped into a dark polo shirt and indigo jeans before carrying his shoes down the stairs to keep quiet.

Anya had a coffee waiting for him in the anthracite kitchen.

"Why the secrecy?" he asked, sipping the coffee. "Perfect temperature."

Anya launched straight into "I don't know why, but the pills are down to forty-five minutes. We need to get a move on."

Wade put the coffee down and grabbed his jacket. "Let's get going then."

They let themselves out quietly. The street outside held a warmth-robbing chill, the street lighting creating pools of shadow.

"I'm ready to go." Anya led Wade through the pools of shadows to a carpark. "It's taken a few attempts."

Wade struggled to keep up with Anya. "Why do you think the pills are no longer an hour?"

"It could be something to do with being close to Paladin." Anya sounded uncertain. "Craig would have known."

Wade suspected Anya had taken more than a few goes as she passed a woman loading the boot of a hatchback with shopping bags. Expert sleight of hand saw her dip into the woman's handbag, emerging with a laminated ID badge on a navy-blue lanyard. Their target lay ahead of

Yesterday Pill   Iain Benson

them, rising above the surrounding buildings like Mount Fuji above Japan. The blue glass gave an icy look to the building. Despite how late it had got, Paladin kept all the floors fully illuminated.

"I found what I needed." Anya read Wade's mind, answering his question before he asked it.

He felt a little intimidated. There seemed to be no point in him talking, as Anya had already had the conversation before. He needed to know some things.

"Any advice?"

"Scout out the target until you know everything you need. Remember, the place has a lot of CCTV, so keep track of time." They reached the front door, walking together past a chaotic jumble of mopeds and up the stone steps. Wade looked up at the curving metal awning as they went through the revolving door. Again, Wade could feel the connection between them, wondering how close they had been and how much his body knew hers, even if his memory did not.

With confidence Wade had to imitate or attract attention, Anya crossed the vast lobby. Wade took in the brightly lit space with a sweeping glance. He took in the islands of seating booths past the entry gates to the security desk. Anya acted like this was something she did every day.

"There is going to be a lot to remember." Anya looked at him, not at the desk. ID card swept over the reader, almost bored. The layout and the processes both came across as routine. The security team barely paid them any attention.

"How do you remember it all?"

Thick glass doors opened with a swoosh, allowing Anya to walk through, closing behind them. Wade noticed Anya had left the ID card by the reader. He picked it up and pressed it again on the reader. The glass doors opened again, allowing him to walk through with the ID card.

"Music." Anya took the pass. "You taught me that. Your favourite song was *Californication* by the Red-Hot Chili Peppers."

Wade reached forward and called an elevator, trying to ignore the

CCTV camera domes all over the lobby. "I don't remember it."

Anya nodded her head for a second, humming, before launching into the song's opening line.

Surprising himself, Wade joined in and took over, the subsequent few lines coming unbidden.

"See." Anya smiled at him as the elevator doors opened. "You remember. It's probably burned into your brain. Now, this is where we part ways. You need floor sixteen. You have thirty minutes. Good luck!"

Wade saw his bemused reflection in the elevator door as it closed. He hit the button again, calling for another elevator. Dome cameras in each corner forced Wade to keep his head down, trying to look nonchalant. Next time, he would bring a hat. At any moment, he could come face to face with a phalanx of armed Paladin operatives. Wade stepped into the lift as the doors opened, looking at his outwardly calm demeanour in the three mirrors. He casually hit the sixteen on the floor list.

As he stepped from the lift, *Californication* started running through Wade's mind, surprising him as he completed each line. What else hid under the blockage in his mind?

Directly opposite, Wade saw a glass wall, the numerals sixteen etched into the glass. Through it, he could see a semi-darkened office filled with pods of desks. Multiple large windows swept in a curve, the twinkling light of Tel Aviv creating a galactic backdrop for any late-night office staff. Wade turned right and headed along the corridor. He stopped at each door, opening, and looking inside. The first two were meeting rooms. After that, as the hall followed the building's curve, he started finding rooms filled with computer servers and terminals.

Wade entered the first one, looking around. He rummaged through the plastic drawers, looking for anything. It could have been a decade since Craig had occupied one of these labs. The next room around had a similar setup, though Wade found a family picture in a thin wooden frame on a desk. Wade realised he did not know Craig's appearance. Two women in the picture looked out. No recognition flashed in his mind for either.

Yesterday Pill   Iain Benson

He put the picture down, frowning. His watch told him he had fifteen more minutes. Time enough for a quick look in each office on this floor. Wade thought he might have been faster had he known what to look for. He opened the next few doors with no great hope. After two more labs, Wade returned to looking into meeting rooms. The second had a light on as he pushed through into a white plasterboard room. The harsh LED lighting reflected in circles off the highly polished table.

Adrian had the furthest seat from the door, framed by a blank display screen. "Close the door."

Wade turned to leave, but the door was closed by a woman standing behind it. She had a shoulder sling and a plaster cast on her left arm. By the window, the broad-shouldered man with a beard from the chalet. Kobe? Wade nodded to them.

He turned back to face Adrian. "Adrian."

"I wondered if you'd come back to Craig's old lab." Adrian swept his good arm around the room. "It took you a while."

Glancing over his shoulder at the two operatives by the door, Wade faced down Adrian. "It's been a while. I forgot where it is."

"We moved it to the basement five years ago." Adrian tapped his plaster cast. "You remember Leah and Kobe?"

Wade made a non-committal gesture as he frantically tried to piece together what Adrian would remember from their encounters. "Vaguely."

Kobe gave a grunting laugh.

Adrian got to his feet and came within a couple of metres. He perched on the table. "You were one of us, Wade. We're the good guys."

"You've said that before," Wade said, before realising Adrian had said it in a timeline Wade had reset. It seemed like something Adrian repeated often. "Cassandra proves the opposite. She is pregnant with my child. 'Good guys' would never consider killing a pregnant woman with such flimsy evidence."

Adrian shrugged. "When you left, what's your memory of our *flimsy evidence*?"

Wade pieced together what Adrian had previously told him now his actual memory had gone. "The System pegged her as being responsible for the end of Paladin. They put a kill order on her."

Adrian had a wry smile as he shook his head. "The System has popped out a few more details since then. It's not the end of Paladin. Do you know what a paradox is?"

"When something happened that cannot have happened." Wade searched Adrian's features for some clue where he headed. "It's a common theme in time travel movies."

Adrian's eyebrows raised, giving him a pitying look with the wry smile fixed firmly in place. He reached into his jacket pocket. Wade tensed, but Adrian pulled out a slim remote control. He clicked it, turning on the television screen. He twisted lithely from the desk to look at the screen, standing with one hand behind his back, holding the remote. Wade looked at a picture of Cassandra, looking to the side, going into a supermarket. Wade had no time reference for the image. All he could tell was she wasn't pregnant.

"She's attractive. If I was a betting man, I'd have thought you and Anya, but I guess I was wrong. Now I will tell you something that I think Paladin should tell all operatives."

"You know I'm not an operative," Wade said. "Anymore."

Adrian remained looking at the screen. He must have pressed a button on the remote as the image changed to a report with dense text. In one corner, larger lettering spelt out Cassandra Roberts.

"I'll give you the crib notes." Adrian turned back around.

"Crib notes?"

"The System receives messages from the future. Messages *we* send after the event."

Wade scratched his chin. "Hence the question about paradoxes. When you stop it, change it. How did the message get sent back?"

Adrian looked momentarily confused. "No. The cuties in the basement tell me that a future paradox is integral to the fabric of spacetime. They happen all the time."

"Cuties?"

Adrian's puzzled look deepened. "QTs, quantum theorists. It was your name for them."

"A decade ago. What has Cass got to do with paradoxes?"

Adrian waved a vague hand at the report behind him by pointing the remote over his shoulder. "The last message the System ever sends is a voice message from Leah."

"What does she say?" Although nearly out of time, this genuinely intrigued Wade.

Leah spoke up. "I relay a message from Cassandra to leave it open and that Paladin and Craig were right about the paradox."

Wade turned to look at her. "Leave what open? Right about what?"

Leah shrugged. "This is all that comes through. Something truncated the message. I sound scared if that helps."

Wade found it difficult to believe Leah ever felt emotion.

"What do the cuties make of that?" Wade asked, turning back to Adrian.

"There are no messages after that point." Adrian clicked his remote, changing to a graph that dropped off at ninety degrees. It looked precipitous, but could have been describing anything.

"Like the first message." Wade shrugged again. "The end of Paladin."

"If that were all it was, we'd accept our end gracefully."

Wade looked at the expensive-looking meeting room with high-end equipment built into the fabric. "A multi-billion-dollar organisation would happily hang up its flip charts?"

"We've discussed the end at board level. That was the decision. It's what Craig would have wanted." Adrian's features became more serious. "The consensus is that even if Paladin ends, there would still be some messages coming through the System. The cuties have concluded that the paradox Leah will mention is a past paradox."

Iain Benson Yesterday Pill

"Talk to me like this is the first I've ever heard of a past paradox."

Adrian sighed. "A future paradox hasn't happened yet. It will never impact us."

Wade nodded, glancing down at his watch. "Makes sense."

"A past paradox happens in *our* past. It causes us to cease to be."

Wade laughed. "Overly dramatic."

Adrian looked serious. "You asked how the good guys could consider killing a pregnant woman? When we weigh that up against all life in the universe, two lives become insignificant. Hundreds of lives become insignificant."

Wade struggled to keep up with Adrian's outlandish claims. "All life in the universe?"

Adrian nodded. Wade searched his face for any duplicity, but it appeared Adrian believed his claims utterly. "A past paradox will collapse back to the point of paradox. We will be gone."

"Cass is only a physics lecturer." Anxious, Wade knew he had to reset. "She cannot possibly be responsible. Whatever the System tells you, it cannot be what you think it is."

"Bring her in," Adrian said. "We will show her the System and the maths behind it."

"And then kill her." Wade could not keep the contempt from his voice.

As he moved to the screen, he twisted his ring and took a pill. As the scene snapped into two dimensions, Wade read the graph's X-axis. He saw it said *Number of Messages*. In two days, it would be zero.

Wade looked at the coffee in his hand. He'd cut it fine.

He put the mug down. "Let's get going."

Once more, Anya led him across the carpark in a curving arc to collect the pass.

"I found what I needed," Anya said as they left the carpark. "It's your turn now."

"Already on it." Wade filled her in on his meeting with Adrian.

Yesterday Pill   Iain Benson

"They're sending messages to themselves from the future?" Anya stopped, her hand hovering over the elevator button.

"That's what he said."

"It sounds like bullshit to get you to bring Cassandra to them."

"I thought that."

"You're going to have to tell me all this again. You realise that?"

Wade nodded. "Where shall I look for Craig's old lab?"

"It was on sixteenth."

Wade shook his head and entered the elevator cab with Anya. "Adrian said they had moved it to the basement."

"Then I've no idea where to look."

Wade looked at the board with seventy buttons, six of them below ground. "I'll start in the bottom basement."

"I'm on sub-two." Anya stabbed the button. "Are you sure you want to start at the bottom?"

"Please," Wade replied.

Anya pressed the sub-six. "I don't think I've been that far down."

Anya headed out when the elevator opened on her floor. Wade glimpsed an ordinary-looking white corridor lit by strip lighting before the doors closed again. He felt the lift descend, stopping with a smooth motion. The door opened onto a battleship grey corridor with red doors punctuating the grey uniformity. Wade set off down the hall, his shoes squeaking on the screed floor. Each office had an access keypad beside it. Wade wondered if there would be two women packing shopping into a car. He tried the doors anyway, discovering them all to be locked, apart from the one that led to stairs. He went up a level.

Sub-basement five was a lighter grey, and the doors were blue. Wade found them locked as well. Wade returned to sub-basement two and headed off, searching for Anya. His time ran out before he saw her. Wade repeated his actions until the elevator.

"Adrian said they had moved Craig's old lab."

"I'm on sub-two. Do you want to start at the bottom?"

Wade shook his head. "They keep all the doors locked. I need an access card."

"Once I'm through the door, you can take mine."

"That was my plan."

They rode the lift down two floors and stepped out together. Anya headed off to the right, with Wade in tow. She stopped by a purple door with a small plaque beside it in English, saying server room four. Anya pressed the pass to the door. The light on the pad turned green. Anya pushed the door open and passed Wade the card. As she disappeared into the server room, Wade headed off around the corridor, looking at the plaques.

The entire floor had nothing but computing power. Wade thought back to what Adrian had said about how the System worked. It sent messages back in time. He guessed the servers were scouring the internet for any news that Paladin could monetise with foreknowledge. The pills allowed Wade to believe this was true. Paladin needed a lot of computer power to find their next job.

Wade took the elevator down to the bottom. This deep into the building, the doors lacked labels, forcing him to try each. The first few wouldn't open, even with the ID card, but eventually, a light turned green.

"Finally."

Wade found the room beyond claustrophobic. He ignored the three concrete walls, enlivened only by a coat rack. What caught his attention the most was the fourth wall. It was half ceramic, half glass. Beyond, constrained by an invisible box, Wade saw a floating, blue plasma sphere. Wade looked at the computer consoles underneath the glass, but the information they displayed held no meaning for him. All he understood was the label. Quantum core temperature.

Wade left, moving down the corridor to the next room. It, too, opened. Inside, Wade found two scientists working on consoles.

One of them turned to look at him. In Hebrew, he accosted Wade. "Who are you? Why are you here?"

Yesterday Pill   Iain Benson

Wade took an involuntary step back, noticing the ID card on a lanyard around his neck. He wondered if it had more access to the other rooms in the basement rooms.

"I was looking for the quantum core."

"That's next door!" The scientist had to have been having a bad day, as he was far angrier than he should have been for somebody coming into the wrong room.

"Do you need a hug or something?" Wade asked. "Nobody labels these doors. They're all the same colour."

The scientist waved a hand and deflated. "We've been trying to build a replacement for the System."

Wade attempted to look sympathetic. "The information ends in a couple of days. We're freaking out upstairs."

"Numerous stability issues." He brightened a little. "Are you a negative energy expert, by any chance?"

Wade shook his head. "Sorry. I'm a mere operative. I don't have the brains for this job."

The scientist laughed and held out his hand. "Sorry for the anger."

Wade shook the offered hand and pulled the man in close, clapping him on the back. "Not a problem. I'm sure you'll keep the System going past the cliff."

Wade clicked apart the lanyard's clasp and caught the ID badge as they separated, and it fell. He surprised himself with his dexterity as he brought his other hand up and shoved the ID into his sleeve.

Pointing back the way Wade had come, he knew he had to leave to use the time he had left. "The core is next door, that way."

Wade nodded and left. In the corridor, he checked the ID. "Thanks for this, Doctor Isaac Levy."

As hoped, the card opened the other doors on the level. Wade checked his watch. If he was quick, there was time to look in each. Wade used all his time up in the first room he tried. Wade had a strong suspicion it was Craig's old lab. He decided it was worth a more thorough investigation.

Wade recognised the layout as similar in shape and size to the other two he had looked in. Although he could see equipment, screens and cupboards, Wade saw no occupants giving a chance to look around. He looked at a map on one wall, fastened to the concrete with masking tape. It appeared to be a section of Ukraine. Red stickers placed all over, with lines drawn in black felt-tip pen. He spent far too long looking at the map, trying to work out the meaning behind the stickers' colours. The glass screen in the centre intrigued him. Computers on both sides looked connected to it. He caressed the keys on a keyboard. The screen came alive: computations, scribbles and handwriting covering it.

Wade traced under a part, leaving a thin line where his finger touched.

"Neat," he said.

Against the back wall, he found a desk. Wade looked through the papers scattered across it. He found no order in the dispersed notes. What Wade recognised were the mathematical symbols recognisable from Cassandra's university lecture notes. Wade realised he knew somebody who could read it.

"I can get out by going back in time," Wade told the notes. "If I bring Cass to read you, I have to get her out again."

Talking to the paper reminded Wade. Glancing at his watch, he realised he was nearly out of time. He glanced at the computer beside the glass. It was output from the System. Currently showing a newspaper story about him disarming the bomb on the train. He scanned the first paragraph, learning the media now considered him an international terrorist, though nobody knew who he was. There were other stories about the bomb exploding that had not happened. Even in those, the papers listed the three of them as terrorists.

"Great," he muttered, taking the pill.

The scene snapped away and back again into the kitchen, where he almost spilt his coffee.

He took a big gulp and put the cup down. "Shall we get going?"

Yesterday Pill   Iain Benson

After getting Isaac Levy's lanyard, Wade headed straight to the lab. Though he had longer to look around, he spent the time looking at the System's output. Stored news stories from all over the world at his fingertips.

Two more iterations taught him System's interface, allowing him to search for things that had yet to happen.

A story in *The Haaretz* caught his attention with Wade, Cassandra's, and Anya's faces splashed on the front page. Tomorrow's date stood out. He almost ran out of time reading it. More iteration followed, each time filling in Anya as they made the journey across to Paladin Tower. He included information from Adrian and what he had gathered from the lab.

"The article said Paladin operatives gunned down the wanted terrorists for the UK attack. Here, in Tel Aviv, while they attempted to detonate an explosive device at Paladin Tower. There were pictures of us."

Anya pushed for the elevator. "It sounds like we'll need a better escape plan. I'll download my information from the server and meet you in the lab."

13

After collecting Isaac's lanyard, Wade spent his time looking around the room's other contents. In a sliding, low cabinet with casters, he found stiff card vanilla boxes. Opening one, he found personal possessions. Awards, photographs. He tried another and took out a framed photo of Anya, Wade, and a third man he assumed was Craig. Craig looked older in a loose, chequered shirt and jeans. All three leant on a red convertible with what looked like a desert behind them. Wade felt it could be New Mexico or Arizona, judging by the sand's redness. They looked happy. Anya nestled under his arm, resting a hand on his thigh. He wished he could remember it.

Short rapping knocks on the door broke his reverie. He saw Anya looking flushed.

"I used the stairs." She pushed past him. "There are more than you'd think."

Wade gave her a brief tour around the room, aware of how little time they had left.

"You're right." She traced a finger across the glass screen and shuffled through the papers. "We'll need Cassandra to understand this."

Wade nodded and took his pill.

The second the scene snapped into three dimensions, he put his coffee down. "I'll get Cassandra."

"It's not safe," Anya said, yet to be convinced.

"You set off." Wade headed for the stairs carrying the coffee. "You'll need your pass."

Anya's understanding was instant. "Anything else I need to know?"

"I'll explain when we catch you up." Wade went into their room and shook Cassandra awake. "Cass."

She woke groggily. Wade pressed the coffee into her hands. "What time is it?"

"Put shoes on, drink that, and come with me. I'll explain on the way."

Within two minutes, Wade dragged Cassandra from the house. She still clutched the mug. "Oh, I need to put this back."

Wade took it and put it on the roof of a car. "It doesn't matter. We need to catch up to Anya."

"What is she doing?"

Wade led her into the carpark, taking a more direct route. He could see her collecting the pass. "She's over there stealing a pass."

Cassandra had to pause by the door as they caught up to Anya. Cassandra was out of breath, with Wade having hurried them along. Anya left the pass on the ID reader. Wade picked it up, opened the gate and put it back. Cassandra approached and dropped the ID on the floor. She attracted attention from the security guards as she fumbled, picking it up.

"Are you okay, miss?" the security guard asked from behind the security desk. Anya glanced at the security guard.

Cassandra waved the attention away. "I'm fine."

She struggled down by crouching and scooped up the pass. She slapped it on the reader, opening the glass doors. As she went through, the lanyard got trapped between the doors as it trailed behind her.

The security guard got to his feet, ready to come over and help.

"Don't you dare help me!" Cassandra glared at him and lifted the pass up and over the top. "I'm pregnant, not incapable."

"She's the Australia expert," Wade told the guard. "They've dragged her in at midnight for an issue."

The security guard sat back down. "Sounds like something they'd do."

Anya held the elevator, taking the ID card from Cassandra as they joined her. "I need sub-basement two."

Wade pressed for sub-basement two. "I need the card after you've used it."

"How do you know where to go?" Cassandra asked as they reached the level.

Wade followed Anya. "Stay in the lift. Keep the door open."

"How long?"

"I'll be back in under two minutes."

He quickly filled in Anya about Adrian and the lab in the basement. Anya listened and nodded. Wade collected the card as she went through into the server room.

Back at the lift, Cassandra was leaning on the door. "I'm going to need some answers, Wade."

"Soon. You'll have all the answers we need." Wade hit the very bottom button. "Do you trust me?"

"Of course."

Wade gave her a tight smile. "Do as I ask, and we'll have the answers we want."

"I feel you and Anya have been holding out on me."

"How so?"

As the lift reached the bottom floor, she gave Wade a long look. "You have lost the little boy lost vibe. You have a more confident air like you now know who you were."

Unaware he'd lost or gained any kind of personality trait, the news staggered Wade. He checked his watch. He needed to be getting a move on in case he needed to restart.

"Wait for me by this door."

"Why this door?"

"It's the door we want."

Wade headed off and retrieved the ID card from Isaac, racing back as quickly as possible. He used it to open the door.

Cassandra looked confused. "Where did you get that ID card from?"

"I used the card Anya took off the woman in the carpark to gain access to a lab where Isaac Levy works. This ID was around his neck. I hugged him and stole it. He will probably notice soon."

Wade opened the door, pushing into the room like a big reveal on a DIY show. Cassandra came in.

Yesterday Pill   Iain Benson

"What is this place?" Cassandra walked around the glass dividing screen. Wade clicked the computer button, bringing the glass to life.

Cassandra made an appreciative noise, looking at the calculations on the screen.

"Do you understand this?" Wade asked.

"It's beautiful." Cassandra traced her finger under a section of calculations. "It's almost like this is real."

"What does it say?"

"Theoretical calculations for wormholes."

"I don't understand."

"It's a calculation for time travel."

Wade switched on the computer, showing the newspaper from tomorrow. "It is real."

Cassandra looked at the newspaper and other news articles that would be happening. She clicked through, seeing a variety of articles that had never happened. "This is amazing, Wade."

Wade nodded. "I used to work for these people."

"You had an idea that was the case."

Wade shrugged. "I know it was the case. I've learned a lot over the past few days."

Cassandra returned to the glass screen, running her finger under a particular section. She rubbed her lower lip with her thumb, her brow furrowed. Wade recognised the expression as her deep thought one. She started muttering and looking down at the computer screen. Cassandra quickly figured out how to manipulate the contents. She pulled it outwards, exposing more calculations, throwing it sideways and nodding with a smile.

While she looked at maths, Wade opened the cupboard and extracted the card box. He found the photo of Craig, Anya, and himself separating it from the frame and putting it into his inside pocket. He was aware of murmuring noises from Cassandra with the occasional surprised 'oh'. Wade found a pale green notebook. He flicked through it, finding partial newspaper cuttings, missing large portions of text. They were of

Iain Benson   **Yesterday Pill**

Paladin hunting Cassandra, plus stories of Craig, Anya, and Wade. Although obfuscated by missing words, Wade found an article that could very well be about the restaurant explosion, except Craig was still alive in it. The newspaper cutting made no sense to Wade.

Flicking through the notepad, Wade found pages of dense handwritten notes. News articles stapled in and a page about Cassandra. He read a message had come through indicating that her discovery about time travel would cause an end to time travel. Underlined three times was the word *paradox*.

He struggled to get his head around how the past viewed the present with messages from the future; Wade was gladly interrupted by Anya's knocking.

She was flushed as she came in. "I used the stairs. There are more than you'd think."

Wade handed her the diary. "Craig should still be alive according to this."

Anya flicked quickly through the pages as though she recognised it. "I remember him putting this together. He said it was to remind him how we changed the future."

She handed it to him. He slipped the notepad into his jacket pocket.

"Anya!" Cassandra joined them by the door. "This is incredible! Paladin uses a stable wormhole to send information back through time."

Anya nodded. "That explains a lot."

Wade felt it was an ideal time to tell her about the pills. "Cass, do you think it would be possible to send a mind back through time?"

Cassandra looked thoughtful. "I would say there would be a lot of problems with that, judging by the maths. Quantum fluctuations mean the world going forward is always different. It should be the evidence physicists have searched for proving the many-worlds theory. However, it appears the quantum state always collapses into what we call reality."

"Anya and I have both jumped back through time." Wade showed her his ring. "Somebody we worked with created this. It allows me to jump

Yesterday Pill   Iain Benson

back about an hour, a day, or a week."

Cassandra twirled abruptly and took the quick steps back to the glass screen. She manipulated using a combination of computer and glass as though she had been using it for years. She circled a section and swished the display across to another area.

"Yes," she muttered, pulling up yet more incomprehensible calculations. "Oh, that's interesting."

"What is it?" Anya went over and looked at the maths before glancing at Wade and shrugging.

She looked a little dubious. "It looks like it would be possible to make a connection between the mind through the time bridge."

Wade could spot her dubiousness. "There is a problem, though?"

"Well, brains are not computers. Their structure changes minute by minute. Imposing your mind now on your mind then wouldn't map too well."

"Would you get a headache?" Anya had a wry smile, taking a box of paracetamol from her pocket.

Understanding dawned in Cassandra's eyes. "Even some memory loss."

"Like me?" Wade raised an eyebrow. Anya flapped the back of her hand against his arm.

Anya shook her head. "Not totally like you. Just things that had happened in the time frame between leaving and arriving. Although, sometimes it would happen, sometimes not."

Cassandra shook her head. "If I'd known, I could have told you that."

Wade shrugged. "It's always reassuring to get it proved by maths. Would you know when memory loss would occur?" Wade's conviction that his seizure and the pills connected somehow only grew with Cassandra's words. But they could only go back a week at most.

Cassandra shook her head. "Infinitesimal quantum changes. Impossible to predict." Understanding blossomed in Cassandra as she put the pieces together. "The rescue? Getting across the borders? The bomb? You two have been jumping back at mistakes?"

Wade nodded.

Cassandra looked annoyed. "Why didn't you tell me?"

Wade took out Craig's notebook. "According to Craig, who helped develop all this, if you knew too soon, it would lead to a paradox that would end the universe."

Cassandra looked up at the ceiling, thinking. When she spoke a moment later, she chose her words carefully, thinking about each idea. "From the calculations, that doesn't make sense. The quantum fluctuations always collapse back into a low energy state. So, say we sent information back to Craig about this. The time as it is now will continue. I'll prove it."

She tapped on the keyboard. Worry flooded through Wade as he had a sudden thought of what Adrian had said. "Are you sure that's a good idea?"

"Are we still here? We are." She looked pleased with herself. "I sent a message back twenty-five years."

"What did you send?" Wade opened the notebook.

"I said: 'Cassandra understands sending time messages. There are no issues with paradox.'"

Wade flicked to what he'd started reading earlier. "Cassandra understanding ends time. Paradox."

Cassandra folded her arms over her bump. "So, he got the message. It is a guess, but the further back messages go, the more the information degrades."

Wade read on. "He's read it as an issue."

"He was wrong."

Anya licked her lips. She looked cynical. "Craig had been studying this for a long time. He wouldn't even tell us how it worked. I guess he was terrified of paradoxes. Why would he be terrified if it wasn't a possibility?"

"Starting point fallacy," Anya said. "He made an assumption and built on it."

Yesterday Pill   Iain Benson

Anya shook her head, her lips compressed. "You could be the one making the starting point fallacy."

Cassandra pointed at the maths. "Somebody else added all this over the past ten years. There is more information now than he had. I'm reading, not inventing."

Wade could tell Anya wasn't convinced. She could remember Craig even if he couldn't. He knew Cassandra better than Anya. He felt conflicted.

"But that's why I didn't tell you. It was the only information I had to go on. If you knew, the universe could end. It wasn't a risk I wanted to take."

Anya tried to conciliate. "If it's any consolation, he wanted to tell you."

Cassandra kept some of her anger, but the direction of it changed. "If this message is the reason Paladin wants me dead, we can get this mess sorted out."

Anya held a different view. "I'm not sure it'll be enough to overturn so many years of their policy."

"What if we close the wormhole?" Cassandra said. "Cut off Paladin's information source?"

Wade recalled what Adrian had said. "That would cause a past paradox."

Cassandra laughed. "A past paradox?"

Wade felt he had insufficient information to argue Adrian's position. "If you closed the wormhole, then all that has happened since could not have happened."

Cassandra pointed at equations on the glass wall. "The quantum possibility has already crystallised. Time is a point. There is no cord to cut. If you prevent your grandparents from meeting, the quantum probability of you still exists now. You cannot unravel time. It's not a string. It's a point. There is no future. The past isn't kept like a library you can visit."

"So, what would happen?" Wade asked.

"Paladin would lose any more information from the future,"

Iain Benson   **Yesterday Pill**

Cassandra replied.

Wade recalled the graph in Adrian's show and tell. "I saw a graph of messages received. They drop off. Stop."

"Then we are already successful." Cassandra smiled. "That's a joke. There is also a story about our deaths. Both might be wrong."

Checking his watch, Wade realised they had passed the cut-off point for returning to his coffee. It was a chilling thought. Any reruns would involve Cassandra.

He remembered the containment device a few doors down. "Is the wormhole a blue, glowing sphere?"

Cassandra's brows knitted together. "I doubt it. The mouth would be invisible. It would be tiny."

"What's at the other end?" Wade asked.

"It's a meaningless question. Some event will have created a wormhole, somewhere in space and time. Paladin cannot send messages before the wormhole came into being."

Wade looked across the room at the map on the wall. "Ukraine?"

Cassandra spread her hands. "It could be anywhere."

Wade returned to the map on the wall, Anya joining him. He could feel her presence like a magnetic field on one side.

"What are these lines?" Anya's finger traced the curves and arcs across the map, with straight lines creating tangents.

"I'm not sure," Wade admitted.

Cassandra left the physics and maths and came to look. "Magnetic fields."

"Why?" Wade looked at how they intersected, finding no pattern.

Cassandra seemed more interested in where there were no lines. "Hmm."

Wade glanced at her. "What is it?"

"Pripyat." Cassandra leaned in. "That name rings a bell."

"Wasn't that where the nuclear reactor blew up?" Anya guessed.

Wade recalled reading about it. "Chernobyl. Mid-nineteen-eighties."

Cassandra squeezed his arm. "That's the one. That could explain it, too."

"Explain what?" Wade asked.

"The energy required to open a wormhole." Cassandra turned around and manoeuvred the screen, expanding out a section. "If this calculation is correct, then the energy from Chernobyl could be enough to create a nanoscale wormhole."

Unable to envisage nanoscale, Wade shook his head. "Nanoscale? How big are we talking?"

"Possibly ten nanometres with the energy Chernobyl gave off."

Wade felt that was going to be hard to find. "That sounds small."

Cassandra scoffed. "It's big enough for electrical signals. Easily. They could put petabits through something that wide."

"But we're not climbing through it to last week?" Anya asked, her tone light.

Cassandra laughed. "No. I'm only surprised it's been this stable for this long. Something in the explosion must have created a zone of negative energy."

"Can you close it?" Wade asked.

Cassandra drew on the glass screen, writing out equations. She pressed a button and looked at the result. "Yes. But we must get to Pripyat. I need to be close to it to close it."

"How close?" Wade asked. He might have no memory, but he knew Chernobyl and Pripyat were out of bounds to random visitors.

"Depends on a few factors." Cassandra did a few calculations on her glass screen. "It would be detectable at around ten metres, but it would take a large surge of magnetism to destabilise the wormhole, even at a few millimetres."

"We'll need a magnet," Anya wasn't asking a question. Wade suspected she was going through a repeat.

Cassandra nodded. "The stronger, the better. Neodymium would be ideal. We use these powerful ones at university. If we could get several of those, we can set up a destabilising field."

"We'll add it to the shopping list," Anya said. "A bag of magnets."

"Are we ready to go?" Wade asked Anya.

Anya checked her watch. "Two minutes. We need to prepare a few things."

"You've been through this before?" Cassandra also understood.

Anya nodded and sighed. "When we leave, we are going to run into a lot of resistance."

While she spoke, Anya started pulling the metal sheets off the computers.

"That metal is too thin to stop a bullet." Wade was wondering what he could do.

Anya gestured at the paper on the desks. "Gather the paper together."

Anya slid the metal into the long cabinet at an angle. She packed the spaces with all the paper in the lab, creating a hopefully bulletproof shield.

"Ready?" Wade asked, standing by the door.

Anya looked at Cassandra. "I'm not convinced that you're right and Craig was wrong, but I trust you. I need you to trust me."

Cassandra glanced down briefly before holding Anya's gaze. "I do trust you."

"Good." Anya stood by the door. "I need you to stay in here until I call you. When the lift arrives, run across and straight into the elevator."

Wade calculated back to where he'd suspected Anya exhibited signs of repeating. "What about you?"

"I'll meet you back at the apartment. No arguments. I don't want to watch you die again."

That statement chilled Wade. "What's my role?"

"When the shooting starts, get out there, hit the elevator button and get back in here."

Yesterday Pill   Iain Benson

Wade could remember that. "Okay."

"On three, open the door." Anya manoeuvred the cabinet into position. "One, two, three."

Wade yanked the door open. Anya pushed the cabinet through and rolled across it, landing lithely on the far side. She gave Wade a reassuring smile that failed to reassure him.

"Close the door."

Wade left the door open to help Anya if she needed it. Bullets gouged chunks in the wall as Anya slid the cabinet down the corridor towards the gunfire. Wade dived across the hall and hit the elevator call button before sliding back into the room. Wade watched half a dozen black-clad operatives with assault rifles firing down the corridor through the crack by the door hinges. Zings and crunches filled the hall as the bullets ricocheted from the angled metal sheets. Anya crouched low behind the rapidly moving furniture. As the cabinet crashed into the phalanx, Anya launched herself over her makeshift barrier. She grabbed a nearby gun, pulling the operative in the opposite direction.

The lift arrived. Wade grabbed Cassandra and pulled her across the corridor into the cab. He kept his body between the soldiers and her as gunshots continued to fill the hallway. Wade's hand hovered over the button. He could not let Anya fight six on her own.

"Stay here. Keep the lift open."

Wade rolled from the lift and into the corridor. He saw the fallen operative scrambling back to his feet. Wade kept the agent between the guns and himself to come up behind the Kevlar clad soldier. Wade grabbed him around the neck and pulled him back. He dug his fingers under the chin strap of his helmet, yanking the headgear off.

Wade pushed him back towards the cabinet with a sharp shove, the operative's head bouncing off the wooden surface. The helmet became a missile. Wade launched it at another operative; he pivoted off the falling agent and up and across the cabinet after Anya. Wade's feet planted into the chest of a shooter, the gun discharging across the ceiling. Wade grabbed the gun and clubbed the owner with the stock. He twisted the rifle around and unloading the magazine into the nearest three. They flew back as the bullets thudded into their Kevlar vests at close range.

The heel of Anya's hand smashed into the remaining operative.

"I told you to get out of here." She was out of breath.

Wade knelt and unstrapped the nearest soldier's Kevlar vest. "I can't watch you die again, either."

Anya smiled, pulling at the vest of another. Although he didn't know much about armour and armaments, Wade grabbed a couple of helmets, guns, and magazines. Laden, they ran back to the lift before the operatives returned to consciousness.

Cassandra threw her arms around Wade and kissed him.

Anya waited for a second before interrupting. "They've packed the lobby."

Wade helped Cassandra into a Kevlar vest. "Where too, then?"

Anya slipped hers over her tee-shirt. "Carpark level on four, but head down to the first floor via the stairs."

Wade hit four, five and six on the floor buttons, before slipping on the final Kevlar vest. Without thinking, he flicked a switch, ejecting a magazine. He looked down in amazement at his hands and swapped in a fresh magazine. "I didn't know I knew how to change a magazine."

Anya flicked out her magazine and pressed the brassy bullets with her thumb. She gave Wade a cocky smile. Clicking it back into place, she shot the camera in the corner. The retort was loud, making Wade wince.

Anya glanced over her shoulder at Cassandra. "Cass, kneel behind us."

Although a struggle, Cassandra got herself and Bump to one knee. Anya and Wade knelt in front of her. They put their guns at the ready, a flimsy barrier between her and potential danger. The smell from the guns almost had a taste, pungent and acrid. The door opened onto an expansive lobby, the glass wall separating the office from the elevators with an etched number four.

Yesterday Pill   Iain Benson

Being cautious, Wade tossed his helmet into the corridor. Gunshots came from both directions. He knew on both sides, black-clad Kevlar plated operatives waited.

With his fingers, he gestured for Anya to fire left, and he'd fire right. She held up three fingers, shaking her hand into two and then one.

At zero, Wade shot the glass wall. The number four vanished into a waterfall of glass shards. They followed the bullet out, diving from the cab. Wade twisted to the right, firing down the corridor at the group of three agents waiting. He felt he had poor accuracy but accurate enough to thud into armour and force them back down the hall. Wade landed with a crunch onto the glistening glass pile, skidding two or three metres into a desk.

The operatives took shelter under their barrage. Wade waved Cassandra out into the smoke-filled corridor while Anya and Wade kept the agents on the back foot. She almost crawled out, reaching them in a low crouching motion.

"Go!" Wade grabbed Cassandra's arm, helping her to her feet and pushing her after Anya, heading for the door marked *stairs*. Anya scooped up another pair of magazines from a fallen operative. Wade fired to keep the agents in their flimsy cover.

Adrian emerged from another elevator, glancing around as they reached the stairwell.

"You two go ahead. I'll catch up." Wade pressed his back against the wall, holding the door ajar with his foot. "Adrian!"

"Wade. You have made quite a mess." Adrian's voice sounded unconcerned.

"Cassandra isn't a problem. Paladin misread the message."

Wade risked a glance back at the sharp, black-suited man striding towards him. Wade fired into the ceiling, pausing the advance.

"It's irrelevant," Adrian said.

"If you let us get on with our lives, Paladin and the System can continue. Don't make us close the wormhole."

"You know about that?"

Wade glanced back. Adrian had a pistol in his left hand. "I know about it, Adrian. I know what it is, where it is and how to turn it off."

"That's a shame."

"We have evidence that Paladin was behind the restaurant explosion and the bomb on the train." Wade was guessing Anya had located the information.

Adrian's tone suggested indifference. "This is bigger than Paladin, Wade. Bring Cassandra in so we can end this shitshow and save the world."

"I can't do that, Adrian."

Bullets cracked into the door, signalling conversation's end. It was his cue. Wade headed down the hard-wearing carpet covering the steps at speed, bouncing off the turns. He caught up to Anya and Cassandra as they burst through onto the first floor. Waiting operatives, guarding the elevators, caught out when they emerged from the stairs. The hiatus lasted seconds, bullets shattering the surrounding glass. Anya led them into the maze of cubicles, unerring in her choices. Operatives followed them, the staccato rattle of gunfire a constant background noise. Wade ducked down, trying to shield Cassandra as they ran past the low cubicle walls.

Wade kept his gaze sweeping to the sides and behind, trusting Anya to monitor ahead. An operative looking for them cut across a side path, but Anya had already led them to the side before he saw them. Beyond the cubicle farm, they emerged onto a brief run to the floor to ceiling glass window wall.

Anya shot at the glass. Starred patterns splattered across the bluish glass. It succumbed and shattered, sprinkling outwards, sucking the noise from the room along with the smell. The gunshots echo attracted the agent's attention. Wade heard approaching pounding feet.

"Through the window." Anya led by example, dropping a few centimetres onto a metal awning that deformed with resounding booms with each step they took.

Wade fired a few rounds back into the office without looking as he followed. Anya dropped a metre onto a second canopy. The drop from that

Yesterday Pill   Iain Benson

canopy to the ground looked about three metres. A fall from that height would cause Wade problems; he knew Cassandra wouldn't make it, the worry for her and their unborn child rising in him as they reached the end.

Anya jerked her gun down. "Wade, you go first."

Wade looked over the edge, a lozenge of green, a bushy box hedging about two metres below.

"This is going to hurt." Wade leapt off, lifting his feet into a sitting position. His theory had been to spread his weight onto the bush. It worked a little, but the pain left him wincing as he rolled off the hedge.

"Cass!" Wade saw Cassandra hesitating at the awning's edge. She sat on the lip, dangling her legs over. "Jump."

Gunshots rang from the interior, prompting Cassandra to jump, more from fear than desire. She wasn't over the bush. Wade caught her in his arms, collapsing and breaking her fall. As he did this, Anya landed in the bush with a grunt of pain. She climbed to her feet.

"We need to go."

Wade walked into the road and pointed his gun at an approaching car, firing a single shot slightly above an approaching vehicle. The white Fiat screeched to a stop.

"Go." Wade used Hebrew to the older man with a white moustache in the driver's seat.

The man, wide-eyed, exited the vehicle, scrambling away. Anya bundled Cassandra into the back seat, following in behind her as Wade took the driving position. Wade hit the accelerator before Anya had the door closed. The car slewed under the sudden acceleration. Bullets from the building punched holes in the bonnet, roof, and road.

"Everybody okay?" Wade did not dare look over his shoulder. In the mirror, he could see Anya almost upside down in the seat. Further back, he saw a rapidly diminishing Adrian standing on the awning, silhouetted.

Cassandra responded, her voice muffled. "I'm fine."

Anya shuffled around to get into her seat correctly. "Same here. Take the next right."

Wade put two wheels through the grass around a fountain, swinging into the on-coming traffic lane and avoiding a slow turning white van. He raced past the parked cars, streetlights creating pools that flashed in Wade's periphery.

He slowed at the T-junction. "Left, or right?"

"There's a car showroom just up on the left."

The Fiat creaked as Wade bumped it onto the kerb.

A few days earlier, Wade had worried about car owners. Now, he used the rifle stock to break open the car showroom window. Alarms blared, flashing a blue alert above the door. While Anya kept a wary eye down the street, Wade knocked out the remaining glass from the door and stepped inside. It took a few minutes to find the car keys in a locked metal cabinet behind the reception desk. Wade shot the lock off. He grabbed a handful of key fobs and returned to the lot at the front.

Anya was standing beside a sleek looking white Tesla. "Did you get this one?"

Wade looked through the fobs and found a Tesla symbol. He clicked it, unlocking the car. "Yes."

Anya climbed into the driver's seat. "Shame we can't keep it."

Cassandra and Wade got in the back.

Once she had fastened her seatbelt, Cassandra leaned forward. "Where are we going?"

Cassandra drove off the forecourt. "To get our cases."

She knew Tel Aviv well, avoiding the main roads and reaching their apartment quickly. The car smelled of cleaning products, the interior metal gleaming.

14

"Are we sleeping?" Cassandra asked as they headed inside the apartment.

"I'm not sure we have time." Wade paused on the stairs on his way to get the bags.

"We have two hours." Anya headed for the downstairs toilet. "I've put the Tesla to charge."

"That's quick," Cassandra said, sounding surprised.

Anya gave a smile. "It's new. We can also do twice the mileage."

Wade gave way to allow Cassandra upstairs to the upstairs toilet. If he had time, he was going to have coffee. He headed for the kitchen.

Cassandra came in first. "I'm tired."

Wade passed her a coffee. "This might help."

"Oh, yes!"

When Anya came down, Wade gave them the bad news. "I told Adrian that we had proof they were behind the restaurant explosion and the bomb on the train."

Anya grabbed her coffee and nodded. "We do. I can release it any time. What did he say?"

"Shortly before shooting at me, he said that this was bigger than Paladin." Wade poured Anya a mug of coffee and shrugged.

Anya snarled. "He'd say anything to get hold of Cass."

Cassandra leaned against the "Once we close the wormhole and end their insights, they will have nothing to help them."

Wade nodded and chuckled. "All we need to do is get to Pripyat."

Cassandra sighed. "Yeah."

Anya got her phone out. "Hey, Ozzy."

There was a pause. Wade could hear Ozzy answering the phone.

Anya had a smile as she spoke to her brother. She put the phone on speaker. "I'd like to book you to deliver some batteries from Tel Aviv to Ukraine."

The reception slightly distorted Ozzy's voice. "Where in Ukraine?"

"We're heading for Pripyat."

Wade could hear Ozzy moving around and yawning. "I can't fly there."

"Where can you fly to?"

Another pause before Ozzy found somewhere. "Odesza. It's on the coast, but they have an airstrip."

"You'll do it?" Anya held the phone between the three of them so they could all hear clearly.

"What sort of batteries?"

Anya looked at Cassandra. Cassandra shrugged. "Neodymium."

"Does that make a difference?" Anya asked.

"If it's like the huge ones that go in a car, I doubt I could fly that far with them." Ozzy paused. "I take it the batteries are a cover?"

Anya laughed. "We need the batteries there. But yes."

"Am I coming to the same airstrip I dropped you off at?"

Anya looked around the kitchen, a questioning look. Wade considered it. A broken fence panel gave entry to that airstrip, but Wade knew Paladin would clamp down. Paladin knew how close they were and that they'd head for Ukraine. They'd have people at every airport, harbour, and border crossing. He wouldn't put it past them to patrol the streets.

"I think it would be dangerous. We need to get out of Israel before Ozzy picks us up."

Ozzy spoke up. "Can you get to Lebanon? Paladin is not welcome there."

"I doubt we'd be welcome there." Anya sighed. "I'm not sure they've forgiven Wade and me."

"What did we do?" Wade asked, momentarily distracted by a nugget from his past.

"When you get a chance, search for news stories about Saghbine Bridge." Anya frowned a little. "I think I might have a way into Lebanon that Paladin might miss."

Yesterday Pill   Iain Benson

"In that case, Annie. Head for the town of Baddaran."

Anya looked puzzled. "What is there?"

Ozzy laughed. "They have an airstrip and lax morals. The latter is more important."

Anya checked her watch. "When can you get there?"

"If I do pre-flight now and set off immediately, I can be there in six hours."

Wade also looked at his watch. It was a little after five. "Bring sandwiches."

Anya rolled her eyes at him. "We will be there in six hours. We may well be coming in hot."

"Please don't," Ozzy said.

Anya was insistent. "Six hours, Ozzy."

"Okay, okay."

Anya put the phone away. She looked at Cassandra and Wade. "We need to leave soon."

"Has Paladin found us? Are you repeating?" Cassandra had grasped the time replay Anya and Wade had been doing.

Anya smiled. "Not this time. But we won't need a full charge, and we need to get ahead of Paladin."

Wade had already decided it was too late for that. "They'll already have the borders under observation."

Anya had a trump card. "Not all of them. There's a tunnel."

Wade didn't understand but went and got the cases, putting his trust in Anya. The sparkle in her eye told him she had a plan. They might not be on a repeat, but she had the confidence that came from being in one. With the cases in the Tesla's boot, more for shielding than clothing, Wade took both bottles of water he'd found in the fridge and put them in the car's cab.

Anya appeared behind him. "You always used to say that hydration is important."

Wade gave a curt nod. "It is."

As he looked down into Anya's eyes, there was a moment that he wondered if his feelings for Anya burned into his brain like *Californication* and driving. He knew he felt something. He pressed his teeth together, trying to shake the desire. She'd already told him it'd been years, and she'd put their time together behind her. Wade said to himself that she no longer had the feelings he could see in the picture weighing heavily in his jacket pocket. He could not escape his real and immediate feelings for Cassandra. They were ever-present.

"Are you ready?" Anya asked, breaking the connection.

Wade raised his eyebrows. "Yes. We must not forget Cassandra, though."

Anya's eyes flicked downward, away from his. "No. We can never forget Cassandra. She'll be down in a moment."

As though the words summoned her, Cassandra appeared in the doorway. Dawn's first rays lit her face. She gave Wade a little squeeze as she climbed into the back. Wade got in the front passenger seat, shuffling to fit in wearing his Kevlar vest and holding two automatic weapons. Anya locked up the apartment.

As Anya climbed into the driver's seat, Wade had a sudden insight. "That's our apartment, isn't it?"

Anya gave him a startled look. "Yes. We'd not been there for a while."

Although irrational, Wade's insides twisted up, like he'd been cheating on Anya with Cassandra. He took a sip of water to push the ludicrous sensation away.

Anya stroked the wheel. "I love this car."

Acceleration threw Wade back into his seat as Anya shot away down the streets, barely slowing as she took corners. They soon left Tel Aviv on a wide motorway, long shadows from the sun peeking above the mountains in the east. They flew along the road, mainly in the outside lane, zipping past early risers. Wade looked out on a landscape that should have been familiar but remained alien. Towns flew past his window, reservoirs,

Yesterday Pill   Iain Benson

and desert. Anya drifted slightly, alerting Wade to a rerun.

"Helicopters on the road ahead." She checked her watch. "The pills are down to thirty-nine minutes."

Wade thought about the reduction in time for the pills. "It has to be something to do with Cassandra closing the wormhole."

Cassandra raised her voice from the back. "It could be a ripple from it. We might see other effects."

"But the world won't end?" Wade asked.

"It hasn't ended," Cassandra said with a laugh. "Think about it. You're feeling the effects. Paladin's information ends, and we are still here now."

Wade bowed to Cassandra's expertise. She made sense. Although, if they failed, that would also prevent the world from ending.

After half an hour, the sea hove into view as they swept around a headland. Anya left the motorway at a small seaside town, moving to a seafront road. She sped down beside roadworks. Wade could see the new road half-built above them, currently inactive, too early for rush hour. Anya left the tarmac to throw up gravel, skidding to a stop under the bridge.

She waited for what felt like an eternity, but only moments passed before a black helicopter swept past.

Wade watched it go past in silence. "How many times is this?"

"Only replay three." Anya leaned forward to look at the helicopter as it disappeared over the houses in a sweeping side-to-side pattern. "They know we're here somewhere."

Once the aerial threat had subsided, Anya edged from under the part-built roadway, thrusting gravel backwards as she got up to speed along the seafront. In the distance, partly shadowed in the morning sun, Wade saw white cliffs. Traffic control humps jolted him as Anya sped over them. Wade saw the tarmac chewed up from a machine gun before he heard the rattle. He looked over his shoulder. No obvious source for the bullets was immediately apparent, as Anya slammed on the brakes, throwing him against his seatbelt. Cassandra grunted from the back seat.

"Are you okay?" he asked.

"I'm fine." Cassandra sounded annoyed, more than hurt.

Above them, the helicopter shot ahead, slewing as it turned. Anya hit the accelerator again, using the car's full acceleration. They sped underneath it, flashes of light from the helicopter's guns hitting the ground behind them. Up ahead, Wade saw parked cars and a looming cliff with a metal gate.

Wade couldn't keep the nervousness from his voice. "That's a cliff."

Anya seemed confident, barely slowing as she took the kink in the road. "That is a tunnel."

Chalk chunks splashed from the rock face as the helicopter swooped after them before pulling to the side over the sea to avoid the cliff. The Tesla smashed through the blue gating, sending it clanging back off the tunnel wall, spinning away. Anya rattled over it with a crunching bump. Only one headlight came on in the darkness, the other damaged by the collision. A display board and bench splintered under the wheels as they rocketed down the tunnel. She squealed to a stop as the darkness became light.

Wade looked out onto the blinding white exposed section.

Cassandra sounded breathless. "What is this place?"

"The Brits built a railway to link up Egypt to Israel." Anya was a little distracted by straining around to peer into the light. "This is what's left."

Wade wondered why she had stopped. He saw the reason for her hesitation when the helicopter hove into view, hovering around, looking for them emerging. Wade admired the pilot's ability, a cable car and cliff creating a dangerous spot to fly.

"How do we get across there?" Wade wondered.

"If this car is as good as they say, we go quickly." Anya hit a button on the dash. "Ludicrous mode launch control engaged. That looks about two hundred metres. Hold onto your seats, folks."

Anya flicked a paddle on the steering wheel. She exited the tunnel like a cannonball, the cable car station a blur. Wade heard the helicopter's guns, but Anya's rocketing speed caught them by surprise, flying

Yesterday Pill   Iain Benson

underneath the skids and into the tunnel on the far side. They smashed through a kiosk. Wade looked back, glad to see the booth was closed. Crashing through benches brought Wade's attention back to the front. Anya's velocity stayed excessive, the old train tunnel's rough walls smoothed by speed. Thrumming from the tyres rolling over rail-sleepers echoed back at them from the wall.

Wade saw a blank wall approaching in their single headlight at speed. A solid white barrier with a door to one side. It filled Wade's vision.

"There's a wall!"

The Tesla hit the wall like a missile, sending the door ricocheting off the wall and bouncing back off the car.

"Border." Anya's face was concentrating with both headlights now out.

The rail tracks remained on this side, a slight glisten from the light at the far end rippling down them. Anya hit the brakes again, the car slewing in the gravel and scraping the tunnel wall. She limped almost to the end; the track emerging into sunlight reflected off the white chalk cliffs. Wade saw the bluff flattened out ahead, well past any customs point on the escarpment above.

The helicopter appeared, hovering, waiting.

"These tracks will slow us down," Anya said.

Bullets tore chunks from the surrounding walls, the helicopter trying to find them. A zinging sound accompanied a rent in the roof. Wade's head immediately snapped back to look at Cassandra.

"I'm fine, Wade."

"Good." Wade climbed from the car, checking the magazine of his gun. Keeping to the tunnel's shadowed side, he advanced to the entrance. He was only going to get one shot.

He gave a snorted laugh. Technically, he'd have as many attempts as he needed. However, it would be one shot at a time.

Staying in the shadows, he kept low and brought the gun up. He sighted along the barrel, trying to see the pilot as the helicopter swayed over the tracks, twisting and yawing slightly. Wade saw Kobe in the passenger seat, clearly visible through the darkened glass.

"Sorry, Kobe," Wade muttered, trying to line up on the pilot.

With a tsunami of air and a tremendous noise, a black streak flashed past the helicopter, swaying it. Another two followed. Wade saw two jets this time, flying close together and low. They left a spray of water as they banked to come around for another turn. Wade could only imagine the conversations going on between the fighters and the helicopter.

The Paladin pilot held their nerve, keeping the guns pointing at the tunnel mouth. The fighter planes swooped back around, their rounds raking the chalk cliff, leaving black marks.

"Please leave." Wade looked at Kobe. "You're outgunned."

Kobe couldn't hear him and refused to budge.

Wade only saw one way the fight could go. He raced back to the car.

"What's happening?" Cassandra asked as he climbed in.

"Fighter planes are shooting at the helicopter." Wade clicked into his seatbelt. "Get ready to leave."

The helicopter exploded, sending waves of flames into the tunnel, brightening it. Repeated booms echoed back off the walls as parts of flaming metal rained down on the tracks outside the tunnel.

Anya swore. "I know Lebanon dislikes Paladin, but that was brutal!"

"They gave fly-bys and warning shots." Wade had a sudden pang. Although he could not remember Kobe, they had to have known each other. "Kobe was on board."

Anya sighed.

"Did you know him?" Cassandra asked.

Wade made a noncommittal gesture, raising his hands. "I don't remember him, but in our run-ins, he seems to know me, so I guess so."

Anya edged forward, leaving the tunnel, speaking almost reverently. "We knew Kobe. He was part of an incidence team, like us. We've worked together."

Yesterday Pill   Iain Benson

In silence, they emerged into the blinding light reflecting off the cliffs. The wreckage had fallen down the rocks towards the sea. Evidence lay strewn all around them, black against the white, a stark reminder of Kobe's abrupt end. Wade watched them pass, like a memorial to those he wished he'd been able to get to know again. The notion they had been trying to kill them was irrelevant in the face of destruction littering the track.

Anya had to negotiate carefully amid the missing rails and disturbed sleepers. After five hundred metres, a gap in the cliff allowed her to leave and join a dirt track. A few minutes later Wade felt more relaxed as they sped along a tarmac highway.

Wade read a street sign as they drove past. "Not only can I speak Arabic, but I can also read it."

Lebanon seemed greener than Wade had imagined. His stomach rumbled as they headed past a town. He drank water instead. As they drove through a small town, Wade noticed they were getting odd looks.

"We appear to be a spectacle."

Anya glanced at him with a wry smile. "We have an expensive electric car and look like we used it in a war zone."

Cassandra added her observations from the back seat. "I can confirm we have bullet holes in the boot."

"It probably doesn't help that we're in Kevlar carrying weapons," Anya pointed out.

Wade tapped his body armour. "I'm leaving it on for now. I don't think Paladin will attack again in Lebanon, but I'm taking no chances."

15

They wound up into the hills. Silent for a while before Anya gave them a little bad news. "I'm not sure we've got enough power to get there."

"I thought it had an enormous range?" Wade was worried.

"Ludicrous mode used up a lot of charge. Also, from the warning lights, I think the bullets have damaged something important."

Wade checked the time. They still had two hours. Outside the car, mountains, scrubby trees, and farms offered no sign of a fuel stop. "We need a charging station."

Anya pulled in and grabbed her phone. She swiped through options. "The nearest is in Beirut. We haven't got the charge to get there."

"How far is the airstrip?"

Anya switched back to her satnav. "About eight kilometres."

Wade looked back at Cassandra. She glared at him. "I can make it."

Wade smiled. "I was wondering about the luggage."

She laughed. "I'm glad your underwear is so important."

Wade looked at the steep rocky bluffs around them. "It's not that important that I'd want to cart it over these mountains."

Anya restarted the car. "We need to get as close as possible, or we won't make it in time."

A car went past, navigating slowly around them. An idea popped into Wade's head. He got out and walked around the back of their car, looking up the road. Before long, a box van came up the road. Wade stepped into the street and pointed his automatic rifle at the driver. The van sped up. Wade raised the gun a little and fired a single shot before levelling at the driver again. This time, he stopped.

Keeping the gun trained on the driver, Wade went up to the cab and spoke to the driver in Arabic. "I need your vehicle. You can come with us, but we're in a hurry."

The driver was overweight, with several day's beard growth.

Yesterday Pill   Iain Benson

"Where are you going?"

"The airstrip."

Anya exited the Tesla. Wade looked back at it: the crushed front wing, a long scrape down one side. Amazing it had brought them as far as it had. She raised the boot and took out the bags.

While she climbed into the cab with the driver, Wade opened the back. The smells of baked goods washed out over them; his stomach rumbled audibly. He lifted the cases in and helped Cassandra up inside amid the shelving of white card boxes.

Cassandra peaked into a box. "Can we eat these, do you think?"

"Are you hungry too?"

Wade lifted out a pastry and bit into it, tasting the almonds, sugar coating his nose.

The van lurched, making him stagger backwards. He closed the rear door, swinging it shut. Cassandra held onto the metal bracket shelving with one hand, a plaited bun covered in honey and sesame seeds in the other.

"This is nice," she said.

The van rattled around, lurching and yawing as it wound into the hills. Wade and Cassandra sat to avoid losing their footing. Wade lost track of how long they'd been bumping along before they creaked and rocked to a stop. Anya's slap on the truck's side echoed on the inside. Light and the warmth from outside flooded back into the back. Wade dropped to the dusty parking area. Stretching off, he could see a runway made from large blocks of concrete, easily four metres square. It looked unused, with lines of grasses delineating the blocks.

Wade passed Anya a pastry and helped Cassandra down from the back after taking the bags.

The van drove off with a skid of tyres, throwing up dirt and pebbles behind it.

Anya waved. "He was nice."

"What did you tell him?" Wade wondered how she could describe a kidnapped driver as 'nice'.

"We're smuggling medical supplies out of Israel."

On the slight breeze, Wade smelled pine and heard Ozzy's plane. He looked over, down the long grey runway, seeing the dot resolve into an aircraft. Within seconds, wheels hitting the concrete sent a squeal towards them. Ozzy rolled to a stop after curling around the back of them to point back up the runway.

He pulled his window down. "Do you need some batteries delivered to Ukraine?"

Anya and Cassandra looked at each other and laughed. Cassandra spoke first. "We forgot the batteries."

Wade sighed and shook his head as he loaded the cases into the plane. "Hi, Ozzy."

"Hey! Wade. It only seems like yesterday."

"Not to me." Wade smiled. The time repeats didn't apply to Ozzy. "A lot has happened in the last twenty-four hours."

With no air traffic control, Ozzy took off into the clouds without preamble.

Cassandra twisted in the co-pilot's seat. "We'll have to get batteries when we land."

Ozzy laughed. "I thought that was a ruse."

Cassandra shook her head. "It's how we stop Paladin. The source of all their information is in Pripyat."

"You had a successful trip to Tel Aviv, then?" Ozzy asked.

Anya nodded. "I have evidence that they put the bomb on the train and that they destroyed the restaurant in the UK."

Cassandra sounded quite excited. "And we know how they get their information and how to stop it."

"I have enough fuel to get you to Kyiv."

Wade grabbed the seat, bringing himself into the conversation. "We cannot ask you to do that. Paladin will know where we're going next."

Ozzy looked at the earnest expression on Wade's face. "I lost my sister to Paladin. I've not seen her for so long. If we end Paladin, I can get

Yesterday Pill   Iain Benson

her back."

Wade wanted to keep Ozzy safe. "That will happen whether you drop us at Kyiv or Odesa."

Ozzy seemed intent on risking his life for his sister. "With me, you will be in Kyiv by mid-afternoon. If you drive, it will be tomorrow when you get there. I want this over."

Wade slumped back, feeling Cassandra's fingers intertwine with his and squeeze. "Fine."

"Annie, could you take over while I re-log the flight-plan?"

Anya grabbed the stick as though she'd won a prize, waggling the wings. Ozzy glared at her. Wade could see him tapping away on the plane's computer.

"Are we heading to Kyiv international?" Anya asked.

"No. There's a Soviet-era airbase used for pleasure flights and parachute drops, that kind of thing. I don't know how easy it will be to sneak out of, but it'll be easier than sneaking out of an international airport."

Anya agreed. "More designed to keep people from sneaking in."

"I will wait for you at the airstrip." Ozzy slapped down the lid on his flight computer keyboard and slid it away. "I've extended my flight log to Kyiv."

"Thanks." Anya gave her brother a tight smile.

Wade looked down at the edge of sea and land. Ozzy took a route that allowed him to hug the coast. They were low enough for Wade to make out details. He had no memory of travelling on a commercial airliner, but had a feeling that would be much higher. Farms appeared as green patchworks, whilst in the distance, he saw mountains and grey rock covered in haze. Cities and towns spread like highly detailed maps, boats visible as dots in the marinas, but cars were invisible on the roads.

On their right, Wade saw an immense mountain. Anya, talking to Cassandra about magnets, saw him looking. "Mount Kiliç. Welcome back to Turkey."

They left the Mediterranean behind as they crossed the Turkish mountains' vast expanse. As they crossed Turkey, Wade tried to look out for the train tracks, but all he could see were mountains as Ozzy climbed to as high as his little plane would go. Off to his left, he saw an expanse of an odd white lake.

"What's that?" he asked.

Ozzy looked over. "Lake Tuz. It's a massive salt pan. They have flamingos."

The pale rock mountains became forested as they reached the Black Sea, the weather deteriorating the whole time. Wade constantly checked on his watch, in case Paladin spotted them. He knew now that Paladin would find them if they appeared in the news or on any internet information or CCTV to which they had access. Ozzy had to book his flight plan, and that was public information. Unless the System had yet to make the connection between Ozzy and Anya and Ozzy's plane, they would be invisible.

As the land returned beneath their wings, they saw the runway for Odesa.

Anya pointed down at the long gash of concrete. "There are Paladin helicopters and their jet at the airport."

Wade peered at the runway. Although they were low enough to make out the aircraft at the terminals and on the runway, he could not identify the Paladin craft.

"How can you tell?"

"They're gunships."

Ozzy looked at the airport, banking slightly to get a better view. "It's a good job that we didn't stop here."

"They will be in Kyiv too," Cassandra said. "International terrorists apprehended at an airport would make the news. Our only chance is that the news stories they've got will have been from all the places we might have chosen or submitted when they lose the wormhole."

"Including where we're landing?" Anya sounded worried.

Yesterday Pill   Iain Benson

Cassandra shrugged. "We didn't choose this. Ozzy did. It might have an impact."

"That's a slim hope." Wade felt a lack of confidence in their chances and rechecked his watch.

"It isn't an international airport," Ozzy said. "There are hundreds of such aerodromes in Ukraine. Paladin cannot watch them all."

"They only need to watch ones where they have a news report of our landing." Cassandra looked glum. As they watched, two helicopters lifted off and sped off towards the coast.

"How do they have news reports of where you will land?" Ozzy sounded confused.

Cassandra had no qualms in explaining. "In Pripyat, there is a wormhole."

"One of those things that connect two places in the universe?" Ozzy asked.

"How do you know about them?" Anya sounded incredulous.

"I watched *Stargate*."

Cassandra became more animated, slipping into lecturer mode. "Yes. It's a shortcut through space-time. Only this one does not connect two points in space, but in time."

"Harika. I'm not surprised they got powerful." Ozzy turned around to look at them as though checking out how truthful they were being. "I don't know how you have kept out of their clutches."

"It's difficult." Anya kept her brother in the dark about their advantage.

They lapsed into silence.

The engine thrum and monotonous landscape lulled Wade into a dopey state. Wade kept having to force his attention back onto their journey. He couldn't nap this close to their target. Visibility reduced as they crossed deeper into Ukraine, snow falling, making the land a white blanket.

Anya pressed a hand against the glass. "The weather is getting worse."

Ozzy checked his computer. "Yes, but we can make it and land before the weather worsens to a point where that's not possible."

Ozzy was correct. Although they could not see the tower, the tower could see them, and Ozzy's calm voice negotiated clearance.

The weather had one advantage Wade had not expected. As they landed, the snow and mist hid their little plane from the main buildings. From their suitcases, they grabbed coats and dropped off the plane.

"We'll be back." Anya hesitated by the door.

"I know you will." Ozzy smiled. "I have your bags."

They trudged through the slush and snow on the grass around the runway to a long wall. Ozzy's plane trundled away towards the hangers, half-hidden in the haze caused by the rain and snow. Beside the airstrip, all three shivered, wet and cold. They reached a crumbling concrete wall topped with razor wire barring a simple exit. They trudged down alongside it, Wade stroking his thumb over his ring, trying to decide if he needed to jump back and try a different route.

Light through the gloom, heralding their arrival at a security gate with silver gates shining in the lodge's light. Wade looked up, quickly spotting the two security cameras that watched the gates.

"If I shot those out, would somebody report it?" Wade pointed at the two cameras that watched the gates.

"I should imagine so." Anya checked the security lodge. "The lodge is empty."

Wade gave a tight smile. "Wait here."

He kept low across the empty lot. He took a wide arc around to reach the side entrance for the small collection of lodge buildings. From somewhere inside, he could hear music playing. Lax security suggested nothing ever happened. Wade reached the wall, the grey plaster crumbling under his fingertips. Grasping around, he felt for the door and gave it a little push.

Unlocked.

Wade slipped around onto a short corridor tiled halfway up the wall

Yesterday Pill
Iain Benson

in small white tiles, some missing, and some replaced in other colours. Sidling to avoid his shoes squeaking on the terracotta flooring, Wade edged forward. A room off to the left held the music's source. Wade glanced around, seeing an overweight, balding man in a blue shirt napping. An undrunk coffee on a small table, next to a small music streamer. With minimal movement, Wade passed through into a smaller annex. Here he found modernity, with CCTV screens and computers, all labelled in Russian. Wade knew it was Russian, making a slightly surprised noise as he read it. One switch turned off the CCTV, and another unlocked the smaller gate. He looked through the rain-smeared window at the just about visible gate.

He left as he'd entered, carefully, quietly, closing the doors slowly to keep the security guard asleep. With the cameras switched off, he walked confidently across the main entrance.

Wade held the gate open. "After you, ladies."

"There is a fine line between chivalry and chauvinism." Cassandra arched an eyebrow acerbically before destroying the affronted façade by giggling.

Their bulky coats hid their Kevlar, but the two assault rifles made them conspicuous.

Wade tried holding it against his body. "Do we ditch the guns?"

"I am loath to." Anya looked both ways down the road. "We need transport. If we cannot find anything quickly, we will have to."

They headed down the street, sticking close to the wall in the shadows. Pedestrians hurried past in the opposite direction, paying them no heed. Winter trees offered little screening from the cars and vans travelling up and down the road.

"I can't carjack another car," Wade said. "There will be a police report Paladin has access to this time."

"Agreed. We need a residential district or a carpark."

Wade checked the long, four-storey buildings behind walls. "This is all offices."

A smattering of parked cars suggested few people remained in the offices. Halfway down, the office entry created a rectangle of white on the grey snow.

Anya handed Cassandra the rifle. "I'll see if there is anything we can use inside."

Although she only went inside for ten minutes, she emerged with a box, almost running.

"How many replays?" Cassandra asked.

"None for this."

Wade lifted the flap on the box. It was empty. "What was in the box?"

Anya was a little dismissive. "Somebody had roses delivered. It is a handily sized box."

They put both rifles in the box, Wade the designated donkey.

"Where to?"

"Hush." Cassandra held up her hand.

Wade stopped walking to listen. Above the traffic noise, he could hear a crowd. As darkness gathered, he looked to where the sound seemed to emanate. A dome of light lit up the drizzle in a gap between two blocks.

Wade recognised the view. "Is that a football stadium?"

Anya tilted her head. "I believe it is."

"Football grounds have spectators," Wade said.

"Spectators have cars," Anya added.

Anya went on ahead, meeting them at the carpark entrance. The carpark had a mosaic of tyre treads in the snow; she led them to a small blue Renault and opened the door. "The jumps are down to twenty-five minutes."

"Unlocked?" Wade's surprise echoed in his voice.

Anya reached into a recess in the dash and extracted the key fob. "With the key."

Cassandra took one look at the back seat. "Wade, you're in the back."

Making resigned noises, Wade slid in, putting the rifles on the seat

Yesterday Pill   Iain Benson

beside him. His knees splayed, turning to pull the seatbelt on was awkward, but with a few grunts, he managed it. Anya and Cassandra had no such issues.

Anya fired up the engine with a coughing grumble. "Next stop, Pripyat."

Wade took a small measure of revenge for the backseat. "Batteries."

Anya clicked her fingers and pointed over her shoulder at him. "Next stop, batteries." With the engine idling, she flicked through her phone. "There's an electronics market in the centre of Kyiv."

She pinned her phone to the charger and set off into the centre of Kyiv. The Soviet-era grey concrete blocked architecture hemmed them in as they reached the city. The market broke the monotony of grey. A mishmash of curved and trapezoid metal skeleton painted bright yellow. Car parking around the corner and below, allowing them to see the structure as a former rail station. Anya found a parking bay near the subway under the busy road.

"Electric charging points." Cassandra gestured to the bays for electric cars. They all had vehicles in them.

"We've got diesel this time," Anya replied. "We don't need it."

Graffiti turned the subway into an art gallery, brightly coloured murals dancing down the tunnel. They joined the crowd heading from the carpark to the other side, a similar number heading out. Wade stomped his feet to shake the snow off his shoes. They rode the escalator into the building, the bright lights reflecting off the glass, hiding the wintry weather outside. The market had two floors, the ground floor stretching off into boxy stalls, the upper storey with more professional looking shop fronts.

"Cassandra and I will go high," Anya said. "You take the market."

"Why not Cassandra and I go that way?" Wade asked.

Anya pointed to the almost exclusively male shoppers. "We'd stand out."

Wade rolled his eyes and headed into the massive market labyrinth.

He would need to jump this time; traditionally searching would take hours. Overtones of solder, grease and hot metal caused Wade to wrinkle his nose and cover it with his jumper. Hundreds of stalls crammed in the cavernous room. Narrow walkways between garish stalls creating a twisting labyrinth. He pushed his way through a barrier of bunting between opposite stalls, creating a web of riotous colour. He decided if he found nothing in fifteen minutes, he would jump back and try a different route.

He found a huge choice of electronics, from transistors to lasers. Wade stopped at a stall selling surveillance equipment.

"Neodymium magnets?" He used Russian, as he didn't know Ukrainian, but with Ukraine's history with the former Soviet bloc, he bet more people spoke Russian than English. The Russian got a snarl, which Wade understood. He apologised.

"Nyet." The store owner had a thick accent. He pointed down the corridor. "Two down, five across. They may have some. Or they may not."

Wade thanked him with a flick of his index finger, a gesture he realised was unconscious while interacting in Russian. He filed it away as an interesting fact about his hard wiring.

As he followed the directions, Wade looked at the contents of stalls, reading the angular Cyrillic characters with ease. The magnet stall owner looked half-starved; he had a shaved head and thick black beard.

"Neodymium magnets?"

"Da." The owner waved at a pile of blue boxes. He switched to stilted English. "How many? What size?"

Wade checked his watch. "I'll be right back with the information."

He took a pill, the busy, vibrant market snapping into two dimensions, replaced by the brightly coloured subway and cold. Wade shivered, glad when they rode the escalators up into the main concourse.

Anya's plan hadn't changed. "Cassandra and I will go high. You take the market."

Wade held his hands up. "I've found them. I need to know how many and what size. And the payment card."

Yesterday Pill   Iain Benson

"We'll come," Anya said.

"Aren't you afraid you'll look out of place?" The derision dripped from Wade's tone.

"The thought had crossed my mind."

Wade led them through the bunting and to the magnet stall, squeezing between other shoppers.

"What's that smell?" Cassandra's nose wrinkled.

The comment amused Wade. "The market."

"They can keep it."

At the stall, Wade picked up battery boxes. "These are the neodymium."

"Oh, wonderful. Anya, may I borrow your phone? I need a calculator."

Anya passed her phone over. Cassandra periodically glanced at the labels on the boxes before returning her gaze to the phone.

"Excuse me." The stall owner asked in stilted English. "Are you looking for something?"

Wade nodded. "She's calculating how many we need."

The stallholder switched to halting English. "What for?"

"I need to close a wormhole!" Cassandra replied.

The stallholder's eyebrows entwined, and he shrugged. Wade stepped in using Russian. "We need them for our trip to Pripyat."

The stallholder shook his head, showing his palms. "Nyet! Nyet."

"I don't understand. Why not?"

The stallholder pointed at Cassandra's bump, shaking his other hand. He used English for Cassandra. "Child. No Pripyat."

Wade stayed with Russian. "Is it still that radioactive?"

The stallholder nodded enthusiastically. "Very much so, my friend. Even when there were lots of tours, they don't allow you to go if you are pregnant or young. It will kill the baby."

Wade turned to Cassandra. "You're staying in Kyiv."

She took an involuntary step backwards. "I am not."

"The radiation is still so strong it will kill Bump."

Anya's eyebrows shot up. "Cass, you're staying here."

The stallholder looked at them as a silent standoff.

Wade was resolute. "You are staying here. I will not risk our baby."

"You need me there." Cassandra sounded much less sure.

"We will work something out." Wade took Cassandra's hands in his and held her gaze. "You will be here in a hotel. Anya and I will take the magnets to Pripyat."

"Okay." She broke their gaze and looked down.

"Get some magnets." Anya looked down the row between the stalls. "I think I saw a stall selling surveillance gear."

Wade saw where she was going. "It'll be like you're with us."

Anya agreed. "We'll be your hands, eyes and ears."

"I need twenty-four." Cassandra pointed to a box, but her tone was flat.

Wade translated and added: "She won't be going now."

The stallholder collected the magnets, putting them in a plastic tube separated by thin black disks. "I worked that out. Keep these away from anything electronic that you want to keep working."

Anya tapped her card, warily keeping it far away from all the magnets. Wade took the tube, putting it in his pocket. He had to take out Craig's diary. Wade looked at the cover, stained with rings from mugs and held closed with elastic bands. He handed it to Cassandra.

"Do you have a pocket for this?"

Cassandra took it, slipping it inside her jacket pocket. "Of course."

Holding Cassandra's hand, Wade led the way back through the pungent crowd to the surveillance stall.

"You're a Russian speaker." Anya gestured to the stall. "We need five-gee earbuds with cochlea microphones. If they have five-gee GoPro cameras as well, that will save us looking. It'd be great if we could have burner sim cards for those. Oh! And charging pads. And night-vision goggles."

Yesterday Pill   Iain Benson

The surveillance stallholder watched Anya reel off her shopping list. He spoke fluent English. "You know your gear, lady. I've got all that. Are you planning a Pripyat raid?"

Slightly taken aback, Wade stuttered. "Yes."

"How are you getting in?"

Anya arched one eyebrow. "I was thinking about driving up to the gate, gassing the guards and driving straight through."

Wade gave a half-laugh. "She's kidding."

"I suggest coming in from the northwest," the stallholder said. "Don't use a vehicle. The guards have sound sensors throughout the forest. They also have mobile infrared cameras, motion detectors and the like. If you see someone in a uniform, run. They're jumpy since the war. If you see someone in street clothes, tell them Nik says you're cool."

"You seem quite knowledgeable." Wade expected him also to sell a city map. "Are you Nik?"

"I am." Nik gave a broad grin and rolled up his flannel shirt sleeve, revealing a tattoo of a hammer and sickle crossed over a mushroom cloud; about a dozen electrons in a Bohr atomic model swept around the design.

"Each electron is a Pripyat breach. I have an apartment looking into Pripyat central square."

"Any advice?" Wade asked.

"Go at night. Keep moving. Stay off the paths. Wear waterproof trousers."

"Sound advice."

Nik appeared quite animated. "There is less security from the northwest. It's further to travel, but a larger area. You'll have to cross the Sakhan, but it's not deep. There are some shelters just past a clearing. We drop off bottles of fresh water there. Oh, yeah. Take water. For you to drink and for leaving."

Cassandra looked puzzled. "Why should they leave water? Is it in case somebody else breaches and has none?"

Nik shook his head. "People live there. We take water for them as what is there is unsafe."

Wade's head tilted as he tried to process that information. "Why would anybody live there?"

"The economy in Ukraine is in ruins. They can't afford to live anywhere else." Nik grabbed some boxes from under the counter. He looked down at Cassandra's bump. "I take it you're staying behind?"

"Yes." Cassandra's mouth turned downwards. "I'd love to go."

"Seriously. It's so dangerous. I'm going to give you two of these." Nik passed Anya and Wade small cards with a black square of plastic attached.

Wade looked at it. "What is it?"

"Dosimeter. If that goes red, get out. If it goes blue, too late."

Anya bought the electronics. "Thanks."

Nik smiled at them. "Have fun."

"Do you have a map of where the motion sensors are?" Wade asked.

Nik shook his head. "They move them. Regularly. They hide them in trees. Keep moving and hope."

Wade gave a half-smile. "We can do that."

"Your English is very good," Cassandra said.

"Thanks. I was in UK when I was young."

They returned to the car. Cassandra's silence told Wade she was upset. Anya fired the engine up and put the heater on before flicking through her phone.

"Let's find somewhere to stay." As she flicked, Anya made tutting noises.

"It doesn't have to be swanky," Cassandra said.

"It needs to allow twenty-four-hour check-in, though." Anya made a few more tutting noises before an appreciative one. "Got one."

Yesterday Pill   **Iain Benson**

16

Anya pulled onto the road, heading into the city. Kyiv bustled with people. Snow coated the pavements, and yet late-night revellers headed in both directions through an icy wind. Lights splashed from shops and restaurants, glistening in the wet snow. From his awkward backseat position, Wade saw a mix of Soviet-style buildings and more modern, sleek-lined concrete and glass towers. Cassandra's bed for the night was an older building, with a modern frontage with a glass arch.

An automated reception left them to their own initiative to check-in. While Cassandra sat on a plush red couch, Wade stretched out the kinks in his hips and back. Anya navigated her way through the hotel reception screen, pressing the options with more force than the touch screen required.

"It's not the Hilton," she said, handing Cassandra a key card. "You're on the second floor, room two-twenty."

The elevator worked, the corridors clean, and the lights were all on. Wade felt that for one night, there was little extra the Hilton could offer.

The plain wooden door opened onto a practical room; a single curtain pulled back, allowing the window to reflect their image back at them as the lights came on. A double bed with brown sheets looked a little firm. Anya dumped her carryall and took out their purchases.

The large TV had internet connectivity, allowing Anya to connect to the receiver for her and Wade's GoPro cameras. Wade slipped the earpiece into his ear. He fiddled with it until he worked out how to clip the cochlear strip to the edge of his bone by his ear.

Wade tried it out. "Testing."

With only a slight delay, the television echoed him. The GoPro looked like a strap over his shoulder. He switched that on, as did Anya. They faced each other. On the screen, the split showed the two of them.

Cassandra maintained her air of resigned, sad disappointment and kissed the tip of Wade's node. "I think you're good to go. Be careful."

"I'll replay if there's an issue."

Cassandra turned to Anya. "Keep me in the loop."

Anya ignored the pleading. "Forget that. Do not, under any circumstances, leave this room. Don't let anybody in but us. If you can't see your door on that screen, keep it closed."

Wade chipped in. "All this is for nothing if Paladin finds you."

Cassandra dropped onto the bed and blew out her cheeks. Wade sat next to her and hugged her from the side.

"We need to go." Anya's brusque interruption forced Wade to separate.

He gave Cassandra a tender kiss, to which she was slow to respond. With a tight smile, he left the room, following Anya.

Driving past a fuel station, Anya pulled in. They grabbed a blister pack of water and chocolate. Getting back in the car, Wade stretched out his legs into the front passenger footwell with a silly grin. He made a sighing sound. Anya glanced at him and shook her head.

Before setting off again, she checked out her phone, zooming in and sweeping around. Occasionally, she muttered under her breath.

"There is a distinct lack of roads in the northwest of Pripyat."

"Nik must have got there somehow," Wade said. "Perhaps head up there and find a path?"

"I can see some paths."

"Head for those."

Anya nodded and pulled away from the fuel station.

Darkness stretched out along the road they travelled, leaving the city's brighter lights behind them. After half an hour, Wade risked terminal boredom by jumping back one dose, discovering it to be a mere ten minutes. After Anya had driven for ninety minutes, he took two doses, putting him back just over an hour as they left the lights of Kyiv behind for a second time.

He gave the news to Anya. "We're down to ten minutes on one

Yesterday Pill   Iain Benson

dose and just over an hour on two doses."

She scratched her chin in thought. "It might be useful. I've often wished we could go back a few minutes. An hour can be too long."

"I've not tried it, but the three doses are probably a day now."

"I'm not sure I want to go back through the past twenty-four hours."

Wade had to agree. He didn't want to see Kobe's death again.

Instead, Wade endured the interminable darkness along the long stretch of road. About a kilometre from the checkpoint to enter the radiation zone, Anya turned off down a dirt track. She checked her satnav. The lights from the car illuminated a dense forest on either side; the path swallowed quickly by darkness.

"I can't see a thing." Anya slowed.

Wade had an idea. "Turn off the lights."

"Jumping back so often has scrambled your senses." Anya laughed. "We would be blind."

Cassandra's voice came through their earpieces, startling them both. "Are you thinking low-level light goggles?"

"I'd forgotten you were there." Wade laughed. "But yes, we'll see better with the goggles."

"They're in my bag." Anya pointed at the bag on the back seat. Wade twisted and pulled the bag over onto his lap. Anya came to a stop.

He rummaged through and took out the goggles.

Instantly the world became a green monochrome vista. The trees looked like stripes against a dark backdrop. Ahead, the world was a solid, bright green until Anya killed the lights. Wade blinked a few times, seeing the path as a dark line between the shimmering strips of trees.

"That's better." Anya set back off, the gritty dirt rattling in the wheel arches as she bumped off down the track. The satnav eventually gave up working out where they were. The real-world path continued even as the virtual one vanished. Wade lifted the phone. Anya came to a stop as he zoomed out on the map to find their ultimate destination.

"I crashed into a log writing off the car," she said, explaining.

Wade realised she had jumped back, stopping the car before reaching the crash point. Wade pushed his door open, feeling the resistance from the scrubby bushes on his side. His breath billowed out in a cloud ahead of him, the cold stinging his nostrils. The Kevlar jacket under his coat added another layer of welcome warmth. Two metres ahead, he saw the fallen log.

"We're not moving that." The partly buried log formed an impassable barrier.

"What's the problem?" Cassandra asked.

"A fallen tree. It's blocking the path." Wade took the assault rifles from the back seat, slinging one over his shoulder. "I guess we're walking from here."

Anya grabbed her bag, slinging it over her shoulder. "Can you take the water?"

Wade nodded and took the blister pack of twelve bottles, wishing he had a bag to put them in. They were awkward to carry, his fingers already cold.

"It's tempting to go back and pack gloves and a backpack."

"That's always a temptation." Anya gave him a conciliatory smile. "The day of your seizure, I was there because I'd gone back a day to stop it. Or try at least."

"Any idea what caused it?"

She shook her head. "You were doing your routine morning check on Cassandra. I thought somebody had shot you."

"You used to check up on me?" Cassandra's voice sounded in their ears. She seemed amused. "I don't know whether that's sweet or creepy."

"Go with sweet," Wade said.

Anya gave a half-smile. "I best not mention the cameras and bugs around your house."

"What?" Cassandra slipped from amused into annoyed.

Wade exchanged glances with Anya. She spread her hands to ask

Yesterday Pill   Iain Benson

silently, 'what?', he responded with a cutting motion across his throat. "We were keeping you safe, Cass."

Wade could see Anya's ghostly features. She had a look of mischief Wade recognised. He waggled his hands to tell her not to say whatever she was about to say.

She said it anyway. "Er, Wade used to watch you pee."

"Wade!"

The three laughed, easing the tension.

The dirt track became a cracked concrete road cutting through the forest. Weeds pushing through the concrete, in places actual trees grew from bomb craters. Autumn's leaf litter remained in piles despite the snow pushed up against the grass at the verges. In the goggles, Wade could see thin lines from power cables. Fresh snowfall left their tracks clearly visible.

Her voice low, Anya checked her map. "There's a path up ahead."

"We need to stay off the road." Wade pointed to their footprints.

Staring up at the trees beside the path, Wade searched for cameras. He'd pepper this area with them. Black voids in the glistening light that delineated the trees attracted his attention. They dashed to the side, keeping low. A mere deer track led through the trees. Using two fingers, Anya gestured down the path.

Anya used a husky whisper. "Didn't Nik say something about microphones?"

Wade nodded. They emerged from the trees into a clearing with scattered bushes. They had a distance the size of a football pitch to cross, with little cover.

Trying to be careful and quiet, they moved from bush to bush. Halfway across, Wade thought he saw a twinkling bright flash of green. Floodlights snapped on, forcing Wade to cover his watering eyes. Pain stabbed into his head. He dialled one dose on his ring and flashed back six minutes.

"Didn't Nik say something about microphones?" Anya repeated.

"We're down to six minutes." Wade tugged at Anya's sleeve. "We need to stay on this road longer. There is a clearing ahead where they spotted us."

Anya followed him down the concrete road, keeping to the treeline. More deer trails ran through the trees. Their map suggested they follow one, so Wade picked a random path. After a few minutes, they reached a pylon on the back of a generator truck, humming slightly. Wade looked up the tower, seeing the powerful floodlights atop it. He held his finger to his lips and gestured with a knife gesture to the right.

He heard the river before he saw it. Through the goggles, the river formed a black, roughly edged slash through the forest, dancing with flashing bright splashes of green. The splashing and gurgling told Wade it was shallow, although it looked like a black ribbon. Wade ran across it, water splashing up his legs. He felt the pebbles and rocks shifting under his feet.

He turned and called back to Anya. "It's freezing."

She tiptoed more slowly across, placing each foot down carefully. "You are right."

She shuddered as Wade helped her up the bank, feeling the chill in her fingers.

Through the goggles, Wade saw the outline of a dilapidated building. Old machines rusted against the walls, the windows jagged panes.

Anya came to stand next to him. "It looks like the set of a horror movie."

"There are more. Over there." Wade pointed to a small stand of houses. At one time, they would have had white rendered walls and red-tiled roofs. Now they fell in on themselves. The trees reclaimed their land from the temporary interlopers.

They walked through the village, the oppressive loneliness pressing down on Wade. He saw another pylon beyond the houses, pointing it out to Anya. She nodded, and they skirted the buildings into a small bus terminus complete with a crumbling bus, collapsed shelters and remains of a pickup truck. Wade almost tripped over a tyre, virtually invisible in the goggles. As

Yesterday Pill   Iain Benson

they set off across the bus station, Wade saw a bright green flash. Once again, floodlights snapped on, brightly illuminating the bus station. Wade looked over from where the green light had come. A tall pole with a camera on it, slowly rotating.

"Are you going back, or shall I?" Anya asked.

Wade dialled a dose, the village snapping into fuzzy green focus.

"The cameras are on tall poles." Wade held his arm across Anya's chest, halting her progress as they reached the bus station's perimeter. "Wait."

After a few minutes, from their shadowed position, they saw the green twinkle.

"Ah." Anya nodded. "Proximity sensors."

They stepped back and pushed into the nearest building, using it to skirt the bus terminus. The house smelled of nature. All the glass in the windows had long gone, but some furniture remained. Wade could identify recent occupants from the minor scorch marks that created jagged black in the light on the brighter concrete. Past the building, a toppled water tower provided ample cover, though it smelled of rust and disintegrated as Wade touched it.

As Nik had promised, they found a water station as they left the village and reached the forest. A wooden crate, with Ukraine for Water Station on the side in bioluminescent paint. He snapped out two bottles, slipping them in his back pocket, and placed the remaining ten on the shelf, glad to free up his hands.

They took the main road into Pripyat from the village. Anya reached up and tapped off Wade's communicator.

"Keep looking forward."

Wade realised what she wanted to say would be for his ears only. Keeping Cassandra in the dark. "What is it?"

"When this is over, I'm going back to Turkey."

"I thought we would."

"Not we." Wade saw her head turn towards him and stop, returning front and centre. "Me. This you and Cassandra thing is killing me."

"I thought you were over me?"

"Did I? I lied." She paused. He'd detected the catch in her throat. "It was easier when you were at a distance. Being with you, working with you again, reminds me of our time together."

"I wish I could remember." Wade touched the picture in his pocket. It brought a lump to his throat, thinking soon it would be all he would have of Anya. "I have a photo of you, me and Craig in Nevada."

"A brief holiday." Wade risked a glance at her. She smiled softly. Anya sensed him looking and frowned at him. He looked forward to the residential scene invaded by trees. "It hurts that you don't remember. It always has. You can live with pain after a while. Being with you makes it flare. The way you laugh, how you risk yourself for Cass and me."

Wade's conflict increased. He sensed his feelings for Anya were as ingrained into his brain as his language skills.

"If I'm candid," Wade said. "Being with you tells me I have feelings for you. I had hoped we could have more time together. No pressure time. You are an important part of my past."

"And Cassandra?"

"Yes. I can't explain it."

"You and Cassandra are having a baby. I need to leave. It's a simple equation. I'll get over you. You'll have Cass."

He was about to object, but she turned her communicator back on. Wade did the same. Through the trees, they saw blocks of flats. No telltale green flash appeared as they advanced, but Wade's alert level rose as he saw a broader light, a suffused glow emerging from the top floor. He lifted the goggles, and the light vanished, hidden by a blackout curtain. With the goggles down, it became clear.

"Somebody is living up there." Wade pointed upwards.

In Ukrainian, a voice from behind made Wade's heart skip a beat. "Don't move."

Wade ignored the instruction and turned around. A kid, only

Yesterday Pill   Iain Benson

nineteen, had taken up a defensive stance, holding a knife. Wade looked towards the trees, where he saw two others. They were not security or army.

As his first port of call, Wade went for diplomacy, but used Russian. "We're on a Pripyat run."

The lad looked them up and down. "You're too old. And armed. And Russian."

Wade switched to English. "Nik told us to tell you we're cool. We got these goggles from his stall. As he instructed, we put water in a stand. My Ukrainian is poor."

The stance softened; the knife dropped to his side. A bandana mask obfuscated the youth's features. He spoke Russian. "Okay. If Nik says you're cool, you're cool."

With the knife lowered and the situation defused, four others materialised from the darkness. Two more in the woods hung back.

"What's with the firepower, chuvak?" The tall one gestured to Anya's weapon with a casual wave of his hand, mainly speaking English. Wade could see another bandana face covering and cap, with loose clothing, but again, no features.

Anya swung her rifle around into her hands. "We're expecting some resistance."

"Kruto." The youth had to be speaking Ukrainian, as Wade did not recognise the word, though it sounded like slang. The nearest he could word he knew to it meant 'relaxed'. "Saw some copters hitting the pads outside the reactor core."

"Black?" Wade wondered if they were Paladin.

"Black gunships." The knife-wielding youth pointed down the road with his blade. "Resistance? You will have good old American shootout?"

"If need be." Wade shrugged. "Hopefully not."

"Shit, man. It is going to be the best day we had here since we made fireworks and the army found us."

Wade gave a half-smile. "You're still here, though."

"We know this town better than them."

Wade pointed to himself, then Anya. "I'm Wade, and this is Anya."

The youth nodded. "I am Hector. These are Yaz, Kita, Dog and Mikael."

Wade took advantage. "What's the quickest way to the reactor core?"

"It is about three klicks that way." Hector pointed with his knife down the street. "In half of one hour, the day will start lighter. You have a big problem then with drones. If they see you, the army will be on you like the flies on a pie."

"Stay undercover." Wade acknowledged the advice with a nod.

"Go in as possible straight a line."

Wade gave another curt nod, and they set off down what looked like a forest path. Above the trees, they saw high-rises, like icebergs in a choppy sea. As predicted, the sun rose, slowly brightening. They removed their goggles, seeing the grey concrete winding around trees.

"That looks like bleachers." Anya pointed at the seating emerging from the vegetation. A partially collapsed roof told Wade it was a stadium. He realised the path curved like a running track, though it was concrete. He thought he saw movement over by the far side.

Nothing more appeared. Wade felt jumpy, paranoid. For good reason. "I think it's a stadium."

A Ferris wheel rose through the trees. In the early light, shining like a ghostly mirage, looking oddly out of place in the forest that surrounded it. Yellow cabs permanently stuck, the struts slowly decaying. They passed under the Ferris wheel, stepping over a discarded ticket-booth door. Beyond, they passed a rusted skeleton of an unidentifiable ride and abandoned dodgems.

The sky looked heavy with clouds. Wade scanned around, checking for drones. They crossed back into the forest and down a narrow path crowded by bushes.

Wade heard the bullet crack as he flew backwards off his feet.

Yesterday Pill   Iain Benson

Beside him, Anya crumpled. A shot onto her Kevlar vest, another through the top of her arm, spurting blood. Wade rolled onto his side, seeing bullets chew up the concrete beside him. Wade needed to know the shooter's position so they could avoid it. He helped Anya to her feet, pushing her towards a building with an exposed stairwell. His leg collapsed under him, sending him toppling to the side. Pain overwhelmed him momentarily.

Crawling, he and Anya made it into the stairwell, climbing over a lip where the glass used to be. He hunkered down. Wetness spread around his waist. Rapid-fire bullets struck concrete, cement, and metal around them. The continuous staccato crescendo made thinking difficult. Chips of conglomerate splashed his face. His vision wavered.

Anya looked pale; the colour had gone from her lips. She whispered, bubbling blood frothing on her lips. "Do it right next time."

"Wade!" Cassandra hissed in his ear. "Go back."

Forming thoughts seemed hard. Wade's vision dropped out of focus. He blinked and looked down at his leg; the dark fabric looked slick. Darkness crept in around the edge of his sight. He slipped down the wall into a sitting position, propped up on the stairwell.

Cassandra was shouting at him, but he couldn't see her.

Wade's thumb ran across his ring. His arm burned as he rotated the design for a single dose. A vague memory made him click it round again to a double dose before pressing it down. He looked down at the fluffy pill.

Wade pressed it to his lips, glad that the pain merged into the two-dimensional screen.

He stumbled as he fell over the door by the Ferris wheel.

"We got shot." He felt his leg. The memory of pain remained, though the physical aspect had gone. "That was close. They got both of us."

"Are you okay?" Cassandra's voice in his ear sounded worried.

"Fine. I jumped back." Wade could not pinpoint the gunshot's source. "Also, a double dose is down to six minutes."

"Do you know where they are?" Anya looked around the bushes and trees surrounding them.

"I'll go up to the roof. Wait here. If anything happens to either of us, we can jump."

Wade pushed through into a corridor strewn with leaf litter and discarded detritus. He picked his way past the remains of chairs and filing cabinets to a stairway heading up. All the walls a canvas, spray-painted with colourful graffiti. Eventually, he pushed his way onto a rooftop. He could see a long way across the treetops. At the roof edge, he looked down. Walking behind an army jeep, Wade counted two dozen soldiers in green fatigues. They were alert, looking around as they moved across the plaza. Wade ducked as one looked in his direction. Almost on his knees, he moved down the rooftop to the corner. He unclipped the GoPro.

"Cass, I'm going to move the camera around. Can you see anything?"

"What can you see?" Anya asked in his earpiece.

"Go back to the left," Cassandra said. "No. The other left."

Wade twisted the GoPro back the way he'd come. Cassandra gasped.

"What is it?"

"Another group of soldiers arriving."

"From which direction?"

"Towards the reactor core."

Wade heard a high-pitched whine. He looked behind him, straight at a drone. "Crap."

Bullets smashed into the parapet. Wade pulled the GoPro down and reattached it. He crawled backwards, staying low. The parapet's concrete crumbled under the onslaught. At the door to the stairwell, he heard boots stomping up.

"Wade!" Anya's voice was high-pitched. "They're here."

Her voice cut off suddenly, followed by the percussion of shots fired.

Wade checked his watch. Had it been long enough? He couldn't remember when he'd jumped back last time. He had to give himself time so

Yesterday Pill   Iain Benson

the pill would work. Wade scrambled beside the stairwell block, bringing his gun around. They'd have to come at him from the front.

The boots reached the gravel. Wade shot the soldier as he came around the wall.

"Sorry, but you won't stay dead." He said the words, but he was directly responsible for somebody's death, and he had to push away the sensations of guilt as more followed. Wade's gun bucked in his hands; the air filled with an acrid smelling miasma hanging in the cold air. The soldiers were close enough that Wade was deadly accurate. After three soldiers, the remaining ones held back.

A whomping sound made Wade look over to his right. A black gunship was approaching.

He dialled two doses on his ring. He had to hope there had been enough time.

The scene flattened out and snapped back.

He was climbing over debris in the corridor. He stopped and came back.

"Six minutes for two doses," he said to Anya, who looked surprised to see him so quickly. "We have to go a completely different way."

Wade set off towards a tall building with a gleaming golden crest, dull in what morning light reached through the clouds. Anya caught him up.

"What happened?"

"There are army personnel beyond that building. They can see quite a long way around that area. It's an excellent spot."

Rather than use the street, they pushed into the tall building, picking their way through the rubbish strewn across the floor. The walls had tags painted across but crumbling away, helped by bullet holes from the war. Fluorescent strips hung from the concrete roof or lay on the floor; the ceilings themselves bare concrete. Rust marks dripped down the walls where water had got to the supporting beams.

At the far side, they carefully emerged back onto the road, going into another office block. The remains of upright pianos, collapsing in on themselves, filled the first room, but the going became easier beyond.

"That road looks well used." Anya looked at the road outside. Although it had cracks running the length, the plants and bushes that had pushed through other streets were absent.

The risk of drones kept them in the shrubbery. They reached a border post in reasonable condition, the red and white striped pole blocking the road. Nobody occupied it, allowing them through. Wade wondered which side needed guarding.

Anya must have thought the same. "Which way is this guarding?"

"I presume the reactor." Wade shrugged. "But I'm not sure."

Movement off to his right made him swing his gun around.

"What is it?" Anya also readied herself.

"I thought I saw somebody."

Anya laughed. "Getting shot makes you paranoid."

17

Wade passed Anya a bottle of water as they walked through a yard of rusting container trucks. She drank in a long draught.

Anya touched the side of a fuel tanker. Her finger punched straight through. "In another hundred years, these will be gone."

"There is less plant encroachment here, though." Grasses had made the first incursion, finding any nook of dirt to grow in, their roots breaking the concrete and allowing the larger plants to establish.

"It's taken only a century for the rest of Pripyat to turn back to the forest." Anya waved a hand back the way they had come. "In another hundred, there will be nothing to see."

Wade glanced at the remains of vehicles in a long line of garages. Plant life dangling over the edges, creating a curtain.

"There it is." Wade pointed ahead at the steel hanger, reflecting the grey clouds.

"I didn't think it would be that big." Anya stopped walking before they left the woods.

Wade realised he'd seen it from the roof at Central Square. Between them and it, permanent and temporary installations, equipment and vehicles and piles of materials. Although Wade couldn't see any people, three helicopter gunships sat idly by the colossal silver edifice.

"Paladin will be all over this place." Anya sounded cautious.

Wade agreed. "We'll have to stay alert."

They followed the path under the overhead ducts and across the road. A black Range Rover turned the corner, speeding up when the occupants saw them. Wade dialled a single dose. The two-dimensional scene flicked in the briefest time he'd seen.

"Paladin will be all over this place," Anya repeated.

"Hold on." He put his hand across her path and guided her into the bushes. They crouched down. As he'd expected, the black Range Rover passed by their hiding spot. They kept the position until the car turned the far corner to continue its circuit.

Anya led the way through the bushes, under the pipes and across the road. Heavy industry around the containment dome mainly kept vegetation at bay. At the margins, nature encroached, unconcerned with the human endeavour beyond. The pair angled for the containers stacked into a multicolour giant block puzzle in one corner.

Even with the lack of sunlight, the silver hanger-like Sarcophagus had a liquid metal quality, dominating the view. Wade saw it even over the containers stacked three high. Anya pulled him back as he was about to step across the gap between two piles. She held her finger up to her lips and pressed back into the container. Wade copied the gesture, feeling the uneven container's corrugated surface press into his back. Two black-clad Paladin operatives walked across the path, their automatic weapons held across them. Though they looked down the path where Wade and Anya hid, they did not look behind them, missing Wade and Anya completely.

Beyond the containers, half a dozen truck cabs parked up. Wade saw the Range Rover's black bonnet before it fully appeared. The two of them ducked under a truck cab.

It took Wade three attempts to get across the forty metres to a manufacturing area. They hid behind huge metal sheets destined to become additional sheeting for the reactor core. The cover the materials offered allowed for rapid advancement, but that halted forty metres from the Sarcophagus.

Wade looked across the blank concrete apron.

"Run?" Anya asked.

She set off, getting two steps before she crumpled, the reverberating gunshot following her slumping form.

Wade took a double dose, stepping back a minute. The reduction in the time the pills sent him back worried him.

"Run?" Anya asked.

"No." Wade held her back. He looked around, spotting from where the shot had come. A staircase ran up the Sarcophagus's entire height, at the top, the glint of a telescopic sight. Two black-clad operatives had the whole yard covered. A mere forty metres from the entrance, and it seemed impassable.

The scope glint meant the sniper saw them. Operatives converged on their location.

Wade took a risk and dialled three doses. The view formed a painting-like quality. A snap, and he returned to the entrance to the containment dome's surrounds.

"Hold on, Anya," Wade said, pulling her into the bushes.

She shot him a glance but crouched into the bushes with him. "What is it?"

"There are snipers on the roof." Wade pulled the bushes back a little as the Range Rover rolled past.

Anya winced, seeing what Wade already knew. "That has everything covered."

"Cass?"

Cass sounded distant, with a rustling noise that grew louder. Wade wondered if she was in bed. "I'm here. What's up?"

"We're struggling to get in the front door. Is there another entrance?"

"There are offices at the back. I can't see anything on the web for getting inside that way, but it might be possible. There are certainly pictures taken from inside the offices from when the trips used to run."

"It'll give me time to catch up to the last jump back." Wade checked his watch. "I took three doses."

"How long?"

"Just under forty-five minutes."

"Shit." Anya's feelings had to be like Wade's. "It's getting shorter quicker."

Cassandra explained it to them. "I think that means you're getting closer to closing the wormhole."

"Closer to ending this." Wade's tone flooded with relief, but he knew it was also closer to never seeing Anya again.

She looked up at him as though reading his thoughts. Given their history, she probably could. She gave a sad smile and set off through the undergrowth, paralleling the conduit piping held above the vegetation. They reached a metal chain-link fence that ran around modern-looking offices. Judging by the lights on inside, these buildings still had occupants. The pipes bent off behind the offices as they reached a concrete wall. A wall they were on the wrong side of, to reach the reactor core.

Keeping close to the wall allowed them to avoid being seen by the sniper, so Wade accepted the current barrier.

When they reached a lake, Wade felt it was probably unsafe to swim in, given the proximity to a nuclear power station. Two groups of four pipes emptied into the pool.

"They'd probably give us entry." Anya pointed to the pipes.

"That water would probably kill us." Wade disliked the water's colour. He considered the electric cables running from pylons into the buildings. "It would probably be safer using those as a zip wire."

They hid momentarily from a Range Rover coming down the road. Two bridges and a thick pipe crossed the runoff pond. The Range Rover on the nearest bridge cut off that route. From their vantage, Wade could make out at least three guards.

"That pipe is too close to the bridge." Wade swung his rifle off his shoulder. "Frontal assault time?"

Anya caught his sleeve. She shook her head. "No."

"What happened?"

"I've not jumped back. Those guards massively out-gun us. The moment we fire a shot, Paladin will be all over us."

She was right. Wade felt relieved that he didn't have to kill anybody. It had been bad enough when he knew he would be jumping back.

"How do we get across?"

Anya looked at the bridge. "We go under the bridge."

Yesterday Pill   Iain Benson

Wade considered the zigzag metalwork framework supporting the road bridge. "We'd need a distraction."

From the woods, Hector chose that moment to materialise. "You need a distraction?"

Both Anya and Wade had snapped their guns around, trained on Hector. He pulled down his bandana and put his hands up, tilting his head and smiling.

"Where did you come from?" Anya looked quite willing to use the assault rifle.

"We have watched you. We have no television or console. You are better anyway." Hector gave a sideways glance up at his hands.

Wade lowered his gun. Anya narrowed her eyes, but instead of dropping her rifle's barrel, she gestured at the bridge and the car on it. "You know who they are, don't you?"

"I know they cramp our style." Hector shrugged and put his hands down. "Since the war, we see fewer tourists. Past six weeks, more army, more these guys. No more tourists at all. We make no cash money when no tourists."

"This isn't a game," Wade told them.

Hector grinned. "Maybe not for you. We call them names them for two minutes, da? You do your thing. They leave. We get back our town."

Anya pulled Wade back and lowered her voice. "I say let them have their fun."

Wade blew out his cheeks. "I suppose." He turned back to Hector and switched to Russian. "Do your worst, but if you get killed, don't sue."

Hector laughed. "Deal."

Hector pulled his bandana back up and took a colourfully painted skateboard from his backpack. He slapped it on the floor. From the bushes, two others appeared. Hector pushed off, giving them a mock salute.

"It's almost like we're destined," Wade said.

"Like the wormhole closes today?"

Wade nodded. "Exactly."

Distraction worked. Hector and his friends skated up to the bridge. Their voices carried over the still air. Three Paladin operatives came to the road, rifles cradled. While Hector occupied them, Wade and Anya scurried to the bridge.

By the metalwork supporting beams, Wade heard one on a comms device.

"These kids say they live here." Wade could not identify which guard spoke. There was a long pause. "The army was supposed to clear them all out. Amateurs."

While the youths occupied the guards, Anya edged along the narrow supporting beam, using the top to steady herself, sidling along. Wade set off, but his extra height made it painful and slow.

He slipped off, falling two metres into the aquamarine water.

He momentarily panicked until he discovered he could stand. The water came up to his waist. As he dialled two doses, his radiation badge faded straight through red and into blue. He took the pill, snapping back to the bridge edge.

"Amateurs," the guard was saying. Worried, Wade set off across the bridge again, nagged by the thought two doses had dropped to thirty seconds. Without the do-over, they would be an easy target for Paladin. Anya reached the far side while he shuffled along, contemplating the reducing time, missed his footing and fell in the water again. A double dose put him onto the bridge; the snapping back of reality caused him to let fall immediately.

Wade climbed to his feet, the water dripping from him, his badge indigo in colour. Thirty seconds had to elapse before he could replay. Faces peered over the bridge, the Paladin operatives breaking off from their distraction to look.

Wade waved before splashing under the bridge, pushing out a turgid wake to avoid the automatic fire. In his head, he counted down from thirty as bullets splashed highly radioactive water on his clothing.

"Zero." Wade popped his double dose, ready for the transition and

Yesterday Pill   Iain Benson

gripping the bridge for support as the world solidified. Anya's progress further down the bridge looked confident, with sliding movements. Wade mimicked her, concentrating only on keeping hold.

They rolled onto the grass on the far side.

Wade looked back. "That water is dangerous."

"I know, but not deep," Anya replied with a smile, telling Wade she too had been jumping back, and he'd thought she'd made the crossing look easy. They lay still, next to one another. Anya's fingers briefly entwined with his, stiffened and pulled away.

As though she could sense that brief contact, Cassandra came into their earpieces. "Don't lie there. Get moving!"

They rolled

"The double dose is now thirty seconds." Anya's analysis confirmed Wade's calculations.

Wade checked his watch and took a single dose. Time seemed to freeze and then continue. "One dose is useless. The double dose is almost useless."

Cassandra also sounded worried. "You need to be careful."

"We will be." Wade hoped he had injected more confidence in his voice than he felt.

Keeping low and alert, they crossed the road to the bushes surrounding a long office block. Wade looked back at the bridge. Hector saw him looking. The youth saluted and skated away, relieving Wade at seeing him safe.

"Cass? Which building do we want?" Anya asked.

"Can you see a long, thin building with a shiny wall?"

Three office blocks surrounded them. One Wade could discount as being in the wrong direction from the Sarcophagus. Both remaining two were long and thin, but only one shined dully. The other he'd describe as dull, with narrow strips of windows separated by white concrete.

"This one." Wade checked the roof and the windows for a sniper. Although the skies looked clear, three heavily armed and armoured Paladin operatives guarded the front door.

"The same issue as the bridge," Anya muttered.

"But this time, we don't have a Hector."

They needed a different way in, or Wade knew they would have a firefight the entire way to the reactor core. The extensive building had no windows, but it had colossal air conditioning ducts. He looked alongside the building. Thick pipes looked climbable.

"What are you thinking?"

Wade smiled. "Do you still have your screwdriver?"

"Of course."

Wade grinned. Hugging the wall, he climbed over smaller pipes on the floor and negotiating protruding equipment whilst trying to stay as quiet as possible.

"Wade, Anya?" Cassandra's voice in their ears caused Wade to pause.

"Yes?"

"There is a tour company that used to show civilians around the reactor Sarcophagus. I've found some information about them."

Anya looked intrigued. "Go on?"

"There is a changing room near the reactor core where you can get paper hazmat suits. You're going to need them. There's no point in shutting off the wormhole, only to never come back."

Wade felt they needed more information. "Do you know where exactly?"

"Sorry. No."

Wade exchanged glances with Anya. Anya had a sudden thought. "Paper suits?"

"According to the website, the dust inside is radioactive. It sticks to the paper and not your clothes. That makes it safe enough to explore the Sarcophagus."

"There is a large margin of error here." Anya looked doubtful. "With the pills taking us back less and less time, this will be tricky."

Yesterday Pill   Iain Benson

Wade thought of his and Cassandra's future if they abandoned closing the wormhole. Letting Paladin have their time forecasting. It did not bear contemplating.

It made sense for him to go on alone. "You don't need to go, Anya. You deserve to be free. I'll go in alone."

She glared at him, head shaking slightly. "Martyr. We're both going. You need me."

He needed her, but didn't want her hurt. Wade sighed and heaved himself up the ducting, using the narrow joins for hand and footholds. At the top, they curved over and formed a bridge into the building. Wade straddled the duct and twisted to look at Anya, arriving unsteadily behind him. She rummaged in her bag and handed over the screwdriver.

Wade levered off a panel. It fell to the floor with a muffled clang in the bushes below.

"It's dark." Wade slid inside. The air smelled stale and cold, a strong breeze coming from the building.

Wade put his night-vision goggles on and switched on the zero-light facility, lighting up the duct's inside. He saw a grating at the end and clanked towards it; the duct deforming under his footfalls.

The grating fell into the corridor with a slight push, the rusty metal crumbling on the tiled floor with a sound like dropped toast. Wade sat and slid out, turning and helping Anya down. His internal sense of direction told him to go left. As they headed down, they looked in each room, searching for the hazmat suits. They found control rooms filled with antique computer equipment, empty spaces, and locker rooms. Unlike the rooms in the Pripyat buildings, these were spotless. Wade wondered if the tour companies orchestrated the disparity for the benefit of tourists.

The corridor ended at a pair of yellow swing doors with porthole windows. They had yet to find the storage room for the suits. Very little light broke through into the corridor itself, mostly seeping in from a single room beyond the double doors.

Anya went into a room with sunlight shafting through a dusty window, blinding them momentarily. "Hazmat suits."

Like forlorn ghosts, hanging from pale wooden shelving around the walls, they found papery white suits. Each came with a filter mask. Although they looked like paper, they felt plasticised and smelled of disinfectant.

"Don't forget your mask," Cassandra said in their ears.

He pulled on the largest suit over his coat and Kevlar armour while Anya kept guard. He took up a guard position by the door as she put on hers.

Wade's voice sounded muffled under the mask. "Where is the reactor from here?"

"You're in the tour area now. I would have thought that there would be a map or something?"

"Do you know where the wormhole will be?" Anya asked. "I must be honest. I wasn't expecting something as vast as this place."

"We're going to have to hope it's outside the reactor's inner Sarcophagus." Wade could imagine Cassandra's thinking face as she replied. "I'm fairly certain it is outside the inner tomb because radio signals can get in and out."

Wade checked down the dark corridor before crossing and shining his torch onto a large map. A blue arrow told him where they were in the large T-shape. He traced his finger along a route to the Sarcophagus.

He memorised the route. "Any clues at all as to the wormhole location?"

"I'm going to say above the reactor." Cassandra sounded unsure. "I could be wrong, but I think it will be above the epicentre. It's a place to start."

Anya rustled out like a snowman. "Do we know where we're going?"

Wade pointed at the axe-head shape on the map. "Here."

"Through that door?"

Wade read the sign in three of the five languages on it. "Reactor. Yes. We want that door."

Yesterday Pill   Iain Benson

Wade went ahead down the staircase. Wearing both night vision goggles, and the mask chafed on Wade's chin. The door clanged close behind Anya as she followed. They had to switch on the zero-light mode for the goggles, not wanting to risk the torch yet. It would use the battery up sooner, but without it, they were blind.

Cassandra's description was accurate. They crisscrossed the ceiling and ran the length of a long, utilitarian corridor. Wade saw what he thought was an imprint of a hand on the wall, but on closer examination found a memorial to those who had died in the accident. Wade gave it a thoughtful nod as they passed. The corridor opened out into an expansive room.

"Are you still getting this, Cass?" Wade asked.

"I've lost video." Cassandra's voice held distortion.

"We've reached the end," Anya said.

Wade took off his goggles and shone the torch to appreciate the massive yellow tanks rising to the ceiling high above. A ladder ran up each to an inspection hatch. From there, wide bore conduits pierced through a crumbling concrete wall painted with nuclear waste warning symbols. According to a sign, they'd reached the pumping room. He closed his eyes for a moment, picturing the map. After the end pump, he found a metal staircase leading up to a mesh walkway, and a door marked for Sarcophagus.

"Up here!"

Anya joined him. "Your badge is red."

Wade looked down at it. "We'll have to be quick."

He pressed down on the door bar, opening the door.

Wade almost gasped aloud as he saw the vast space into which they emerged, but he stifled it as dozens of Paladin operatives guarded the roller doors and office.

An operative saw him, raising an automatic weapon and shouting, but Wade didn't hear the words; he took a double dose. The snapback and his hand felt the door bar's cold steel.

A double dose had dropped to seconds.

Anya's brows creased. "What is it?"

"Dozens of Paladin operatives."

"Ah."

"What do we do?"

Anya swapped places with Wade. "Let me have a look."

A brief pause, but the door remained closed.

Wade spotted the rewind. "What info did you find?"

"There is an immense pile of concrete."

"I think that's the cover for the reactor."

Anya nodded. "There's scaffold all over it. I think we can get to the scaffold and use it to hide."

"We need to go up, anyway."

"Timing. We will need perfect timing."

"Do you want to do it, or shall I?"

"Rock, paper, scissors?"

Anya shook her head. She muttered the opening line from *Bat Out of Hell*.

"You've already done it." Wade recognised the song. "And I guess it's a long one, as that's a long song."

Anya nodded her head. "A triple dose is two and a half minutes."

Wade readied himself. For Anya, this could be the hundredth run through. She turned and pushed through the door, keeping low. Wade followed, repeating her movements. They crossed the space to the scaffold, running up the crumbling concrete wall. Wade glanced around. For one brief second, all the operatives looked in directions other than theirs.

Anya sat with her back to a corrugated concrete wall. Wade joined her.

"Why is Anya singing Meat Loaf?" Cassandra asked.

"She timing our runs based on the song lyrics."

"I see. I have video back now."

Wade saw a huge rusting chain off to the side and wondered why anything needed to be so big. In the other direction, he saw a stack of

Yesterday Pill   Iain Benson

offices. Old sheets of metal plates constructed into a sheet over the offices, the lines between sheets an orange stain.

Anya started moving, singing under her breath. Although he knew why, he found it as disconcerting as their escape from the restaurant.

Together, they sidled along the wall to the offices. She kicked a metal plate at the exact moment someone accidentally discharged a gun. Around the cavernous containment hanger, angry voices berated the accidental shooter. The space's vastness swallowed their anger.

Anya crawled through the hole.

Wade followed. Inside, metal grating stairs climbed, with an observation deck on each level looking out into the cavern.

Anya climbed rapidly, Wade feeling the burn in his lungs and knees as he followed. Their steps thumped on the metal.

Anya stopped, holding up her hand as she muttered "battering ram". She explained while still concentrating on the song lyrics. "Heat sensor sweeping the level above."

She set off again, creeping.

Almost catching Wade off guard, she increased her speed. Wade found her ability at finding the small chink in the almost air-tight Paladin set-up nothing short of remarkable.

They reached the top floor. Wade risked a glance to the Sarcophagus floor. The Operatives looked insignificant. Tiny far below them.

"You need to open the panel in the roof." Anya pointed at the metal sheets riveted together. She held out her screwdriver. "I can't reach."

Using the flat screwdriver blade like a lever, Wade broke the rivets.

Anya stepped forward at the exact moment and caught the metal plate before it could clang on the flooring and alert everybody to their location.

Wade boosted Anya through the hole. She lay flat, her hands helping him through. He rolled onto his back, feeling the metal underneath him buckle and bend with his weight. They were still several metres from the Sarcophagus roof, though they were now level with the concrete original.

Anya rolled onto the concrete, still singing. Wade followed.

Keeping on her hands and knees, she moved across the surface. Without looking behind her, she hissed. "Don't put your hand there."

Wade instinctively froze.

Where he'd about to put his hand, the concrete looked crumblier. He placed his hand to the side instead.

"How do we find the wormhole?" Wade knew they could not see it.

"The concrete tomb's centre will be right over the reactor core." Static caused Cassandra's words to break. "The wormhole's magnetic field should pull them into place."

Anya pulled the tube of magnets out from her bag. She handed half to Wade, and he started placing them on the concrete. Anya moved across the flat, crumbling surface and placed some down.

Three of Wade's magnets spun slowly. "It's here."

Silently, Anya nodded and brought her magnets to the three that were spinning. They placed them down, so each of them turned, beginning to form a lazy spinning circle.

They worked efficiently and quickly, moving each magnet until it, too, rotated. It formed a perfect circle.

One by one, the magnets rose from the ground, hanging in the air like a magician's show, the speed gathering.

"Wade!" Wade stopped watching. Urgency in Cassandra's voice sending a spike of fear through his guts.

"What is it?"

"Somebody is banging on the door!" A pause, they heard through the communicators a splintering crash.

Then, silence.

Yesterday Pill   Iain Benson

18

"I am disappointed." Wade's head snapped around at the voice.

Adrian had climbed the staircase up the concrete tomb.

"You're too late, Adrian." Wade waved his hand at the magnets, now forming a sphere around a spot that glowed with iridescent light.

Adrian's gun pointing toward Anya. Wade and Anya brought their rifles up. Adrian had to know he couldn't stop them now.

"Dismantle it, for the sake of everything you hold dear." Adrian lowered his weapon, but his finger remained alongside the trigger guard.

"No." Wade kept his muzzle pointing at Adrian. "While this wormhole exists, Cassandra and I can never be safe."

Adrian looked down at the ground and sighed. "What happened to you, Wade? Once, you believed in what we do."

"Then you went after Cassandra. You threatened an innocent person based on a half-heard comment."

"It is one person against every life in the universe." Adrian looked abashed. "The equation is simple, if brutal. We were right to go after her, as you are now proving."

Wade glanced at the sphere of magnets. At their heart, the wormhole sparkled and coruscated. It would soon be over. Paladin would have no reason to continue their witch hunt.

"Do you not feel it was a self-fulfilling prophecy, Adrian?" Anya asked. "If you had not gone after her, Craig would not have recruited Wade and me to help find her and keep her alive."

Adrian shrugged. "There is truth in what you say. We made decisions. I believe they were the right ones."

"Wade!" Cassandra's voice held an urgency in Wade's ear. "Leah is here!"

"Are you safe?" Worry flooded through Wade.

"Yes! She wanted to show me the maths from the quantum techs at

Paladin."

A seeping dread filled Wade; his breath stilled. "And?"

Anya and Wade exchanged glances. Adrian got a call, holstering his weapon and taking out his phone.

"Paladin's calculations are right. You need to break up the magnets."

Cassandra and Wade dropped their guns. Wade grabbed a magnet.

The shock coursed up his arm and threw him backwards with a jarring thud against the brittle concrete.

Flakes of grey flew up as he landed. A hole opened. Anya lay on her back opposite the spinning bronze globe of magnets. Inside, the light from the wormhole grew exponentially. Lights flashed across the Sarcophagus's underside; a flickering blaze as the neodymium flashed by the wormhole's radiance.

"I see you both got the same message I did." Adrian pulled out his gun and fired at the spinning mass. The bullet visibly slowed on its approach, falling with a dull thud on the concrete.

Wade dialled three doses on his ring.

The snapback was seconds, the two-dimensional scene a mere flicker. Wade watched the bullet slow a second time.

His mind was a whirring, conflicting mass.

"Cass, are you sure?" Wade quickly asked.

"Positive! The paradox resets the universe back to when the wormhole formed. Nineteen eighty-six."

"Shit." Wade scrambled around to Anya.

"What can we do?" Anya's voice cracked.

"Dial three doses," he told her, doing the same.

Anya did as Wade instructed.

Wade dialled three on his.

Anya passed him her pill. Wade held it next to his own.

"What are you doing?" Adrian asked.

"Cass. I love you." Wade told her. He looked at Anya. "And I've

Yesterday Pill   Iain Benson

always loved you, Annie."

"Wade?" Cassandra's voice wavered, enhanced by the interference.

The globe was a blur.

The light from within, a second sun, blazing across the silvered Sarcophagus.

Anya threw her arms around Wade. "I love you too, Wade! Do it right this time."

Wade took the double dose of three.

The globe froze.

Wade saw sparks in mid-arc. Anya's word's echoing in his mind.

The scene furled at the edges, blocky and breaking up.

Had he left it too late?

With a rush, his universe shrank to a single infinitesimal point. The wormhole, the only light he could see.

An eternity of darkness swallowed his essence.

With a rush, the light returned.

He lay on his back. He could feel a hard stone beneath his back. His head was a smashing pounding of pain. Pulsing waves crossed his brain, counterpointing his heartbeat.

Above him, morning illumination filtered through leaves, creating a dapple of light and shadow across his face. He could smell the earth, fresh from a recent rain shower.

He shivered. The concrete felt cold.

A face appeared in his wavering vision. He saw a woman with loosely curled blonde hair cut into a long style that framed a look of worry and concern.

Like a tongue searching for a tooth, he tried to think where he was, who he was.

A thin cotton veil held back everything he thought he should know.

"Are you okay?" The woman asked, bringing him back to the present.

Was he okay?

He had no answers.

He turned his head. Across the road, he saw a dark-haired woman, also looking concerned. She looked like she wanted to run over.

Did he know her?

Did he know either of them?

He shifted position, raising himself onto his elbows.

Waves of nausea washed through him.

He vomited on the pavement.

"I'll call an ambulance." The woman was already reaching for her phone.

An echo. A distant voice called a single word.

He had a memory of that single word through the fog of his petrified mind: "Wade."

It connected to the woman across the road.

With a rush, everything came back to him.

"No. I'm fine." His voice cracked in his own ears.

"You collapsed." Cassandra, that was her name. "You should go to the hospital."

Wade managed a wan smile. "Really, no. I am fine."

He looked across the road at Anya, concern creasing her features. He waved.

Checking for traffic, she crossed the road and knelt next to him. "Wade?"

"Anya." With her help, he sat up.

"What happened?" Anya asked, supporting him.

"I collapsed. It's nothing to worry about." Wade looked at Cassandra. "Cass. Please, don't worry. I have a lot to tell you both."

"But." Anya's voice filled with a hesitancy and uncertainty he rarely heard from her.

Wade smiled at her. "We're going to do it right this time."

Printed in Great Britain
by Amazon